HAWAII FOR TWO

A NOVEL

CHRISTINA BRAVER

THREE BS PUBLISHING LLC

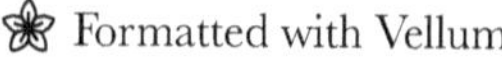 Formatted with Vellum

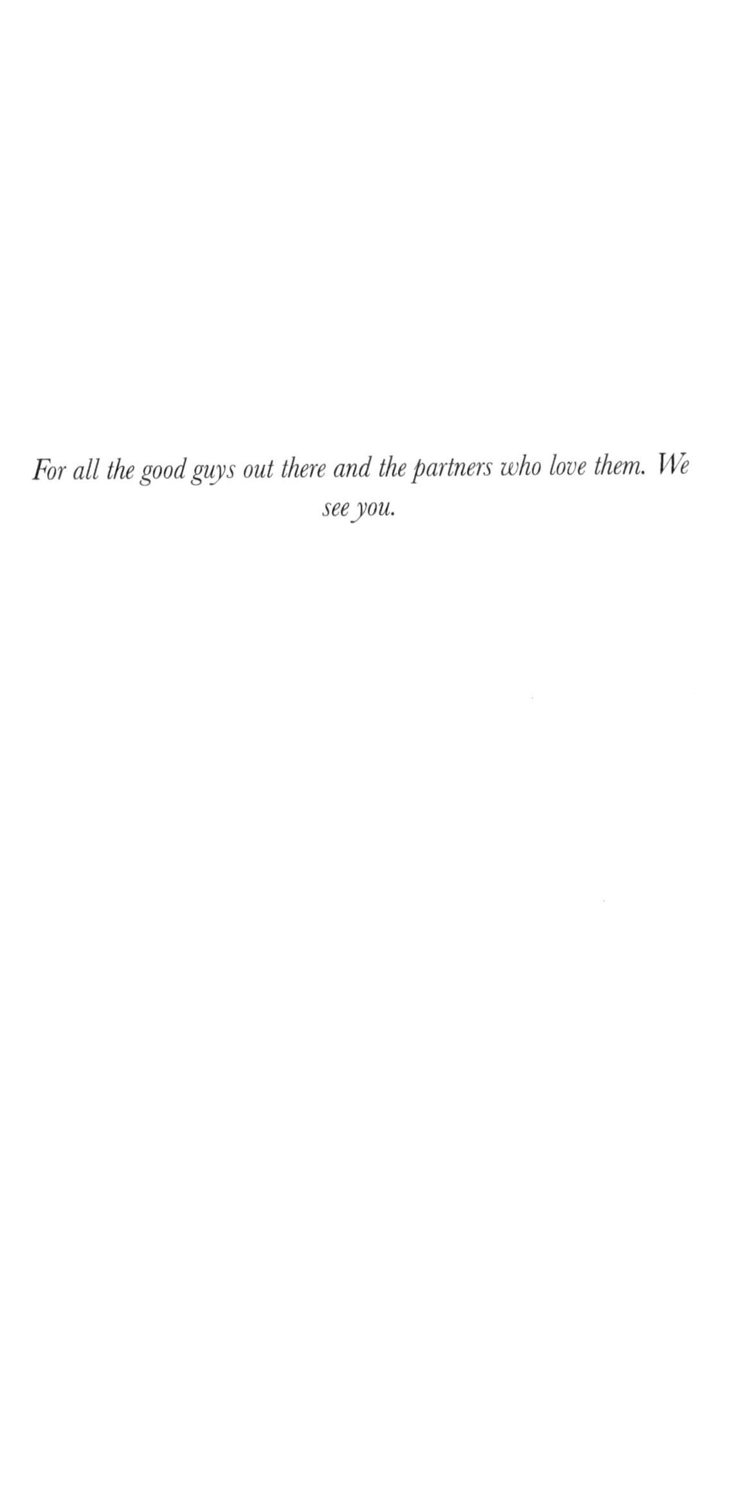

For all the good guys out there and the partners who love them. We see you.

1

KATE

Damn, it was cold. Too cold for June. Souls tired of clouds and rain shuffled inside the crowded coffee shop wearing sandals and bright spring colors under sweaters and fleece-lined hoodies, me included. Another *June-uary* in the Pacific Northwest.

A week in Hawaii sounded necessary, even if it was with my family.

Pushing through the door, I brushed past Kimberlee with two E's Van den Berg, on her way out with her usual posse, the skinny nurses of Harborland Hospital. If there was a calendar, these women would feature.

She smiled her cool acknowledgment, not quite pity, not quite condescension, like a queen gracing a loyal peasant. It didn't matter that it had been months since my ex dumped me at the first flutter of her sooty lashes or that she dumped him not long after. What mattered was he dumped me for her, and she dumped him. By the transitive principle of mathematics, as well as the brilliance of reality TV logic, *she* dumped me.

I refused to let getting dumped by either of them make me feel small.

"The usual?" asked the barista, a big grin on his familiar face.

"Thanks, Pete. Wait … shouldn't you be in school?"

"Senior ditch Friday," he said in a high voice before clearing his throat and continuing in a deeper register. "It's a good day to pick up extra hours. I'm eighteen now, a man. It's time to get serious." He straightened to his full height, and I had to tilt my head to meet his gaze.

A cough rumbled behind me.

"Well, don't work too hard. Do something fun," I said, readying my card to pay. "Take a risk before the stakes get too high."

I stepped aside to keep the line flowing, and in no time, Pete strode over to the pickup area with my vanilla cold foam latte. "Uh, in the interest of that risk thing—" he cleared his throat again "—let's go out."

I blinked, sure I'd misheard.

"You're pretty. I like you. Let's go out. We could get dinner. Take a walk. Whatever you want. There's no law against it anymore." He grinned.

A man's low chuckle behind me caught my attention.

Oh, no. Nope. No one was mocking this boy, er, man.

"Pete, I'm—"

"Don't say flattered." He leaned closer and lowered his voice. "You're what … twenty-five?"

"Twenty-eight," I said with a squint and a smile.

Pete barely faltered at our ten-year age gap. "No problem. It's dinner. Nothing serious."

I held his gaze and whispered, "Is this a booty call?"

Pete's eyes rounded before he ran a hand through his shaggy brown hair, and the deep voice said, "It's whatever you want it to be."

Oh, Pete. This guy had a future in breaking hearts. He was lanky, but his sturdy shoulders said he wouldn't be forever. With bright hazel eyes, patches of dark stubble on a sharp jawline, and that confidence, women of all ages would soon line up to have dinner with him.

"Pete, you have me thinking. And you're the first man to do that in a while."

A hesitant but satisfied smile lit his face.

"I can't. Thank you for the invitation. Honestly, it was perfect. But … the age difference is a problem for *me*."

He nodded silently and glanced down before meeting my eyes again. There was no embarrassment or feigned casualness, just sincerity and sweetness. "The offer is out there if you change your mind."

With a half-smile, Pete confidently returned to the register, having handled that about as well as a person could. Wow. So, good ones were still out there. Fingers crossed for one closer to my age.

The girl who'd been working next to Pete snapped her gaze back to the customer line, trying to hide the fact she'd been watching our exchange, and I recognized the barely disguised look of longing from my own awkward teens. She wanted to be the girl he asked out. I silently vowed to help make that happen. Dating was a challenge at any age.

Latte in hand, I scanned the crowded space and found the only vacant seats were at a large high-top table stretched along the side wall. Folks with headphones and laptops sat mostly at one end, tapping lightly on their keyboards.

I sat at the other end and pulled out my phone. My flight to Kona in the morning was still on time, and I swallowed against the pit in my stomach.

My younger sister was getting married. I was expected to be there. No exceptions.

I usually limited my time with my family to three days max. That was long enough to smile, not rock the boat, and not stab one of my sisters in their sleep. Three days. This wedding trip was a week.

Thankfully, my best friend Kristen was coming along as a buffer. My excuse to head to the beach when the urge to cause bodily harm grew unbearable.

"Is this seat taken?" a voice asked, deep and silky like chocolate so rich you had to lick every bit of it from your spoon.

Next came the scent of cardamom and leather. I sucked in a breath of manly deliciousness before turning to find Levi Abrams, exuding confidence and untouchable mystery packaged in broad shoulders and a trim build that said he knew how to use his body. All six-feet-plus of it.

He worked at the hospital, but not in patient care, and wasn't overly talkative beyond "excuse me" and "hold the door." He made cargo pants look good, rode a bike to work spring through fall, and wore hiking boots like regular shoes. Throw in tousled dark hair, and it was no wonder Levi caught the eye of most women and some men, garnering a sort of *great white whale* persona among the nurses.

Plus, he regularly had lunch with an unknown, stunning woman. That was the *challenge factor*, irresistible to top competitors in the game of love, or at least the game of sex, like Kimberlee.

Not me.

"I'm sorry?" I replied, nearly getting lost in the way the green of his fleece pullover highlighted the blue-gray color of his eyes.

He smiled, and the shine landed smack in my belly along with the dimple on his left cheek, winking through dark scruff and threatening to make my panties ignite.

He leaned in slightly, blocking my view of anything but him. "I asked if anyone was sitting here. All the other seats are taken."

"Oh, right. Please." I scrambled to pull myself together and shift my backpack out of the empty space at the head of the table.

"Thank you," he said, gliding onto the stool like it was made for him. "Unless you're saving it for Pete's break,"

What? I frowned. "Don't mock."

"Hey, respect," Levi said, raising a hand. "Asking an older woman out, especially one who's pretty and sophisticated, takes guts. I'm impressed. If you find yourself at the plate, man, why not swing for the fences?" He sipped his coffee with that shine still beaming.

I furrowed my brow, replaying his words. Yes, I was older than Pete. *Pretty* wasn't a word I heard often, though it had been said. But *sophisticated?* No one had ever called me, Kate Wells, sophisticated. Certainly not compared to my beautiful and effortlessly sophisticated sisters.

The urge to hide my unpainted fingernails, with their rough and ragged cuticles, prodded at me.

Medical-grade hand sanitizer wasn't easy on the skin. Particularly when I used it ten times a day. "I'm hardly sophisticated," I said, digging in my bag for my favorite coconut-scented lotion. It was like a mini-tropical vacation.

"I disagree. You could have laughed like it was a joke. Tried to let him down easy that way. Or you could have told him he was dreaming, *hacked* him down that way." He shuddered. "Instead, you took him seriously, didn't placate him with clichés about the right girl and someday. Your rejection was honest but kind. *That's* sophistication."

Suddenly nervous about receiving what might have been the best compliment ever, I vigorously smoothed the lotion over my hands. "Thank you."

"You're welcome." His smile lingered before he pulled out his phone, and I exhaled a breath, happy to let the awkward feelings die along with the conversation. Me with the *great white whale*. What a joke.

"Vanilla cold foam latte. Can't say I've had that one before," he said.

"Oh … It's a special order." I held the drink in question. I could talk about this. "The cold foam isn't too sweet, and it cools the hot drink to the perfect temperature."

"Good to know. Dark roast drip, black," he said, lifting his cup. "I'm a simple guy."

I flashed a grin, a little confused. Levi Abrams was telling me about his regular coffee order. Why?

Yes, I was smart and competent. People trusted me with their lives, and if Levi was having heart palpitations, I'd spring into confident action. But this casual talking thing … with Levi *effing* Abrams, was outside my wheelhouse.

Both of our phones dinged with a text, startling us and breaking our eye contact. We each glanced at our screens with chagrined smiles.

Kristen.

Kgirl: Hey. Got a minute?

Me: Sure. Packing?

Me: Throw some stuff in with your bathing suit. We'll be at the beach most of the time.

Kgirl: That sounds great.

Those three dots danced and paused and danced again. I noticed Levi focused on his screen, a deep crease in his brow.

Kgirl: Here's the thing. I can't go.

Me: To the beach? Okay. I don't care what we do as long as it's not with my sisters.

Kgirl: I can't go to Hawaii. I met someone.

My fingers froze above the screen. She wasn't coming? My stomach lurched with a sudden sinking feeling. I had to swallow. Wait. She met someone?

Me: Have you been taken against your will? Answer my next question wrong if you need me to call 911. What was the name of my childhood pet?

Kgirl: Patches. Your cat.

Right answer.

Kgirl: I know I never do things like this. It's reckless.

Kgirl: But I'm almost thirty. And what I'm doing isn't working. I'm going to be reckless for a change.

Okay …

Me: Who is this person?

Kgirl: His name is Chris. We met yesterday, and he's amazing.

Kgirl: He asked me to go camping with him this week in Yellowstone. Yellowstone!! It's fate.

Kristen wasn't a big camper, but she didn't need to stay at the Four Seasons either. She'd wanted to go to Yellowstone National Park since about birth but hadn't made it yet. It's popular and nearly impossible to get into in the summer months.

Me: Wow.

I didn't know what else to say. I was happy for her, a little stunned, and a lot disappointed. It was a lot to process.

Kgirl: You're worried about the trip. But you'll be fine.

Kgirl: Tell those bitchy sisters of yours to fuck off. You look amazing. You worked hard on that body, and you're rockin' it.

I huffed a smile and smoothed my hand over my belly. My hips still flared, and my ass remained substantial, but my arms had more definition, and I'd felt stronger the last time I helped lift a gurney into a medevac chopper. It wasn't a regular occurrence, but as a traveling nurse for the small islands off the coast of Washington state, it happened.

Kgirl: Meet some bronzed stud and have a fling. Bring him to the wedding and make everyone jealous. [Winky face emoji]

Me: A bronzed stud?

I glanced over to see Levi texting, vigorously tapping away.

Kgirl: Yes!! Why not? Maybe this reckless thing is what we've both been missing. It'll be great.

It would not. The wedding and my family for an entire week on my own weren't survivable. I barely made it through seventy-two hours at Christmas, and that was with a bunch of cookies and alcohol.

Kgirl: When a hot guy asks you to do something reckless, say yes.

I frowned.

Me: Send me a photo of this guy's license right now. If I don't hear from you in a week, I'm calling the police.

Kgirl: I will. But don't worry. I've got a good feeling.

Wasn't that what people said about serial killers?

Me: Kris!!!????

Kgirl: He could be the one. And I never say that.

Kgirl: I'll text next week. I promise.

Great. She found *the one,* and now I was on my own. I sighed, resignation taking over as usual. I could diagnose a patient, perform CPR, or stitch a gaping wound all on my own because I had to. This was no different. Nothing to do but face it. Get through it. FUCKING Kris.

2

LEVI

"Fucking Chris," I said with a sigh. It was louder than intended, because it echoed. Or had my coffee companion said it too?

I looked into her wide brown eyes.

"Kris? My Kris?" she asked with a frown that was kinda cute on her, drawing my eye to her mouth and the cupid's bow there. Dark hair, thick and shiny, fell below her shoulders, framing her face and highlighting a sparse string of light freckles across the tops of her cheeks. Her ears were unadorned as were her fingers. And she had that mysterious *more* factor.

I had to give it to Pete. He had good taste. Possibly too good. I don't think even I would have *swung for the fences* that much when I was his age, and I rarely turned down a challenge, especially then.

"No, my Chris. You have a Chris?" I asked.

"Yes. At least I did. My friend Kristen and I were planning a trip together, but she bailed."

"Huh. Must be something with Chrises," I said. "My buddy invited me on this epic Yellowstone camping trip he won at a charity auction. Biking. Hiking. Guided rock climbs starting tomorrow. But he met a girl, and she's going instead." I waved my phone with the text screen still open.

My new coffee friend stared as if she didn't believe me.

I took the chance to stare back. She was subtly beautiful, like if you didn't take a moment, you might miss it. Once you noticed though, you couldn't unsee it. The rich jewel tones of her sundress and cardigan brought out the creamy gold of her skin and the vivid dark color of her eyes. There was something there in those quiet depths, and I definitely wanted to figure it out, figure her out.

Puzzles were my thing. I loved puzzles, and people were the best kind.

She told Pete she hadn't dated in a while, and she didn't reject him because of a husband or boyfriend. Good news for me.

I shrugged off my disappointment about Yellowstone, ideas already forming about how I could spend some of my now free time with this enticing puzzle. "I'll find something else to do. At least I won't be at work, right?"

"Right," she said, still sounding dazed.

I sipped my coffee and raised my brows, silently questioning her continued staring.

As if she were waking from a dream, she sat taller and cleared her throat. "Let me get this straight. You have a friend named Chris. And you two were going camping in Yellowstone starting tomorrow?"

"Yep."

"But now Chris is going with a girl he just met?"

"So, it would seem. Can't compete with *the one*." I smirked.

Chris met a lot of *the ones*. He always fell too fast and too hard. I told him these things took time. You can't know a person, know you can count on them, after a few days or weeks. Hell, even years. But he was in love with love.

I liked love. And women. One day I woke up and pretty girls were everywhere. *Everywhere.* I wanted to be the prince of romance, with stars in my eyes, for one special woman. But the reality of finding that woman turned out to be harder than I'd imagined. I had the stitched-together pulverized heart to prove it.

I knew guys who took that kind of pain and turned it into an excuse to diligently fuck and dump as many women as possible, or worse, write some seriously disturbing shit on an underground message board. That was not my style. Instead, I took things as they came, kept them light. I spent time with women when I could and enjoyed it as long as it lasted. It was a solid approach. It had been years since that vital organ of mine paid the ultimate price.

The brunette beauty slowly shook her head, a small grin playing across her full lips. She didn't appear to be wearing lipstick, or any makeup, and I wondered if, as the legend went, their dusty rose color matched the color of her nipples. I hadn't conducted conclusive research, but based on past observations, I was a believer.

I wanted to know about my pretty coffee friend's nipples.

She set her coffee aside and leaned in conspiratorially. "Here's the thing. My Kris, or Kristen, was spending the week with me in Hawaii starting tomorrow. But she just texted to say she couldn't go because she met a guy, and he invited her on *his* trip to Yellowstone."

My lips parted as an incoming text dinged on her phone.

She glanced at it and showed me. "Is this your friend?"

A photo of Chris's driver's license filled her screen. What the hell?

"Yep, that's him." I shook my head and huffed as reality set in, then extended my hand. "Levi Abrams."

"Kate Wells," she said with a firm shake as our stunned smiles grew. The subtle coconut scent of her snagged my attention. Did she use that lotion every-where? Did her hair smell of sweet treats and sunny days too?

A moment passed with us staring at each other before we both grinned, and I glimpsed unease in her eyes.

"Is he a good guy?" she asked.

"Chris? Yeah. Really good. He won't hurt her, if that's what you mean. It'll probably be the other way around."

"Why? Kristen's a sweetie."

I quickly added, "It's not about her. Chris goes all in early and then gets his heart crushed. But he keeps getting up." I shook my head in awe at the sheer number of times I'd witnessed it.

"Kristen's heart has taken some punches, too. Maybe this time will be different for them both."

Her expression relaxed, and the silence stretched for a beat. I took the chance to admire the curve of her jaw and the column of her neck. I wanted to know what her skin tasted like, warm in the sunshine and heat of the day.

"So now what?" she asked.

"I could go to Hawaii with you," I teased.

She huffed. "Right."

"I've got the time off already." I shrugged one shoulder, realizing it was true.

"Funny joke. You're hilarious."

Was I joking? A smile lit her eyes, and I wanted to see it again. And there were worse things than spending a week in Hawaii, especially with a beautiful woman. So what if we just met. It wasn't like I never did anything impulsive or never took risks. And it almost always worked out great.

I matched her grin. "Actually, I don't think I am."

"Levi, come on, you're serious?"

"Why not? Based on our friends, we're both good people. Are you a bad traveler? Do you whine when you don't get your way?"

She scoffed, "I'm a great traveler. I almost never get my way. And I don't whine."

Her little scoff was almost as cute as her frown. All the parts of my body were quickly getting on board with this plan. Warm ocean water and scented evening breezes. Her in a bikini by the pool, every glorious curve right there. Kissing those dusky pink lips … and other pink places.

"Think about it. What are the chances you and I would be here together at this moment? Seems like the universe demands it. And Hawaii is always great, right?"

She demurred, "I've never been."

"What?" I clutched my chest in exaggeration. "I have to go now and show you around. Which island?"

She hesitated, but I caught the small curve hinting at the corners of her tempting mouth. "The Big Island."

"That's my favorite one!"

She smirked.

"I'm serious. It's got it all, and I can be your guide. Show you the best beaches. Best places to ride ATVs. Now, I'm pumped. There's a lot to do. I'm not sure where to start, but I'll figure it out by the time we get there. What time's our flight?" I unlocked my phone and opened a web browser, ready to check on plane tickets.

"You seriously expect me to take you on my trip?"

"Yes."

"But we just met. And I'm not trying to become a cautionary tale on some infotainment news show."

She was right. I held up a hand. "Okay." I set my phone on the table and ticked off the points of my argument on my fingers. "One. I work in the IT department at Harborland Hospital, so I can pass a background check. My coworker Nicole has known me for years and would vouch for me. You can call her.

"Two, I've never been convicted of a crime." Never convicted. An important distinction.

"I don't complain about taxes because we all gotta do our part. I open doors for women not because I think they can't, but because I like it when they smile at me. And I have a sister plus a tween-age nephew. You can ask them about me. Tweens never lie."

She huffed a laugh then met my gaze with a sober expression. She was thinking.

It felt like an interview for a job, one it surprised me to admit I really wanted. Talking with Kate was easy and fun. Uncovering all of her mysteries while she looked at me with those deep brown eyes and the blue of the Pacific behind her would be a great way to spend my vacation.

"My dad is a cardiac surgeon in Seattle," I continued. "You can call his office. My sister's fiancé is an elementary school teacher, so he's legit. He'd vouch." I lifted my phone and gestured to her. "Who do you want to call first?"

Kate leaned closer and placed an elbow on the table but didn't take my phone. "You'd really go with me?"

"Absolutely."

"No matter what?"

I tilted my head to the side. "I like adventure. And I'm pretty good at reading people. I'd be able to tell if you were dangerous."

"I'm not. But …"

I smiled at her hesitation. Everything about this woman said good, sweet, and tough when she needed to be. All wrapped in a soft and sexy package. I got more sucked in by the second.

"But?" I repeated, drawing out the word.

"It's a wedding." She paused for effect.

"Okay. As long as it's not yours."

She scoffed louder this time, "No, *definitely* not mine. My sister's."

I noted the emphasis on definitely. "So, it's a family wedding. Do you have other siblings?"

She nodded. "Another sister. Older."

"Ahh, let me guess. She's married, and you asked your friend to go because you didn't want to be the odd one out."

Kate shifted in her seat.

"I'll go as your date. Problem solved."

"My family … doesn't have good boundaries.

They'll say anything. With me, it's a game of twenty questions like 'why aren't you dating?' and 'have you gained weight?' Or offering sage advice like 'makeup is an investment in your face value' and 'women who don't need anyone do needlepoint' like if I'm too independent, I'll always be alone." Her sigh was heavy with frustration.

"Sounds like bullshit advice. Don't hide who you are, Kate. The right man will love it."

She rolled her eyes, and I chuckled. "I know it sounds like a line, but it's also true. I have a sister, remember?" I shifted closer. "Do you really want to face all those questions on your own?"

"No, but …" Her eyes flashed with uncertainty.

I spread my arms as if to say *here I am*. "Then take me. I can help. I like to help."

She gave me the side-eye. "You're pretty smooth. Hopefully not serial killer smooth."

My pulse ticked. She was gonna do this. "Call my people, Kate. Check me out. I'm no kind of killer, serial or otherwise."

She worried her bottom lip and stared into my eyes. I did not imagine biting that plump, rosy lip or the cupid's bow above it. Definitely. Did not.

I gave a final push to convince her. "I know what it's like to be the odd one out. A lot of my friends are newly married. I want to help, and I'm suddenly free for the week. Being your date for a wedding in Hawaii sounds great. Unless you changed your mind about giving Pete a shot."

She chuckled, and I flashed my flirtiest grin. It had about an eighty percent chance of conversion from flirting to touching. I was putting it all out there.

"Having someone to do things with away from my family would be good," she said. "Save me from saying or doing something I can't take back."

"Your hero has arrived, Kate. All you have to do is say yes."

Something flashed behind her eyes. Then a blush rose with her smile as she looked to the side and gave her head the tiniest shake.

3

———

KATE

HE WASN'T COMING. THERE WAS NO WAY LEVI ABRAMS, legendary unattainable *great white whale* of Harborland Hospital, was coming with me to Hawaii for a week. With my family.

However, he had given me his information so I could change the name on my companion ticket after I called his sister. I wanted to be reckless, like Kristen, but not suicidal.

She was as friendly and guarded as you would expect when your brother said he was going on a trip with a stranger. But her son had been effusive with praise for his uncle, and something in my middle settled.

He'd had to get back to work after that, so we tabled the rest of the get-to-know-you conversation for the plane ride. I hadn't asked about the gorgeous woman he had lunch with and hadn't confessed that I knew him from the hospital. I'd do both of those things today. Maybe.

Did I want to learn about the woman? He volunteered for this trip. He said the word "date." They must have broken up.

Levi, with all his earnest arguments and putting himself out there, didn't seem like the cheater type, but then what did I know? No one had ever cheated on me. They always ended it before they had the chance to cheat. At least I had that.

We'd agreed to meet at the local airport. It was small but had daily direct flights to three Hawaiian destinations this time of year, including Kona. Hawaii was a thing for us Pacific Northwest folks yearning for sun.

I'd given it a fifty-fifty chance he'd actually go through with it. He'd texted earlier this morning that he was running late, and as I boarded and found my seat with no more texts from Levi, I was down to twenty-eighty.

"Can I get you something to drink?" the flight attendant asked, leaning in. "A Mai Tai? Get in the Hawaiian spirit?" Her expression was bright, like her shiny, gold name tag.

A Mai Tai before noon *would* make getting stood up easier.

"Sounds perfect," I said, and she went to make my fruity cocktail. Settling into the seat, I stared out the window and tried to breathe. The baggage handlers and those little cart trains whizzing around the tarmac were surprisingly distracting from thoughts of facing this week alone.

I'd get through it like I got through everything else; I'd just do it. If things got rough, I'd make a run for it. I wasn't a runner. My sturdy Nike trainers were too clean for a serious exercise enthusiast. But running had to be better than jail.

"Trying to ditch me?"

I spun my head at his voice, and Levi stood in the aisle smiling. His dark hair was messy like he'd had his hands in it more than once, but his gray-blue eyes glittered. He showed.

He showed! My heart jumped with relief. Or was it the sight of him in worn jeans and a navy long-sleeved T-shirt, his dimple flashing?

This was really happening.

Well, not *really*. It was fake. He'd been the odd single before, and he liked to be helpful. He was a nice guy, and that's why he'd offered to be my date. And because he loved Hawaii. Also, our friends were making a love connection, and we'd likely see more of each other in the future. It made sense for us to become friends. This was a friendship-building trip.

But … a week in Hawaii with Levi *effing* Abrams. Gah! Eat your heart out Kimberlee Van den Berg, with her perfectly proportioned backside and full tits bouncing in her scrubs. Levi had been in her sights for a while, probably before my lying ex, but Kimberlee wasn't the one with him on this plane now.

I bit the inside of my lip. "You were late. I thought *you* ditched me."

Levi leaned in and met my gaze with a smirk, his cardamom and leather scent hitting my nose like a drug. "Not a chance, babe."

That one word in his growly, low voice sent a zing through my body. It'd been said before, but it never felt like that.

Okay. I needed to have a strongly worded conversation with all my girl parts later. This was fake. *Fake.* No more zings. Anywhere.

Levi rose and removed a book from his bag before shoving the well-used satchel into the overhead compartment. I only glanced for a second at the light blue, worn spots along the fly of his jeans while he did. Possibly two seconds. Shoot. I needed to include my eyes in that no-more-zings conversation.

He took the aisle seat next to me and buckled up.

The book in his hand was a battered paperback copy of an old adventure series. Either he liked to reread books, or he liked to buy used copies. My kind of reader. I ignored the warm feeling rising in my belly. At least it wasn't a zing.

"Are we going to be a *babe* sort of couple, um, fake couple?" I asked.

He furrowed his brow. "I'm kind of a nickname guy, but if you don't like babe, we can pick something else. Honey?"

I shook my head.

"Pumpkin?"

I squinted.

"Sugar lips?" He whispered close.

I rolled my eyes at his playfulness. "Babe is fine."

Levi grinned, and the flight attendant, Patricia, arrived with my drink. "Would you like a Mai Tai as well, sir?"

"Absolutely," he said with zero hesitation.

Her warm expression melted even more.

The plan was to tell people we'd been dating for a couple of months and hadn't gone public yet. We'd have to share a room in the rented house where the wedding was being held, but I'd requested the one with two double beds for me and Kristen. All good there.

We'd have some meals with my family, but as a

couple, we could slip away to the beach without too much drama. It might even be better than if I'd brought Kristen. Everyone was so worried about my dating life that they'd probably push us to spend more time alone.

"First class, huh? That was a pleasant surprise." Levi said as Patricia left to make his drink.

"My dad was a pilot for the airline. I still get a few perks." I shrugged one shoulder.

We both made quick work of the Mai Tais and settled into our roomy seats before the crew started their flight safety routine. The alcohol warmed my veins, and I relaxed.

"So, let's talk," Levi said once we were airborne with two fresh drinks in our hands, because why not.

"Right. Our backstory." I shifted in my seat to face him.

He chuckled. "No, well, yes, but I'd like to get to know you for real first."

I licked my lips as my stomach fluttered. "Okay, but let's start with you. You mentioned IT yesterday. What exactly do you do?"

"I maintain the hospital's firewall and security protocols. There are four of us in the department, but we each have different areas of expertise. I'm the security guy."

I nodded, more than a little impressed. That was a huge responsibility. If there was a breach and patient data was leaked, the fines could be in the millions.

"Sounds like a big job."

"It is, but I'm good at it. So, it's not too bad."

It wasn't bragging. It was true. He liked his work.

I could relate. I was good at my job, too. Being a

traveling nurse wasn't for everyone, but it was my one thing, and I loved it.

"So, how does a person get into IT security?"

A shadow passed in his eyes briefly. "I studied computer science in college. But … I got the best training messing around with my friends in high school."

"Like playing video games?"

"Not exactly."

I cocked my head to the side, curious. "What?"

"Promise you won't judge?"

"Is it nerdier than holing up with a bunch of unshowered teens and playing Xbox all night?"

"Probably."

"Okay," I said, drawing out the word.

"We were hackers."

I frowned, and he held out his hands in defense.

"Strictly white-hat stuff. We didn't hurt anybody. We were young and cocky and mostly did things to see if we could. If we succeeded in breaking in somewhere big like a bank or something, we left a digital note telling them how we got in. Companies pay professional hackers a lot of money to find their weaknesses, and we did it for free."

"You broke into banks?" I said, shock and unease clear in my voice.

"No," he blurted. "That was an example. I never said I broke into a bank."

"Levi …"

"We did minor stuff. Not big enough to get caught."

"Like what?"

He shrugged a single shoulder. "There was this golf club north of Seattle, pretty well known, that didn't allow women to become members. So, on the day of their big pro-am event, we changed their website photos from bucolic golf course shots to golfer memes highlighting their misogyny. If they wanted to practice 1950s sexist policies, their website should reflect that. Truth in advertising."

I eyed him.

"We fixed it the next day, but it got people talking, and a year later, I heard the club had changed its policies. So, a happy ending."

"You aren't wanted, right? I'm not harboring a felon or taking one across state lines? Because that would *not* go over no matter how happy the ending was."

Levi grinned. "No, I'm strictly legit. But … if you ever did need something … I'm not saying I couldn't do it." His expression turned all *Godfather-y*, and he stroked the stubble on his firm jaw.

I punched his shoulder lightly and shook my head.

"So, what about you? You haven't mentioned what you do," he said.

The overhead announcement stopped me from answering and revealing my secrets. "Pardon the interruption folks, but if there is a doctor or nurse on board, please ring your call button. This isn't an emergency, but the captain requested I ask. Again, if you are a doctor or a nurse, please ring your call button."

I bit my lip, pressed my finger to the button, and the color drained from Levi's face.

IT WASN'T AN EMERGENCY. A toddler seated in the back had spiked a fever, and the new parents were concerned about giving her more medicine. I checked the dosage and instructed them on how much to administer, then helped them make ice packs to cool her. By the time I returned to my seat, the little girl's fever had lowered, and the first-time parents were nearly giddy with relief.

I shifted past Levi and sat.

"So, you're a doctor," he said with an expression I couldn't read. Was he disappointed?

"Nurse practitioner. I'm one of Harborland's traveling nurses. I work the smaller islands that don't have local care. The work of a doctor with a fraction of the professional clout."

The tension I thought I saw dissolved.

"A fraction of the debt too, but still," I added and grinned.

Levi looked at me with a question in his eyes. "You come into the hospital, then?"

I nodded. Time to fess up. "For meetings or to check on a patient, and … I recognized you yesterday."

He raised his brows.

"Only that you worked at Harborland. So, I knew you could pass a background check."

"At least I had that going for me. Still, you should have said. It would have been nice to know the pretty girl noticed me first."

I squinted at him. That was his takeaway? Not that I should have been more upfront? There was more to say, but this was enough for now. I didn't want to push my luck.

"You're so smooth with the flirting," I said instead.

"It's a gift. Is it a problem?"

"No. My family will be surprised, though. You aren't the typical guy I go out with."

Levi angled toward me this time and rested one broad

shoulder against his seat. His shirt showed a bit of wear in spots, and I'd bet it was soft. It smelled like leather and clean laundry. "What *is* the typical guy you date?"

"Oh, you know, the nonexistent kind."

Levi's brows shot up, and I wanted to pull the words back.

"I mean, it's been a while. Not that there never was anyone." Sheesh, I sucked at this casual talking thing. "There was a fisherman a couple of years ago who cooked a lot of fresh fish." I grimaced. "I don't like fish. There was an auto mechanic, and my car never ran better."

He chuckled. "Is that a euphemism?"

"What?" I barked a laugh. "No."

"So, what happened?"

I considered how much of the humiliating truth to reveal. Right now, I was anything Levi wanted me to be. Hundreds could want me, and I was simply choosy. I could only be interested in hookups with no strings. I was a fantasy, not a woman dumped because she wasn't worth the effort, because she was bad at sex. Every truth revealed threatened the fantasy version of me, and I wasn't ready to let it go.

"Do you really want to talk about my past rela-tionships?"

"As your boyfriend,"—he quirked a single brow above his dancing blue-gray eyes— "I think it's some-thing I should know."

Jeez those eyes. And *boyfriend*. No zings, girl parts. No zings. They didn't listen.

I went with the reason my exes *said* things ended, because what sort of asshole would tell the truth? "My job is important to me. If I'm needed, I go. It's what I do."

"And the guys had a problem with that?"

I sighed. "Among other things. Maybe I do value my work too much. It's fine. I'm fine."

He blinked at me in the silence that descended before his expression brightened. "Not this week. This week, you're going to be way better than fine. With this boyfriend—" he waggled his brows "—your *job* is to have fun."

I gave him a side-eye.

"What? I'm thinking of swimming and hiking. What are you thinking about?" He brushed the hair back from his forehead.

"Your flirt game is like professional level. You may want to reel it in before I swoon."

"Would you swooning be so bad? In fact, I'd like to see you swoon. Challenge accepted."

"Levi."

"Okay, okay." He relaxed back in his seat. "I'm just glad you aren't a doctor. That could have been a deal breaker."

"Why?"

"I only know one doctor who's a decent person, and that's my friend Jonah," he said.

"I thought you said your dad was a cardiac surgeon."

"He is."

4

LEVI

THANK FUCK THE SEXY, SOFT BRUNETTE WASN'T A doctor. Most doctors I knew, including my father, were entitled assholes who only cared about themselves. Plus, hospitals still had a hierarchy, and working in a hospital in anything other than patient care had a sort of second-class citizen tag.

I had a hard rule. No medical staff. I didn't need to prove myself professionally to anyone, especially on a date.

But not noticing Kate was a miss. I'd included nurses in my rule, but now that I'd seen this one, I couldn't unsee her. And the universe, or fate or whatever, was giving me a second chance.

I had a week with her on a beautiful tropical island. Vacation flings happened. And Kate seemed like she could use one. I knew I could. Today's sundress, paired with another matching cardigan, sealed the deal.

Her small breasts sat high and firm, with the top of her dress hinting at the shallow valley between them. I loved that valley. I wanted to press my nose to it and inhale her sweet scent. Something about her just did it for me.

I'd even confessed to being a hacker in high school, and that was more than I'd shared with any woman in years. Not even the ones I'd shared some pretty intimate things with. Women I'd tasted and heard scream my name. Our unusual circumstances had to be throwing me off.

Her soft brown eyes were guarded as she tried to hide the hurt when talking about her exes. It made me want to rush in and treat her gently because somebody somewhere hadn't. She'd trusted the wrong people and paid a price. I could relate.

We kept talking, covering the basics about our families, our college years, and more. First date stuff. I told her about mountain biking, my favorite hobby. Kate didn't seem to have much room for hobbies with her work.

"Traveling to a doctor's office isn't reasonable for most of my patients. It's easier for me to go to them," she explained. "And there are perks, like baked goods and casseroles."

"It sounds very wild west."

"It can be. I've delivered a few babies."

"That must be a rush," I said, unable to keep the admiration out of my voice.

"Yeah. And a little terrifying. A lot can go wrong, and there's only so much I can do in the field. I'm never happier to hear the hospital transport team's arrival than after an emergency birth. Those helicopters are fully equipped."

"Impressive," I said as Patricia served our breakfast. You had to love first class.

"I hope you're not a vegetarian." Her words were quick with alarm as she examined my tray. "We had to stick with Kristen's order. If you'd rather have my vegetable frittata, you can."

"I'm not a vegetarian, and if I were, I wouldn't take yours. That's a dick move, boyfriend or not."

"Well, you *are* doing me a favor here. The least I can do is give you my breakfast. Escorts get paid a lot to do this."

I choked on my laugh. "I'm not an escort." I scooped up a bite of eggs and sausage. It wasn't too bad.

"No, no," she stammered. "That's not … it's just. I appreciate what you're doing, especially if you recently broke up with someone."

I paused with my fork halfway to my mouth again and faced her. "Why do you think I broke up with someone?"

"Oh, well"—more stammering— "I've seen you eating lunch with the same woman a few times. But then you're here … as my date, my fake date." Her eyes went wide, and she gasped. "Oh, you didn't break up. Right. This is fake. And if I looked like her, I'd be pretty secure, too."

I chuckled, watching her brain switch topics so rapidly. "Kate, I'm single. The only woman I have lunch with these days is my sister. You talked to her on the phone. And if I *was* with someone, I wouldn't go on a date to Hawaii with someone else, fake or not. I'm seriously worried about the men in your past."

She blinked, and the smile she tried to hide told me she was pleased with my relationship status. Kate was interested.

Her shoulders relaxed. "She's gorgeous. I thought you were dating a supermodel."

"No, not dating my sister. Not dating anyone, and I haven't had a girlfriend in years."

She looked at me with a puzzled expression.

"And as for doing you a favor, I volunteered. You're taking me on your trip to paradise. If anything, you're the one doing the favor. Plus, I'll be saving you from your sisters, and I like to do some saving. Makes me feel important." I winked at her.

Her smile grew as she glanced at me through thick lashes. "I'm not a vegetarian either. This just sounded good."

"Then enjoy it. You want some of mine?"

She laughed. "No, but thanks."

My first assessment of Kate was dead accurate. She was good and sweet and tough, wrapped in a soft and sexy package. Getting sucked in by her was inevitable. There was no way to fight it. So, I'd make this the best fucking vacation fling ever, for both of us.

Our conversation continued after breakfast until she yawned, surprising herself.

"You can take a nap," I said, grinning. "I think we covered enough ground to take on your family. Plus, I have my book."

"Flash that dimple and Patricia will bring you anything you want." She waggled her brows at me.

She liked my dimple. I made a mental note and looked closer. It wasn't jealousy in her bottomless brown eyes, but maybe possessiveness. I didn't hate it.

"I'm not on a *date* with Patricia, so I'll reserve the flashing of dimples … or anything else for you."

Kate rolled her eyes, but not before the tiny pulse in

her neck let me know she'd heard my tease, and *she* didn't hate it. More good news for me. This date kept getting better and better.

I grabbed my book as Kate settled and closed her eyes for the last leg of the flight. After about twenty minutes, she rolled from her position facing the window and shifted her body toward me. I'd rested my arm on the wide console between us, and as she curled into a ball, her head came to rest in the crook of my elbow.

Her hair fell across my skin, and her cheek was soft as silk. It made me wonder about the softness of her body in other places.

Held captive and happy about it, I closed my book, ordered a beer, worked word puzzles on my phone with my free hand, and let Kate sleep exactly as she was until the announcement of our approach to Kona woke her.

"Are we there?" She sat up, rubbing her eyes.

"We are," I said gently and flexed my fingers to encourage the flow of blood back to my hand.

"Oh, goodness," she said, trying to surreptitiously wipe a bit of saliva that had pooled at the edge of her lip. "I slept on your arm."

"You did."

"I'm sorry."

I smiled at her sleepy expression. I wasn't a bit sorry.

THE SUN WAS MIDDAY BRIGHT, the air warm and salty as we descended the stairs from the plane onto the tarmac. The airport had fewer than ten gates, so the trip to baggage claim was short. The line at the rental counter was longer, but this was Hawaii. I'd rather stand in line here than do most things somewhere else.

I used my phone to check all my favorite outdoor adventure businesses. This trip would be epic. Loaded into the Jeep she rented, we headed to the house where we were staying the week with her family.

"Is our time packed with wedding events?" I asked.

"No. We should be able to get away each day for at least a while. My sister texted the itinerary this morning."

"What do you want to do first?" I asked.

"Shower."

I grinned at her. "That's fast. But I'm into it if you are."

She shook her head but didn't take her eyes off the road. "Is flirting like a second language with you?"

"You're my girlfriend, and I like to flirt with my girlfriend."

She gripped the wheel tighter. "You're right. Okay. I'll try to get used to it."

"Do you really not like flirting, or have you been around men who were bad at it?"

"Not sure. I never knew Pete was flirting. Maybe there were others."

"Kate, I'm sure men fall all over themselves to get your attention." I was one of them.

"*That's* a bit much, but thanks. I'll be prepared next time. For you, I mean. Your flirt game."

"Good, because I'm just getting warmed up, *babe*."

The curve of Kate's smile grew. She liked that idea. Yep, better and better.

"Where is this house?" I asked, studying the large navigation screen on the dashboard as we wound through a neighborhood of small homes among densely packed plants and flowering trees.

"Near the top of this mountain, I think."

A text notification dinged, and Kate glanced at the screen then handed the phone to me. "Can you answer that? If I don't respond, he'll keep texting even though he's probably already called the airline and gotten all our flight information."

A group chat titled *Hawaii for Ten* was highlighted.

Dad: Did you land? The airline said you landed.

"He wants to know if we landed," I told her.

"Tell him we're up the mountain and almost there," Kate instructed, and I typed out the response.

Another ding.

Dad: The code is 0421#, Jill's birthday, if you forget.

"He sent a code," I said as we rounded the last curve and turned onto a black, paved driveway with an ornate iron gate surrounded by more thick trees, banana plants, and greenery as if it were a portal into the jungle. Easing forward to the box, she punched in the numbers, and the black iron bars swung open without a sound.

Kate flashed an anxious smile, and we rolled forward on a long strip of dark asphalt caged in on both sides by jungle until it opened to a manicured lawn carefully bordered by a low row of bright pink and orange flowers. The white stucco house with a turquoise metal roof was immense. A long single-level ranch that stretched across the hillside.

The circular drive wound around a large palm tree and colorful bushes planted at the center. A thick canopy of trees surrounded three sides of the house and waved in the light breeze along with the palm trees dotting the tiered landscaping. It looked more like a resort hotel than a house.

"Kate, is this your family's place?"

A bark of laughter escaped. "Um, that's a no. A hell no." She double-checked the address and looked around. "This has to be it."

She switched off the car and reached for the door handle. I'm not sure she blinked, taking it all in.

"Katie!" called an older man, rushing toward us with his arms wide. He was tall and a bit soft in the middle, with a salt-and-pepper beard.

"Dad," Kate said, her smile just for him as she stepped into his embrace. A petite woman with long black hair and sun-kissed skin stopped next to Kate's dad and reached out for a hug.

"Aloha," she greeted and placed a flower lei around Kate's neck.

"What is this place?" Kate asked the woman I assumed was her stepmom based on her description earlier.

"The house belongs to a client of Steven's," she said, like it was a secret. "It's unbelievable. Plus, there's a cleaning service on call and a chef who lives right up the hill." She gestured to the lush green expanse behind us. No other houses or structures were visible through the surrounding trees, thick like the walls of a fortress.

"This must have cost a fortune," Kate said.

A blond man in his thirties stepped forward in brightly colored board shorts and a short-sleeved button-up shirt left open like a jacket. "It's on me."

"That must be some client, Steven," Kate said, giving the man she said was her brother-in-law a cool hug.

"Oh, he is. Of course, I'm not at liberty to name names."

"I wouldn't dream of asking." Kate's voice was high and breathy in a way I hadn't heard before. I didn't like it. I preferred the sultry timbre of her regular voice.

"Just don't look too closely at the *Marvel* movie posters in the screening room for similarities." He waggled his brows.

First impression? Steven was a bit of a douche.

Kate turned to me. "Everyone, this is Levi Abrams … my … boyfriend."

There was a beat of silence as the group rotated in unison to face me. I smiled and stepped forward. "Mr. Wells, Sir. It's a pleasure to meet you."

"Call me Phillip," the man said, shaking my hand and sizing me up as any father would when meeting a boyfriend he hadn't heard of before. He wrapped his arm around the petite woman next to him. "This is my wife, Mei.

"Ma'am," I said with a nod.

"None of that." Without warning, she reached out to wrap me in a quick hug. "Aloha to you too," she said and gave me the same lei treatment. She kept her focus trained on me but spoke to Kate. "I thought you were bringing Kristen."

"Change of plans." Kate's expression was bright but uncertain.

I pulled her close to my side and tried not to react to how right she felt there. "We work together and were keeping things between us quiet. But I finally talked her into going public. When Kristen offered to let me take this trip instead of her, I couldn't resist."

5
___

KATE

Levi looked like there wasn't anywhere else he'd rather be as he shook hands with everyone. And I kinda loved him for it. My family didn't even try to hide their surprise that I'd brought a man to an event for the first time, especially one as handsome and confident as Levi. My fake boyfriend was killing it.

"So, you're a doctor," my younger sister Jill said with a smirk that only accentuated her innocent, pixie-like beauty because of the contrast. "Well done, Kate."

"Sorry to disappoint you," Levi said, his voice strong. "I'm in IT. Information systems security. Not a doctor."

"But just as essential," I said. "If he doesn't do his job protecting the computer systems, everything from email to operating room lights could be at risk. He and three others basically carry the place." When I turned to Levi on the last part, his eyebrows rose, and a surprised grin curved his lips.

"I get it," Dad said. "You can be the best pilot in the

world, but if the mechanics don't do their part, it doesn't matter."

I smiled at my dad and Mei, the two people in my family I actually liked.

"Come in, come in," Mei said. "Let's get you settled, and then you can come out to the lanai and tell us everything."

Strolling inside, Levi gestured to me, and we both toed off our shoes by the door, adding to the sizable pile already there. "Hawaiian rule," he said.

When I looked up, it was like Dorothy stepping into Technicolor Oz. This house was perfection down to every detail. Thick, muted rugs covered cool, tiled floors in shades of beige and white in several spots. What had to be a hundred feet of the back wall was completely open to the view. The steep hillside down to the town, the shore, and the blue Pacific in the distance.

The long, rectangular great room featured multiple seating and dining areas. Those outside were closer to the steps that led down to an infinity pool with a hot tub and sun deck to the left of it.

The decorations were beachy but not kitschy, with touches of turquoise and aquamarine. Definitely upscale. Rich teak accents complemented the cabinets in the large, modern kitchen, which featured a wrap-around breakfast bar for twelve.

"This is *Hawaii for Ten*?" I asked. "We should have called the group chat *Hawaii for Twenty*. This place is enormous."

"Isn't it perfect?" Jill practically vibrated with glee. "The wedding dinner will be here in this space, obviously. We'll have the furniture moved out."

She strode through the broad expanse of luxury and

gestured to the large swath of green to the right of the pool and the gazebo at its edge. "The ceremony will be there with chairs fanning out on the lawn. We'll have high-top tables there for the cocktail hour. Flowers and tulle bunting in the breeze. After all the waiting, everything is finally coming together." She clasped her hands in front of her and glowed. "Don't you love it?"

She looked like a puppy whose dreams were coming true, mixed with Maria from *The Sound of Music*, alive in the hills.

"It's perfect," I said, keeping my voice light. And it was for her. With my older sister Janie and my mom involved, it would also be wildly over the top. Not my style, but definitely everything Jill could want. The bigger, the better. All eyes on Jill.

Janie strode into the room, her leopard-print maxi dress billowing behind her. She lifted her hand to her golden highlights, and I noticed a thick cuff bracelet had replaced the thin bangles that had once constantly chimed from her wrist.

"Kate, how are you? You look tired," she said and pulled me into a hug. "Rough flight?"

"Not at all."

She fluffed my hair like I was an awkward teen again. "I've got some eye cream to help with those bags and we'll get you a nice blowout for the pictures. I've already had the spot above the mantel in our formal room cleared for a family portrait. I want everything to be perfect."

Same ol' Janie.

I glanced behind me at Levi, standing with our bags. "Janie, this is my boyfriend, Levi Abrams."

My sister's gaze snapped to his, and she wove around

me, driving toward the man with focused intensity. "Well, hello. Kate didn't mention a boyfriend." She turned back to me. "Good for you."

Yes, a woman's greatest accomplishment, landing a man.

"It's nice to finally meet you. I've heard good things," Levi said without missing a beat.

"Oh really? What have you heard?"

Levi's grin was pure charisma. "That you're a dedicated wife and mother who makes beauty look effortless. Your fashion sense is impeccable, and you'll do anything to make your sister's wedding epic."

For the record, I said none of that, but Janie was eating it up with a spoon. Maybe I *should* pay Levi. He was a pro.

"What did she say about me?" Jill asked, practically bouncing on her toes. "I'm dying to know."

Levi faced her. "That you're a talented marketing rep who will make the most beautiful bride ever."

"Kaaaaate," Jill said. "Thank you. That means a lot to me." She put her hands over her heart.

"Levi Abrams?" Janie asked. "Any relation to the Hollywood Abrams? You certainly have the charm."

Levi appeared humble yet confident. "No."

"Oh well, it's probably for the best. Steven would have drilled you for information. He's in entertainment law, and his firm has been trying to land that account for years." She shot a glance at her husband standing by the wet bar.

"I heard you brought the kids. Where are they?" I asked.

"The game room with April." She looked at Levi. "Our nanny. Can't have a family photo without them.

Amelia is seven. Carter is five." With a sigh, she said, "They'll be in the pool soon, swimming off some of those chocolate-covered macadamia nuts that seem to be in bowls on every surface in this place." She waved her hand around the room. "At least the chef has agreed to use only organic ingredients for our meals. It's a vacation. I can tolerate some sugar, but non-organic food is a bridge too far. I know, as a nurse, you must agree, Kate."

Oh sure, if it were free or money grew on trees. Before I could work up a response that wouldn't start a fight, Steven handed my sister a white wine spritzer and guided her out to join my dad and Mei in the deep-cushioned chairs by the pool.

"That's Janie," I said to Levi with my eyebrows near my hairline.

His smile relaxed into one I'd seen before, the one he gave so easily on the plane, and some of the tension in my shoulders released.

"Mom arrives today too, right?" I asked.

"Her flight lands in a couple of hours," Jill said.

Well, at least Levi was getting a little time between meeting Janie and meeting my mother. Those two were so similar that meeting them in short order would be like a one-two punch.

"So, which way is our room?" I gestured to the broad hallways on either side of the large, open space.

"Oh, so, about that." Jill flashed a bright smile at Levi and motioned for us to follow her down the hall on the left. "There's been a minor change. Since Janie and Steven brought the kids and April, after all, they wanted the room with two beds. It's across from their suite."

"But that's the room I chose," I said sharply.

"I didn't think you'd mind. And with your man here, it's even better." She flashed a knowing grin at Levi.

"I mind," I said, my voice rising. We'd been here five minutes, and already Jill was calling the shots. I usually tried to get along, but that was *my* room.

"Kate," Levi said, calm as could be, while the blood rushing in my ears made him sound a mile away.

"Jill …" What did I say here? I'd told Levi we'd at least have separate beds, but I didn't want to give Jill any reason to doubt us.

"Kate." Levi again.

"I liked that room," I said, ignoring him.

She huffed and spun to face me, her expression resigned. "We have this house because of Janie and Steven. They wanted it. What could I do?"

Right. I sucked in air through my nose and silently chanted *just go with it*.

"Good news for you, though," Jill said, oblivious to my unease. "You guys get one of the primary suites on this side. It's *gorgeous*. But Dad and Mei have the other one, so keep it down." She winked at Levi. "Mom is in the other wing with Janie's family."

"And you?" Please don't be on our side of the house.

"Troye and I have the guest house below the pool. It's … very private," she said with her hand next to her mouth, like sex was a normal confidence between us. She stopped at a set of wooden double doors with an ornate design carved into the dark stained panels.

"The room is smaller than Mei and Dad's," she said, grasping the handles dramatically. "But the lanai has the same view Troye and I have, and the sunsets, Kate. Oh, my god … the sunsets"—she gasped—" they're spectacular."

Delightful. Me and my fake boyfriend can look at the same view, not having sex, while my sister and her fiancé bang it out below us.

This was not what I promised Levi, and I couldn't make eye contact as Jill pulled both doors open with a whoosh.

A giant king bed sat against the wall and looked out on a private outdoor seating area and the vast hillside beyond. Creamy walls, wood accents, and crisp white linens glowed in the sunlight and contrasted with the deep green of the trees and the royal blue water in the distance.

The floor was engineered hardwood with grain colors ranging from dark gray to an earthy brown, and it was covered with a plush, pale rug. From the artful seashell photos on the wall to the teak bowls displayed on the dresser, this room was perfectly appointed.

"This is amazing, babe," Levi spoke low into my ear and placed his arm around my waist like he had out front. I liked it. Boy, did I like it. A pack of butterflies took flight in my belly, and it was way more than a zing. His fake flirting was totally selling it and lighting up my body for real. I needed to get a grip.

Jill took both my hands in hers. "I'm glad you came, Kate. I was worried this might be … tough, but then you bring your man, and you seem like the same old Kate again. I couldn't be happier. Every dream about my wedding had you in it. You had to be here."

I rolled my lips against the rise of mixed emotions and mustered a brief smile before breaking free from her grasp.

"Your sister is right," Levi said boldly, changing the vibe in the air. "You and me, this room—" he flashed his dimple all slow and sultry "—sharing a bed was always my preference, even in the same house with your parents."

"Well, then." Jill chuckled. "I'll let you two … get settled." She waggled her brows and strode toward the door with glittering eyes.

When she was gone, Levi said, "She's …"

"A lot," I offered.

"Not what I expected."

"She's used to getting what she wants, more so now with the wedding."

He considered me, then took two strides and leaped onto the giant bed like a big kid, surprising a laugh out of me.

"What are you doing?"

He scooted to the top of the bed, lay back with an arm behind his head, and patted the pillowy white comforter beside him. "Giving your sister what she wants. Join me. This bed is awesome."

"What?"

"She expects us to be doing *something* in this bed." He grinned. "We can't let your family think I'm such a quick release that we're out there in minutes. Come on. Check it out."

I hesitated.

"At least help me mess it up."

This trip was so far outside my comfort zone I couldn't even see it in the distance. What was I thinking? Oh, right, I wasn't. I was being reckless.

In for a penny … I rallied. I may not be a pro fake flirter, but I could flirt. I put a hand on my hip. "Maybe I'm so amazing, you can't help but be quick."

The truth was more like I was so difficult that my

lovers usually came before I could. But he didn't need to know that. He was nailing *fake boyfriend*. I'd nail *fake girlfriend*. And Levi's girlfriend would definitely be hot in bed and give him all the sass about it.

He laughed. "Babe, I wouldn't be surprised."

I shook my head at his pro-level response and glanced at the brightness of life and color outside. When I looked back at Levi, he was like a dream. A flirty, hot, way-out-of-my-league man and a pristine bed. Nothing more reckless than that.

With two large, determined strides, I leaped onto the bed exactly as he'd done.

"Nice!" he shouted and pulled me next to him.

"Whew, it's been a while since I did that."

"And how did it feel?"

Euphoric. I sighed and stared at the wood-paneled ceiling. "Really good."

Too good, dammit. I liked Levi.

"Stick with me, babe. There's more where that came from." That's what I was afraid of.

6

———

LEVI

Kate felt good next to me, her head resting on my arm, inches from my chest, her soft body close, and the sweet scent of the flower leis thick around us. The suggestion that sex with her would be so amazing I couldn't hold back? Yeah, I believed it even though I had lots of practice holding back.

Her sister Jill was interesting. Based on Kate's description, I expected someone more genuine. Janie might be direct, but at least she was authentic. Jill was playing a part.

And she thought a family wedding could be so "tough" for Kate she might not have come? Why? Being the odd single at a wedding wasn't Kate's idea of fun, but she didn't seem like the type to let that stop her. Was Jill just underestimating Kate, or was it something else?

"Kate—" I started, not sure how to ask my question.

"I think I need that shower," she said abruptly, rolling off the bed. "Let's unpack."

I tried to read her but came up blank, which was unusual for me. There was definitely more going on here, and as much as I liked a good puzzle, if Kate wasn't talking, I'd have to respect her space and wait. Resigned, I nodded and helped her wheel our suitcases farther into the room.

She strode toward the en suite and froze. "There's no door."

I'd paid little attention to anything but Kate and the view since we entered the room, so this was the first time I'd noticed the large cased opening on the other side of the bed. Stone tiles in muted gray filled the space curving behind the wall that held the bed's headboard. A marble-topped counter with two sinks and multiple bouquets of exotic flowers rounded to the left. On the right was a large soaker tub and a double-sized rain shower, both butting up against a wall of dark wood shelves and drawers that parted to reveal a walk-in closet.

To the left of the closet was a door, which I assumed was the toilet. The only door that was necessary.

"What's the problem?" I asked Kate, her face broadcasting her distress.

"I promised you two beds. There's only one. And now, there's no bathroom door. This isn't what you agreed to, Levi."

"Kate," I said with a chuckle and leaned forward to catch her eye. "I'm good. We'll figure it out. We'll take turns in the bathroom. And if you're uncomfortable sleeping in the same bed, that sofa on the lanai looks fine to me. I love sleeping outside. But if you think *I* have a problem being in that cloud-of-a-bed with a beautiful woman, you'd be wrong."

Her expression was skeptical. "I'm not uncomfortable sleeping in the same bed with you. It's just … we're strangers … and I don't want to make this weird … for you."

"We're hardly strangers. I know you're not a vegetarian. I know you like coconut lotion *and* how you take your coffee. I know about your job, and I've met your family. You've met mine. I know how you drive, for fuck's sake. We're in like fifth date territory here, and in record time."

She chewed the inside of her cheek.

"You know all those things about me, too, except the driving thing. I'm great at it, by the way."

She huffed a laugh.

"We know each other well enough to sleep in the same bed. We could even cuddle." I lowered my head and grinned. "You've already fallen asleep on me. The natural next step is cuddling."

She rolled her eyes and crossed her arms over her chest, her expression bright but cautious. "Fine."

Was that fine to the bed or fine to the cuddling? Or cuddling with a silent but implied *naked* as well? A man could hope.

"This isn't weird for me," I said. "Stop worrying. Go shower. I'll sit out there on the lanai and not peek. Though I'm tempted." I winked.

"Ugh," she replied and walked to her suitcase. "I may never get used to your fake flirting."

Good. I didn't want her to get used to it, because I never said this was fake. That was all Kate. Now, I needed to convince her.

I DIDN'T INTEND to fall asleep, but I'd stayed after hours at work, making sure all systems were good. Then I'd been up late unpacking my Yellowstone gear and repacking for Hawaii and up early to catch the flight. And the mountain bike maintenance podcast I'd been listening to was not nearly as entertaining as the fantasy images of Kate in the shower.

That damn coconut lotion. I wanted to bury my nose in her neck and stay there. Wanted to bury my face somewhere else. Would she taste sweet like coconut?

When she lightly shook me awake, I was finding out in my dreams. I glanced at the fly of my jeans, hoping my semi-hard dick wasn't obvious.

"Hey. The shower's all yours," she said like a secret. Yeah, I liked her real voice, but it didn't help the jeans situation.

"Oh." I sat up. "Thanks."

Kate left to join her family by the pool, but not before I caught my first glimpse of her legs in shorts. Her supple calves and thick, rounded thighs looked soft. I wanted to smooth my fingers along the skin to find out exactly how soft.

I jumped into the shower and dressed in light blue shorts and a navy T-shirt, then finger-combed my short hair. My stubble was going on two days, and I considered shaving but decided not to. This was vacation.

Barefoot, I walked out the wide-open back wall of our room and around to the pool area. Two young kids splashed in the water while a woman I hadn't met sat at the edge, watching and giving instructions on swim strokes. That had to be Janie's kids and the nanny.

"Levi, have a seat. What can we get you to drink?" her father asked.

Glancing around the table, I said, "I wouldn't turn down a beer if you have it."

"Coming right up."

"I can get it if you point me—" I started.

"Nah, son. I'll wait on you today. After that, you're on your own."

"Sounds good, Sir." I gave him a single nod, and he strolled toward the kitchen.

A man in a branded golf shirt sat close to Kate's sister, Jill. "You must be the groom." I leaned over to shake his hand. "I'm Levi."

"Troye." He raised his chin and stared at me while we shook hands.

Who the fuck are you?

I'm with Kate. What's it to you?

I released his hand and took my seat next to Kate, not sure what to make of that silent exchange. I'd met a few overprotective brothers, but Troye wasn't her brother.

"Hey," I said, keeping my voice low and placing my hand on the back of Kate's chair as I angled to see her face partially hidden by her sunglasses.

"Hey," she said with a quick smile.

Something was up. "What'd I miss?"

"We were talking about all things wedding," Mei answered.

"And all things you and Kate," Jill added with a mischievous gleam.

"Great. Me and Kate is my favorite topic." I looked at her with a playful expression. She removed her glasses and showed me her beautiful, dark eyes, streaked with gold at the edges.

"Look at her face," Jill said. "Kate was all 'it's new,' and 'there's *nothing* to tell,' but that look isn't 'nothing.'"

"What look?" Kate's laugh sounded hollow.

Jill leaned in and whispered behind her hand, "*That look. Like you've already enjoyed the comforts of your one bed.*"

Troye cleared his throat.

"Well, it was a long flight," I said with a wink at Kate. I rested my hand against her nape and let my thumb smooth along the delicate skin where her shoulder met her neck.

She inhaled, and I swear her eyes darkened. Kate liked to be touched there. And she liked my dimple. And her eye roll was usually followed by her acquiescence. I was picking up on all her little tells.

Troye set his bottle on the glass table with a loud clatter as Phillip returned with my beer.

"Thank you," I said and tipped it to him before taking a sip.

"Are we still on the great seafood debate?" Phillip asked as he sat.

"I'm telling you, no ceviche," Janie leaned in and replied, her wineglass dangling from her fingers. "I don't care what the caterer says, raw seafood is asking for trouble."

"Janie, it's *my* wedding," Jill declared, then glanced at Troye. "I mean our wedding."

Troye worked up a grin for his fiancée before glancing toward me and Kate.

"Do what you want," Janie said. "But I don't want to hear about how you puked your entire wedding night." She sharpened her gaze on the pool. "What is April doing? That is not a butterfly stroke." She stood, scraping her chair legs on the tile, and strode toward the young woman.

Steven sat back like the picture of relaxation and

gave his head a slight shake. "Neither of our kids is bound for the Olympics, but don't tell Janie."

"My sister was a swimmer in college," Kate told me. "She won a state title and almost made the Olympic team."

"And has the body to prove it."

I choked on my sip of beer and looked at the man who was definitely a douche.

In front of her dad, man?

She's my wife. We fuck. He knows.

"If you need the Heimlich, Kate's right there," Steven said. "Fake dying always gets her attention."

He gave Troye a too-big grin, which the man returned with a grunt. "I really was choking, asshole."

Steven laughed. "Right. You'd been eying her all night, and your move was choking on a carrot."

"It wasn't a move," Troye ground out.

"This is how you met Jill?" I asked.

"No, Kate," Steven barked.

"Kate?" I looked at the woman, and those beautiful eyes went wide, a hint of hesitation on her face.

"You didn't know?" Steven asked.

"Troye and I used to date," Kate said, setting her jaw.

"Date? You were engaged." Steven again.

Kate had been engaged to the man her sister was marrying? There was the *more* I suspected. And it explained a few things. It certainly explained why her sister thought this would be "tough."

"It doesn't matter now. Everything worked out the way it should." Kate grasped my hand like a lifeline. Something pleading flashed in her eyes, and I threaded our fingers together for the first time, temporarily distracted by how good her hand felt in mine.

I liked her. And she'd been engaged to the man her sister was marrying.

Her *sister*. Fuck. How did that even happen?

I wanted to hurt Troye for betraying her. Wait. Did she still have a thing for him? That thought made me want to do more than hurt him.

7

———

KATE

Shit. Shit. Shit.

Was he mad? He looked a little mad. Was he one of those guys who seemed calm on the surface, then went bat-shit later?

But this was fake. There was no need to go bat-shit. Yes, I should have told him about Troye. I didn't. I'd apologize, and we'd be fine.

I knew he'd find out, but I didn't think it would be so early. Wasn't it rude to discuss past partners of a soon-to-be-married couple, especially if the past partner was sitting right there? I thought I'd have more time to devise a plan to tell Levi that Troye dumped me and moved on to a slimmer, sexier Wells girl.

Troy's expression was like a caged tiger since he walked in from playing golf with someone … I didn't care enough to remember who. He still had the fit body, the light brown hair cut to a sharp edge the military would envy, and the slightly longer incisors that made him appear a bit vampire-y. I'd been cordial, but we no longer knew each other. Did he think we'd chat like old friends?

Our friendship was in the past, and it was possible that friendship was all we'd ever had. We dated, yes, but his proposal was an impulse. He didn't even have a ring. He was moving, and he wanted security. I said yes for the same reason. Grad school was finished, and our futures were wide open. When he left Seattle to start his physical therapist job with Portland's pro hockey team, and I signed my contract with the hospital, an engagement felt like a placeholder. It wasn't.

My family has seen him plenty since he started dating Jill, but not me. I stayed a few days at Christmas and, blaming the demands of my job, was gone by the time Troye made it to Dad's for New Year's.

It wasn't a broken heart that kept me away, though I'm sure they assumed it was. I needed a clean break. Jagged edges tended to bleed longer. Seeing him around the *Yule log* each year did not sound like the clear separation we both needed to move on. Plus, I could do without yet another reminder of how I didn't measure up to my sisters.

"Sorry," I whispered to Levi, finally alone by the drink cart after the conversation at the table switched back to wedding details, and Mei and Dad helped corral Amelia and Carter to the side yard for a game of bocce. "I wasn't sure how to bring it up."

"You could have just told me." His eyes flashed, and his voice carried an edge. "Is there more to the story?"

I knew what he was asking. "I'm not …" I paused and put my hand on Levi's warm, solid forearm. The same one I'd used as a pillow earlier. "Let me be clear. There is nothing between me and Troye. We weren't a good match, and that hasn't changed. I don't want him, and there is no plot to win him back." I shivered at the idea. "Until today, we haven't spoken in more than two years."

Levi's expression warmed. "Glad to hear it because, as your *boyfriend*, I might have had something to say."

The tease in his tone settled my stomach, and I relaxed. "It's embarrassing. First, he's with me, then he's with my *sister*. Not right away, but still. It's a little too eighteenth-century-England."

Levi chuckled.

"I really am sorry. I should've told you. What a day of surprises you've had."

He wrapped his arm around my shoulder, pulling me to him. Tentatively, I settled my arms around his middle. Our first hug. Despite noticing the multiple sets of eyes on us, I closed mine and went with it, moving my hands along his strong back and sinking into the earthiness of his clean scent.

"We're all good." His warm breath blew across my ear with the whispered words. "I usually like surprises, but—" he pulled back, his seductive gray-blue eyes searching, and I got a bit lightheaded "—any other secrets I need to know?"

Another shiver, but this time, it was for a different reason, and I shook my head to cover it up. "No. Nothing."

"Good. This is you and me now. We got this."

"Hello!" called a voice from the front, startling me back to reality.

Jill jumped up and jogged inside, and Janie followed, motioning to April to bring the kids.

"My mom," I said to Levi as they passed us, and he

released me. I gestured in their direction. "Let's get this over with."

"I'm here. Let the party begin!" Mom shouted and gave out enthusiastic hugs.

"Oh, Kate. You've lost weight," she said when she released me. "Keep it up. I know there's someone beautiful in there waiting to burst free."

"More beautiful than she already is?" Levi asked, stepping to my side. "I can't imagine."

Take that, Mom.

"Oh." Her eyes landed on his chest before rising to his face. The effort it took for her not to scan the rest of him was obvious. At least she was controlling herself, which was new.

"Mom, this is my boyfriend, Levi Abrams. Levi, this is my mother, Cherie Wells."

"Ms. Wells—"

"Call me Cher," Mom said, her smile a little extra. "It's nice to meet you."

She turned to me with an elbow nudge and lowered her voice. "Good for you, Kate."

The door opened, and a man entered with two roller bags. "Cher, honey. Where do you want these?"

Janie, Jill, and I froze, our eyes fixed on the man who couldn't be much older than Janie. His dark hair was cut short, revealing the beginnings of male pattern baldness, but with his light beard and muscles on display in a tight T-shirt, it worked. My mom was fit, but a man twenty years younger was surprising, even for her.

"Oh, Sam, drop those anywhere and come meet the girls."

With an easy expression, he strode over, shifting the

car keys in his hand to the pocket of his casual pants. He reached out to greet Jill first. "The lovely bride."

Jill giggled, and I barely contained my eye roll.

Moving around the group, he offered greetings with no visible trepidation. Sam seemed genuine and grounded. What was he doing with my carefree bulldozer of a mother?

"Phillip," he said, greeting Dad like they were old friends.

"Good to see you again, Sam." Dad shook his hand. "Glad you could make it."

They'd met before? That was … considerate. How novel of my mother. I exchanged a glance with Janie, who raised her brows, indicating even she hadn't known about this development. Okay …

Turning, Mom looked around the luxury house. "This place is impressive." Her billowy pants and top flowed behind her as she swanned outside, the rest of us following. Her long hair, dyed a deep red, swayed as much as her hips.

"It looks like cocktail hour," she said.

"We're having POG," Mei said, nodding to Amelia and Carter back at it with the bocce set. "But ours has vodka. I'll get you a glass."

"I'll get it," I offered. Mei didn't need to wait on my mother.

I squeezed Levi's hand, a silent apology for momentarily abandoning him, and turned on my heel toward the kitchen. As I pulled the pitcher of spiked passion fruit, orange, and guava juices from the fridge, I heard footsteps behind me. Mom.

"I can get it," I said.

"I know, but I can help. Mei said there were snacks

prepped. We didn't eat much on the plane, so I thought it was a good idea, with cocktails."

I smirked. "How responsible of you."

She searched in the open fridge. "No one is more surprised than me."

ONCE WE'D SETTLED outside again and discussed Mom and Sam's recent trip to New York like they were just another happy couple, Mom turned to me. "So, you two, tell me your story."

My eyes shot to Levi. I'd avoided giving Jill any details earlier when Levi was showering because we hadn't finished fleshing out our fake history. And we still hadn't.

"We met at the coffee shop near the hospital," he said without missing a beat. "A guy was hitting on Kate, and who could blame him?" He winked at me. "She wasn't interested and let him down easy with so much grace I thought, there's a woman I'd like to know, even if I might not have a shot. So, I introduced myself." His smile was familiar and playful and impossible not to return.

"By the end of our conversation, I'd convinced her to take a chance. And here we are."

Huh. That was basically true.

"We've seen each other a lot since then. I can't seem to pry myself away."

Good Lord, the man had game. And his expression when he said that last part would make anyone swoon.

"It was the same with us," Jill told him and glanced at Troye. "Once you feel a connection, it's hard to deny."

The man shifted in his seat, knocking his knee against the table.

So, he was uncomfortable with comparisons to me and my new boyfriend. Boo, fucking hoo. When folks saw me at his effing wedding to my waif of a sister, there would be nothing but comparisons.

"Falling fast is new for you, Kate. I'm surprised," Janie said.

"Being with Levi just gets better and better." Another truth, and this time, *I* winked at him with a little smolder, and the curve of his lips ticked up like he was fighting it. If everyone thought I was talking about sex, that was fine with me.

By the time we sat down to dinner in the enormous rectangle of a room, the conversation on other topics flowed easily, in no small part due to the now-empty drink pitcher. The sunset was as spectacular as promised. The orange ball grew larger as it descended, then melted into the sea with a shimmering burst of yellow at the final moment. As bright pink streaked the sky, the warm evening air was scented with cooling earth and plumeria. Dad and Mei shared stories from their recent travels and the French cooking class Mei was inspired to take.

"Do you like to travel, Levi?" she asked.

"I do. Mostly to places with outdoor sports. Like here." Questions about his cycling and work followed. I listened, intent on learning as much as possible. It was clear in the way he shared about his sister and nephew that they were close, and I wondered what it would be like to be *close* to Levi. To lean into his care and strength any time I wanted.

"Dessert is limoncello gelato," the chef announced,

halting the conversation. He served the ladies first. Janie declined, of course. He looked at Levi.

"No, I couldn't," he said. "That was the best Mahi Mahi I've ever had. I'm stuffed."

He'd eaten most of mine along with his because I didn't want the chef to know my objections to fish. The poor man had enough to deal with in Janie.

"Kate will eat yours," Janie smirked above the edge of her wineglass. "She never skips dessert."

I beamed at my sister. "Jealous? I grew up with you. I know how much you love sweets. Does being a size four *really* feel better than ice cream tastes?" I savored the tart sweetness on my spoon, as if it were a lover, and made a little "mmm" sound in the back of my throat.

Clearly, the day was getting away from me if I was intentionally pushing Janie's buttons.

Her eyes narrowed before she flashed a fake smile and took a gulp of wine, letting the subject drop. Fighting with Janie on the first day did not bode well for my *just-get-through-it* mantra.

"Oh, that reminds me," Mom said. "The appointment for our dress fittings in Mauna Lani wasn't on the itinerary. It's first thing in the morning, so we should still have time to do some shopping after and have lunch."

"Girls' day," Jill squealed, and my stomach dropped.

"I'm good. I brought a dress."

"No," Janie said, taking back the upper hand she'd momentarily lost to me in the ice cream discussion. "We're having photos made, and since Jill and Troye aren't having a wedding party, we all agreed wearing a color that coordinated with the men's gray suits would be best."

We all agreed? No, *they* all agreed.

"A friend in LA recommended a woman here on the island, and she fit us in … for the right price," Janie said.

I furrowed my brow. "To make four dresses in a couple of days?"

"Of course not. She's almost finished with them."

"Finished? When did you plan to tell me?"

"We're telling you now," Jill replied. "And the dresses she made are gorgeous. You'll love yours."

Images of past dress fiascos flashed through my mind. Styles that looked amazing on Janie and Jill never worked on me. They were lithe, slim, with light coloring like Mom's. I was curvy with my dad's dark eyes and hair. Clothes that dazzled on them were out of place on my pear-shaped body. As a teen, shopping together had been, in a word, painful, but everyone else loved it, so I sucked it up and went along.

"What color?" I was almost afraid to ask.

"They're all shades of coral. It's beachy and summery. And we found a slightly darker one that should work for you," Jill said.

"Orange? You want me to wear orange?"

"Coral," Janie stated emphatically.

I felt Levi shift in his chair beside me.

"Dark coral *is* orange," I replied in a flat voice. Whatever. It was a dress. Except the wrap dress I brought for the wedding was a beautiful shade of deep emerald that enhanced my coloring, and the style high-lighted my curves. I looked great in it.

Maybe it was petty, but I wanted to look great at the wedding of my sister to my ex. I did not want to look like a tangerine with a sunburn.

I chanted *just go with it* in my head. Get through the week.

"I think you'd be stunning in orange," Levi whispered without a hint of sarcasm.

"No one looks *stunning* in orange."

His eyes were bright. "You would."

"Thanks." I rolled my lips and leaned close. "You're a good guy, and as a boyfriend, you're killing it."

He shifted, and the scruff of his jaw brushed my cheek with a zing. "That's the plan, Kate."

8

LEVI

After dinner and the discussion of orange dresses, the need to *get through it* rolled off Kate in waves, and my job here was clear. I'd promised to save her, give her a break from her family, and show her all the fun things the island offered. That started tomorrow. She said I was "killing it" as a boyfriend, and I intended to keep killing it. I'd make everything *tough* about this week easier.

Finally, sitting alone on the loveseat at the edge of the pool deck, we let the quiet night settle and watched as the inky dark sky filled with pinpricks of light. The day had been a roller coaster, bouncing between fun flirting, major confessions, almost cuddling, lingering glances, standoffs with exes, and judgy family comments. Good thing I liked roller coasters.

Kate giving her sister the verbal smackdown about ice cream was the highlight of the evening. Especially the way she licked her spoon while she did it. I tried not to stare, but fuck. What was I supposed to do when all I could picture was her mouth doing the same thing to my dick? And her little *mmm* sound. Jeezus.

I pretended I hadn't been thinking about it for the last hour.

"So, is Janie generally grumpy, or *is* she jealous of you?" I asked, my eyes still turned to the stars.

Kate huffed and rolled her head from side to side along the back of the sofa like it was all the movement she was capable of. The day was catching up with us both. "It's not jealousy. She's been low-grade pissed at me since our parents' divorce."

"Did you break them up?" I joked.

"No. That would be Raul. Or maybe it was Paul. I forget."

"Ah."

"The months before the divorce, me, Janie, and Jill just wanted a *normal* family, whatever that was. We thought if we did everything right, Mom and Dad could work things out. It couldn't hurt, and it felt like something we could control. Janie jumped in as de facto leader, pushing us to do better. Especially me. I needed to get better clothes, better friends, better grades. Then, when she left for college, I was busy making dinner, helping Jill with homework, and signing permission slips because no one else was around to do it. Doing everything perfectly was no longer on my radar."

"You took care of Jill?"

Kate nodded. "When Janie came home the summer after her freshman year, Dad had moved out. Unfortunately, her habit of *helpful critique* was unchanged."

"What about Jill? She must have appreciated everything you did?"

Kate shrugged. "I'm not sure Jill realized it. She's the baby. She's thin and pretty. Things work out for her.

She probably expects they always will because they always have."

Shit. Were her sisters ever in her corner?

I wrapped my arm around her shoulders and looked for a brighter subject. "Your parents seem happy now."

"Yeah. I don't see my mom much, but Dad's happy. He and Mei are great together. All he wants to be is her rock, and she lets him." A genuine smile appeared on her full lips. "What about your parents? You said they're still married. It's good then?"

I flopped my head from shoulder to shoulder, weighing my words. "Me and Ione, we don't have a great relationship with our parents. We play along and visit on the holidays, but it's all surface. It's one reason she and I are close. Dr. and Mrs. Abrams know what's best. Either you're on board, or you aren't. We aren't." I gave her a side-eye. "But I think they're happy, or as happy as either of them can be."

A few beats passed while I exhaled and rested my head on the back of the loveseat, silently staring at the sky again. "Thank you for bringing me," I said finally.

She huffed a laugh. "You're still glad you came, even with my family and the Troye blindside?"

I looked at her, not wanting there to be any doubt. "Absolutely. Your sister is marrying a guy who once made promises to you. No one needs to face that alone."

"I would have looked pathetic."

"You could never look pathetic, Kate. You're living life on your terms. It would have looked like you didn't need him. For some dudes, that's a kick to the balls."

She glanced at her drink. "I wish I'd kicked him in the balls." Her tone was menacing.

"Agreed, and I'm a dude. I don't say that lightly."

We both laughed.

"I am sorry he hurt you," I said.

"Me too." She squinted at me. "But then, looking back, I think he did me a favor. Sure, I'm alone, but at least I didn't settle for comfortable or convenient. I think real love is more than that."

I couldn't have agreed more.

The night air grew thick as the kids went to bed, and Kate's parents and partners went in shortly after with goodnight waves in our direction. Janie and Steven changed into swimsuits to soak in the hot tub while Jill and Troye stretched out on one of the double lounge chairs close to the pool.

They both glanced at me and Kate several times. I couldn't read their lips, but I knew they were talking about us. I didn't give one fuck. I was here, and Kate didn't want Troye. That was all that mattered to me.

I fought a yawn, and Kate stirred against my chest where she'd fallen asleep again.

"Hey, sleepy girl."

"What?" She sat up, rubbing her eyes with one hand.

"Let's go inside."

I pulled away and stood, reaching back for her hand to help her up. She let me thread our fingers together like I did earlier when she grabbed my hand the first time, and I had to fight the urge to bring hers to my lips. It was too soon. But every touch built our connection and got me closer to showing Kate there was nothing fake about this date.

Troye's eyes followed us as we rounded the pool to the back of the house. Jill and Kate exchanged good nights, and I lifted my chin to the man. He returned the gesture, but he was working hard not to care about my hand holding Kate's.

What an asshole.

In our room, the lights from outside cast shadows as Kate switched on her bedside lamp. "You can take the bathroom first. I want to grab a glass of water from the kitchen." Her voice was thick with sleep. I tried not to be captivated by it. I failed.

"You go first. I'll get the water and take the long way back." I winked. "No rush." I headed for the door.

"Levi …"

"Yeah?" I turned back.

"Thank you for being here. It's already easier because of you."

"I'm here all week, Kate. And I'm only getting started."

THE TIME DIFFERENCE meant I was up with the sun the next morning. Unfortunately, I hadn't woken to Kate wrapped around me like every rom-com movie promised. She'd rolled closer from where we'd started the night before, but not enough. I wanted to wake up to her sweet coconut scent, but I could barely make it out. I refused to lean over and sniff her like a creeper.

Instead, I left her to sleep and dressed in my running gear.

The air was cool and damp as I headed out beyond the gate to explore. I climbed first, saving the downhill run for the way home. As the air warmed and the world came awake, my mind cleared. An hour later, I returned to the house with a sweaty shirt and a head full of plans.

I refilled my water bottle and searched online for

snorkeling companies I'd used before. I checked on availability and hit the jackpot on the third try. Consulting the itinerary on the counter, I made a few more plans. This would be an epic week. Nothing tough about it.

The chef arrived, and after breakfast, including the best avocado toast I ever had, Kate's sisters, her mom, and Mei all headed to the large SUV that came with the house. Phillip volunteered to drive and promised to stay out of the way of the "girls' day." It was obvious he didn't enjoy being away from Mei.

"Are you sure you'll be okay here? Take the Jeep and go into town if you need to," Kate said, her words coming quick as she grabbed her purse and shoved her feet into flip-flops.

"I'm sure. I'll take a swim and sit in the sun. A little *me* time."

She chuckled and shook her head.

"Seriously, I'm good. It'll give me time to finish up the plans I'm making for us this week. Plans to take you away from all this at least a little each day." I flashed my dimple with a wink, and a quick smile of relief flashed across her features before she jogged out the door.

Steven, Sam, and Troye must have gotten lost somewhere because I spent the morning blissfully alone, swimming laps and then listening to podcasts on the pool deck in the sun. It didn't last.

"You and Kate, huh?" Plopping down on the edge of the outdoor lounge chair next to mine, Troye jumped right on the back of that elephant in the room.

"Yep," I said and tapped an earbud to pause my show.

Troye rested his elbows on his knees. "So, we're

clear, I love Jill. The only feelings I have for Kate are platonic."

"I hope so, or you'd be a real dickhead." I kept my focus on the trees and hillside below.

"You've been together a while?"

"Yep," I repeated, popping the P as I removed an earbud. Troye clearly wanted to *chat*. Fine, I had a few questions for him too.

"And things are good?" he asked.

"Great since the word go." I kept my tone casual.

"Huh. Okay. Glad to hear it."

I didn't believe him. "Why are you asking? You're marrying her sister. By the way, how does that even happen?"

Troy's expression hardened. "I care about Kate, her happiness, as a friend or … a brother."

"You're not her brother," I said, noting the fact he didn't answer the last part of my question.

"No. I know. But … Jill and I were worried about Kate and all of this, our history. Then you showed up, proving everyone has moved on, water under the bridge. It's a load off."

"I'm happy to help." I tried not to sound like a dick, but this guy pushed my buttons.

He hesitated. "Look, I know things with Kate … can be difficult."

"There's nothing difficult about Kate." I frowned. Kate was the opposite of difficult. "Maybe you were difficult."

"Is that what she said? That it was me?" Kate actually hadn't told me specifically why they split, but Troye was way too interested for it to all be "water under the bridge."

"Why does it matter? It's like you said, everyone's moved on. Kate and I are awesome. No difficulties anywhere. If you care about her *like a brother*, that's all you need to know."

Troye clenched his jaw and nodded. "Good. Then … good."

What the fuck were we talking about?

"Gentlemen," Sam said as he approached with a rolled mat under his arm, oblivious to the ton of awkwardness that had settled between me and Troye. "Join me for yoga?" He gestured toward the gazebo at the edge of the lawn.

"I'm in the middle of a podcast," I replied and pointed to my earbuds, hoping Troye would take the hint too.

"No thanks," Troye said to Sam, who nodded and strolled to the side yard as the music playing in the background switched from indie-rock to pop with a loud burst in volume.

Steven strolled past us in a pair of swim trunks and threw a pile of towels on a chair at the edge of the pool. "I've got you set up here, April," he shouted behind us.

I turned as Kate's niece and nephew jumped onto Troye's lap and legs. "Uncle Troye, come play basketball in the pool!" Carter demanded.

"In a minute. I need to catch my breath." He feigned being knocked sideways by the two small humans, making them giggle and changing the vibe. Thank fuck.

April strolled past with a wave and headed toward the chairs. I'd learned at dinner last night that she'd recently earned her degree from UCLA and was working as a live-in nanny to save money for grad school.

Steven helped her unload the stuffed swim bag she carried, his eyes roaming every inch of her exposed skin as he said something to make her laugh. Bold, but then douches gotta douche. April was pretty, and young, and Steven was married.

She appeared to be either unaware of or unfazed by Steven's added attention as she found a bottle of sunscreen and gestured toward Carter.

"He's a walking sexual harassment case," Troye said with a frustrated exhale. "It's assholes like him always trying to get away with something that make everything harder for the decent guys."

Decent guys … like Troye? Sure.

9

KATE

Levi: Name 4 cool things that are orange.

Me: ???

Levi: 4 things that are orange and also cool. Like oranges. They are delicious and good for you and orange.

I smiled at my phone.

Me: Peaches, apricots, pumpkins, kumquats.

Levi: Kumquats for the win!

Levi: But you forgot sunsets and basketballs.

Me: Basketballs are awesome?

Levi: Of course. All you need is a basket on a pole and you have a sport, exercise, and competition. Awesome.

Me: I only play basketball in the pool.

Levi: Oh, it's on Wells. You're going down in pool basketball.

Levi: Did I forget to tell you I played a little water polo in HS?

Yes, he did, and now I pictured high school Levi shirtless in a swim cap and goggles.

Me: Not scared. I've been playing my entire life. Growing up in AZ, every house had a pool, and every pool had a net.

Me: Did you bring the Speedo?

Levi: You wish.

I chuckled, and Jill looked over from where she sat next to me. "Something to share?"

"Levi." I lifted my phone.

"I like him," Mei said from the front seat. Yeah, I did too.

Levi: How's shopping?

Me: Finished. We're heading back.

Levi: Is the dress all you thought it would be?

I rolled my eyes inwardly but couldn't contain the laugh bubbling up. Laughter after shopping with my sisters. That was new.

Me: Soooo much more. [Devil emoji]

Levi: Describe.

Me: They were all different, but mine was a sheath, like Janie's, plain and boxy. Too loose on top, threatening to flash the girls. Stretched to nearly splitting at my hips. Shocker.

Me: Jill suggested I not sit while wearing the dress. Janie said actresses do it all the time.

Me: #notanactress

Levi: Just stand for hours?

Me: Yep.

Levi: Tell me that's not the plan.

Me: No. Mei suggested adding a fuller skirt and a thick band at my waist.

Thank God for Mei.

Me: Gotta highlight the waist and above because these hips don't lie.

Dots danced and paused. Oops. Was that too much?

Levi: Needed a minute there. No, babe, they sure as hell do not.

I bit my lip. Maybe I wasn't so bad at flirting—fake flirting.

Me: What's the plan for the afternoon? I need a break. Lives may be at stake.

It was visions of his smile this morning with the dimple and all the ways I wanted him to *take me away from all of this* that had gotten me through. They gave my brain something to do besides imagine smacking a sister with a bolt of tulle.

Levi: I've got the perfect first adventure set up.

Me: Where are we going?

Levi: Wait and see. [gift box emoji]

"Snorkeling?" I asked as Levi led me down the gangplank toward The Frog Man snorkel tours. He wore blue striped board shorts and a plain white T-shirt, which clung to the lean muscles of his upper body. But it was the polarized aviators that transformed him into a cologne ad. Some guys looked douchey in those glasses, but not Levi. He was like *Oh hey, I always look this good, and I happen to have these sunglasses on too.*

"Have you ever been?" he replied.

"No. Is it hard?" I pulled at the loose cotton swim cover I wore with a pair of cutoffs over my new purple bikini. Most people considered me adventurous because of my work. Not true. Regardless of my recent *reck-lessness.*

"Not even a little," he said. "All you do is float on the surface and watch the show below."

The crew walked us through instructions and the safety routine, and then we, along with thirty others, were off. Levi snagged two seats on a bench at the front of the crowded catamaran, and I set my beach bag on the floor there as others found seats on the netting between the pontoons or stood near the side.

Before he sat, Levi whipped off his T-shirt, and oh, there was his chest in broad daylight. I'd caught glimpses of it in the dark last night as he climbed into bed, but this was different, better. Lean muscles moved and shifted, drawing my eye to the lack of hair and tattoos. Just bare skin and flat nipples. I stealthily swiped at the corner of my mouth to check for drool.

"Need to even out my tan," he teased and reclined against the wall of the boat. "Join me."

I stared at him for a beat, the bright sunlight making his features stand out in shadow. His strong jaw and long lashes. His nose with an exaggerated bump like it had been broken more than once. The shadowy scruff that would likely be soft soon if he let it keep growing. Levi Abrams was male perfection, and many pairs of eyes were sneaking peeks at my fake boyfriend.

With a confidence I didn't feel, I stood and pulled off my swim cover, leaving the shorts on. I shoved both of our garments in my bag and leaned back next to Levi to soak in the sun as the boat powered through the deep blue water.

"Dolphins off the starboard side!" one of the crew members shouted.

Levi and I turned to see three dorsal fins rise and fall in the waves, easily keeping time with the boat.

I scrambled to open my camera app, and when I looked up, Levi snapped a shot of me.

"Hey," I said, grinning.

"Needed a photo."

"You'll miss the dolphins."

"I got the pic I wanted." He flashed that dimple and set his phone down before reaching into the bag between us for a bottle of sunscreen.

I snapped shots of the animals playing beside us, and when I turned back, Levi was rubbing the white lotion on his chest. He squeezed a small puddle into his palm and smoothed it over his shoulders and muscled arms.

It was a sex-dream-inspiring vision. Levi looked good rubbing lotion on himself.

"Want some?" he asked, holding out the bottle.

I blinked. Um. Yes …

"This sun is strong. You don't want to burn on the first day and ruin all my big plans for the week."

"No. No, I don't," I said and held out my hand. I wanted to ask about those plans and if any of them were naked. They wouldn't be. Levi was a good guy who said nice things and was doing me a big favor in exchange for free travel and housing in Hawaii. He was flirty and fun and could have any woman he wanted. We were friends. There was no reason to expect anything different. However, my imagination was struggling to keep up with the facts.

I pulled myself together and smoothed sunscreen on my chest and arms, but I needed to lose the shorts to do my legs. As casually as possible, I stood, unbuttoned, and slipped the cutoffs down. I stuffed them in my bag and quickly applied lotion to my ample thighs and hips.

Levi cleared his throat as I sat. "You … um—" he gestured to my chest "—have some streaks."

I looked down. "Oh, thank you," I said and rubbed the thick white lines at the edge of my top into my skin.

He pulled on the back of his neck and looked out at the water.

"You okay?" I asked.

"Sure," he replied. "You want me to … um, get your back?"

"Oh, yes. Thank you."

He took the lotion from me, and I lifted my hair, securing it in a bun with the elastic on my wrist. He rubbed his palms together and then smoothed his hands along my shoulders. My nipples reacted, standing at attention when he dipped his fingers under the bikini strap at my nape. I liked his hands on me too much. Blood rushed south despite our *friendly* arrangement, and my suit bottoms were damp in seconds.

When he finished, I faced him. "Now you?" I wasn't certain I could handle touching Levi's skin in my current state of arousal, but I wouldn't miss the opportunity. Unless I actually orgasmed while touching him, the situation in my bikini bottoms couldn't get any worse, and the chances of me orgasming anywhere were slim to none.

"Right," he said as if surprised and handed me the bottle before giving me his back. Faint tan lines circled his biceps, and I wanted to smooth my lips along the silky, pale skin on the underside. Instead, I concentrated on keeping my breaths even and applied the lotion down to the waist of his board shorts.

Touching Levi was as wonderful as you'd imagine. He was warm and hard, and from behind, I could make out the tapered shape of him, the indent of his backbone, and the symmetrical dimples above each scapula.

And though I'd never tell Kimberlee Van den Berg I knew how the muscles of his back felt shifting under my touch, I'd still know. Every time she looked through me in the hallway like I didn't matter, I'd remember, and smile.

"Thanks," Levi said when I'd dropped the lotion back in my bag.

"No problem." Except for the problem of my hard nipples and wet pussy. The cool ocean water couldn't come fast enough.

We reached our spot near the dark rocky cliffs along the island's edge, and the crew gave us more instructions as they handed out gear. Other snorkel companies were in the same bay, and people of all ages dotted the surface wearing life jackets or floating on colorful pool noodles rising like Vs around them. It did seem straightforward, and my excitement bubbled up. I could do this.

"You want to be my buddy?" Levi stepped beside me at the back of the boat, where other passengers were already sliding into the glittering water. His eyes held their usual flirty gleam, and I decided to practice more flirting of my own, learning from a master.

"I don't know," I answered. "One of them could be a good buddy." I gestured to a group of guys with backward hats and gold chains, laughing loudly on the opposite side.

"Huh, you're into college guys. Maybe Pete has more of a shot than I thought."

I chuckled and shook my head. "I may need to make a change in my dating life, but not a Pete-sized change or a college guy-sized one either."

"Change? Have a heart, Kate. You've hardly given me a chance."

I lightly pinched his arm and elbowed him away from the box of snorkels.

With life jackets on, Levi helped me secure my mask, and we put on the flippers.

"You ready?" he asked.

"As I'll ever be," I said and sucked in a breath for the short jump off the back ledge of the boat.

Cool water electrified my sun-warmed skin and Levi-warmed blood. Coming up for air, I blew the water out of my snorkel and turned my focus to something safer than a bare-chested Levi. The sea bottom below.

Dappled sunlight danced across the sand while colorful fish darted between rocks. The only noise was the ripple of water and the sound of my breathing.

Swimming slowly, I skimmed the surface as the current helped to carry me from one rocky outcropping to another until a hand grabbed my ankle, and my head popped up.

"You're supposed to stay with your buddy," Levi said, pulling me to where he treaded water.

"Oh, I got distracted. Did you see that angel fish?"

He smiled, his snorkel dangling on the side of his face. "I did, and I also saw some turtles headed that way." He gestured toward the shore, and I realized how far I had drifted from the boat. Oops.

"Lead on," I said and followed him.

Under the water, Levi stayed close and touched my hand or arm before gesturing to various fish, like an eel making Ss in the sand or a strange ugly one that looked like something left behind from the dinosaurs. He held two fingers to his eyes, telling me to look, and on his other side was a turtle floating leisurely around the rocks, dipping down and then coming up, waving his flippers gently in the current. He was the most peaceful creature I'd ever seen.

Keeping a safe distance, we floated and watched, Levi looking back to make sure I was staying close. I liked it, being with him like this.

With a huge gesture, he pointed behind me, and I spun, thinking shark, but it was another turtle, not ten feet away. I froze at the feeling that he was checking me out as he slowly moved past me, coming close to my body like he didn't have a care in the world.

"I thought he was going to bite me," I said after he passed, and we popped out of the water.

"He wouldn't hurt you. They're super curious by nature. Your suit is shiny and they like that, so he was probably coming to get a closer look."

"At my ass?"

Levi shrugged. "Hey, shoot your shot."

I splashed him, and a few drops of water landed in his dark scruff, then dripped down as he laughed, totally unfazed.

The next spot had a sudden drop-off at the edge of the coral, and the dark water had an ominous vibe compared to the colorful and sunny reef. This time, I stayed closer to shore with the starfish and anemones. And Levi.

"That was wonderful," I said once we'd climbed back on the boat for the last time. I grabbed two towels from our bag and handed him one.

"I'm glad you liked it. Today was a good day with the turtles." His bicep flexed as he ran the towel over his hair and then his chest before pulling on his T-shirt. I barely saw anything else.

What would it be like to kiss him? Would he pull me

close and press his firm body against mine? Would he reach back, like guys did, grab his shirt by the collar, and yank it over his head in one move, revealing all that muscle to my questing fingers?

The heat in my blood surged again. At least this time, my suit bottoms were already wet.

"Um, do you know when I pay?" I needed to get a grip on things before I embarrassed myself.

Levi grinned. "I paid already. I asked you, Kate. I pay."

"Levi—"

"Want a beer?" he interrupted, flashing that sexy dimple. "I'm gonna grab one."

"I don't expect you—"

"Kate." He raised his brows with a playful warning.

"Sure. Thanks." I nodded. And that's how I found myself soaking in the afternoon sun, floating on a catamaran off the coast of Hawaii, casually drinking a beer next to Harborland Hospital's *great white whale*.

10

LEVI

Purple was my new favorite color. Kate, wearing that tiny bikini, sealed my fate. My mouth went dry when she bent to remove her jean shorts because, fuck me, her body was sexy. That suit did nothing to hide the curves I wanted to explore in every way possible.

The whole sunscreen thing was next level. Kate allowing me to touch her silky skin, and taking my time while doing it. I tried to touch her as much as possible after that.

I stared down more than a few guys checking her out, especially from behind. Those suit bottoms covered little of her generous ass and the faint dimples stretching north from her thighs. Women thought those bumps were ugly, but on Kate, I loved the pattern of tiny dips like a topographic map leading straight to the promised land. I wanted to run my fingertips over them and then my tongue. Drove myself a bit nuts thinking about it.

Dinner with her family featured another stunning sunset, as Kate described our day. I barely contained my smile, watching her enthusiasm as she talked about all the fish and the turtles, their size, and the peaceful way they swam. She deserved to be enthusiastic. She deserved to be filled with light. She deserved an epic fling. And I was here for it.

I wanted her, and the look in her eyes when I toweled off on the boat said she wanted me too. It was on, but epic took time, and I refused to rush.

The evening was pleasant with a notable absence of digs at Kate, thank fuck. Steven was so impressed with our adventure that he suggested taking the kids snorkeling later in the week, but Janie just gave him a sideways glance, to which he responded with a knowing chuckle. Their relationship was hard to read sometimes, with Janie's quips and Steven's roving eye, but for some reason, I was about ninety percent sure that whatever they had, they were both genuinely happy.

Still dressed in our suits and shorts from earlier, Kate and I sat at the edge of the pool, kicking our feet in the warm water and sipping aged tequila like scotch, the golden color shimmering in the light of the tikis that edged the outdoor space.

"Wanna float with me?" Kate asked, nodding to a long, thin raft. She stood and pulled off her loose, white top, then unzipped her shorts before letting them drop to the tiled pool edge.

Once again, I said nothing as I watched, and my dick decided to join the party. Realizing her family was still milling around, I jumped up, whipped off my shirt, grabbed the float, and slid into the water before the situation in my trunks became obvious.

Kate piled her hair on top of her head and slowly descended the stairs like a fantasy. I grabbed each of our glasses before gently guiding the raft to her.

She stretched out in the water, resting her elbows on the float from one side while I did the same on the other. It brought our heads close together and gave me a perfect view of the rounded swells of her small breasts and that damn sexy valley in between.

I looked away, searching for something to take my mind off thoughts of her nipples. Troye and Jill rattled chairs as they sat at the outdoor table, reminding me how curious I was about what he thought was *difficult* about Kate.

"Can I ask about you and Troye?"

She chewed the inside of her lip. "Sure. What do you want to know?"

For starters … "How long has it been since you were together?"

"About three years," she said with zero emotion. "We met in grad school."

"And Jill works for the same pro hockey team?"

She nodded. "In marketing. Troye helped her get the job not long after he got there."

Uh-huh.

"Don't get that look. He got her the interview as a favor to *me* before he and I broke up that fall. They didn't start dating until nearly a year later."

Okay. "So, what happened?"

She swallowed.

"If you don't want to talk about it—"

"No, it's … I'm not good with long-distance, or long-distance isn't good for me. I didn't know that then, so when he asked me to come to Portland, and I took my dream job at Harborland instead, I thought *no problem*. Troye and I weren't kids, and Portland wasn't that far. My contract was only a year. I'd get experience, and dream jobs closer to him would open up. Other professional couples made it work."

"But it didn't work."

"No." Her tone was flat.

"Why?"

She hesitated. "Are you sure you want to talk about this?"

"If you want to tell me. I mean—" I looked around at the privacy being alone in the pool provided us "—this is boyfriend time. Couples talk about this stuff."

Doubt flashed across her face.

"Or they should," I added.

She sighed. "Sex."

"Good sex can't hold a bad thing together." I learned that from experience.

"And bad sex obviously can't."

What? I lowered my voice. "Bad sex? Did Troye have some kink you didn't like?"

"No."

"You?" That idea sent a charge to my dick.

"No," she repeated with intensity.

"Then how was it bad?"

"Me," she said and gulped the rest of her tequila, squinting as she swallowed.

"You?"

"Yes, me. It's always me." She let out a whimpering groan and lowered her forehead to the raft.

"Kate, I'm sorry, but I'm gonna need more information."

Her head snapped up. "How about you share something embarrassing now?"

"How about *you tell me yours, and I'll tell you mine?*"

She sighed. "How far back do you want to go?"

"All the way."

"I need more truth juice for that," she said handing me her glass.

I took it and stood in the waist-deep water. "I'll be back."

With two refreshed drinks, I returned and handed one to Kate. She gulped half the glass in one go and didn't look at me. "I lost my virginity in high school. I've had sex with a total of seven men. Some were more casual than others. Troye was the most serious."

"And sex with them was …"

She stared at me.

"I don't want to hear about dick sizes or whatever. I'm curious why you think it's always been you."

Kate licked her lips. "I can't believe we're talking about this. I barely know you."

"Not true, Kate. We've slept together. No cuddling yet, but I'm hopeful."

She laughed. "You like to cuddle?"

"I do, but we're talking about you right now."

She rolled her eyes. "I've always *liked* sex. With my first couple of boyfriends, it was easy, but then, it got … harder."

"What got harder?"

"I didn't always …" She held my gaze and lowered her chin with a silent message.

"Come?"

She nodded. "And when I couldn't, my partners … didn't like it or took it personally, were disappointed or frustrated. It was a problem."

I had to push down the part of me that saw her issue with orgasm as a challenge. That wasn't what she needed. She'd already had the caveman making her pleasure all about him.

"Did it start with Troye?"

"No, before," she said, her voice small.

"And it was a problem for him?"

She smirked, "I hadn't learned to fake it yet."

I frowned.

"I had to," she added quickly. "Troye was the first serious relationship to end because I couldn't come. When I started sleeping with the next guy, I didn't want to risk it."

The fuck? "He ended your engagement because you didn't orgasm?"

"Shit," she mumbled and looked away. "I did sometimes, but he wanted it every time. Expected it once we were long-distance, thinking our time apart would heighten the physical intensity. It didn't. He would probably say it was just the breaking point, but I think it was more than that."

Something here didn't sit right, and it wasn't the fact that Troye was a complete asshole. "Kate. You said it used to be easy. What changed?"

She looked at the raft, and suddenly, I wasn't sure I wanted to hear the answer to that question. Or I didn't want it to be true. But if I ever got the chance to worship all her curves, I needed to know what not to do.

"I had a hookup in college. It wasn't … good, and it sort of broke something. The next time I had sex almost a year later, it wasn't like before."

Anger simmered, but I kept my voice calm. "Did he …"

"No, no, not really."

"Not really?" I raised my eyebrows and fought to keep the outrage at bay.

"I said yes. I never told him to stop. I wasn't drunk. I thought he was into me. He'd been so sweet, telling me I was pretty, and he was *so* hot. Way out of my not-skinny-girl league. I wanted it. But when we made it to his dorm, he was sort of rough, or at least not sweet anymore. He finished quickly, and that was it."

"He kicked you out?"

"Not exactly."

"That sounds like 'not really,' Kate."

She didn't meet my eyes, staring at the water instead. "He was like, 'thanks,' then pulled on sweats and opened the door for me. I was still naked in his bed with the sheet pulled over my chest. I asked him to close the door so I could get dressed, and he was like, 'I gotta pee, see you around.' And he left."

Asshole. "You didn't finish, and he kicked you out."

"We had classes together and, based on the snickers and shoves from his friends the next week, I'm pretty sure I was a bet. Sleep with the fat girl."

Motherfucker. I wasn't a violent man, but I wanted a name and a location. Perhaps he needed a nasty computer virus. I had a few options in mind. Make no mistake, that movie *Revenge of the Nerds* was a cautionary tale. Don't fuck with nerds or the people we care about.

"I'm fine. I'm healthy," Kate said. "I eat what I want, including ice cream. I wasn't letting that little shit get the best of me. But … it was a while before I could finish again. With a partner, I mean. I finish myself whenever. But with a partner … it's still difficult."

She swirled the tequila in her glass and took only a

sip this time. I stayed quiet, not sure what to say yet, and not wanting to say something stupid.

"Okay, *boyfriend*. Enough about me. What's your number?"

I shook my head to clear the red mist of outrage along with uncertainty. "The number of people I've had sex with?"

"Yes. What are we talking about here?"

"It depends on what you call sex. I lost my virginity in college, and my dick has been inside the pussies of three other women."

Her expression sobered, and she blinked. It wasn't an unusual reaction. Most people expected me to have a higher number. I was almost thirty and single, and not a hermit.

"You look confused," I said.

"My number is higher. That's a first. And you're …"

"I'm …?" I ducked my head to catch her eyes.

"Hot," she sputtered. "Not an asshole. An independent adult with a job. You can talk to women, flirt. You should have numbers in the low double digits."

"Who says?"

Her eyes went wide. "Everyone?"

"Well, I don't give a shit what *everyone* says. It's my dick."

She said nothing and stared.

"It's simple. I don't have intercourse with a woman unless I have feelings for her, and I've only had serious feelings for four women. The number of women I've given an orgasm to, or received one from, is a different number. One I don't actually know, because I don't keep track. Counting them isn't the part I'm interested in."

She huffed a small laugh and looked away.

"There are lots of ways to make each other feel good. But I guess by *everyone's* standards, my number is four."

She met my eyes with her bright ones. "You keep surprising me, Levi. I'm sure no one ever faked it with you."

"Honestly, I don't know. I hope not," I said, trying not to imagine it. "I'd rather her tell me it wasn't working, and either we'd find something that did, or we wouldn't. But the idea that she thought she *had to lie* to get it to stop … shit." I shook my head. "That would be bad."

Kate was quiet.

"Hey, you had your reasons. I'm not judging you. I'm judging them for making you feel like you had to protect them. I'm not that guy."

Her grin was subtle. "My last boyfriend said it should all happen *naturally*. Which meant no vibrators. It was so important to him, and he said he'd never had complaints before. So, I made all the right sounds during foreplay, which was real. Then, when I sensed him getting close, I'd fake it. He was happy. I was happy enough. It was meant to be a short-term plan until I figured my shit out, but I never did."

I figured it out. She had a bunch of fuckwads in her past. Especially Troye. He dumped her because he didn't know how to make her come. And worse, he and the other fuckwads let her think it was something wrong with her.

There was nothing wrong with Kate. Women were all unique. The thing that worked for one didn't always work for another. But that was part of the fun. Trying *all* the things until you found the right one, like a sexy puzzle. My favorite kind of puzzle.

Kate took care of people. She took care of her family, her patients. She protected the fragile egos of her fuckwad exes. Who took care of her? Who protected Kate?

Nothing hurt more than knowing the people who should have cared about you didn't.

Our drinks were empty, and our fingers were wrinkled as everyone headed inside. I told Kate to take the bathroom first again because the truth was, I needed a minute.

I pulled the raft out of the water as Janie turned off lights and straightened chairs.

"Want some help?" I asked.

"No, I've got it." She studied me. "I'm glad you're here. Jill and I were worried about how Kate would handle this."

I bristled. "You and your sister underestimate her."

Janie stared for a beat. "You may be right, but you should know before you get too attached, her career always comes first, even before family. Troye needed more. Maybe you don't."

"Oh, it was Troye who needed more?" I huffed. "How would you know? Did you ask Kate?" I'd bet my new mountain bike she didn't.

Her brows rose, probably surprised I'd challenged her.

"Kate is good. Kate and I are good. And as far as her career goes, I'm glad she's loyal to her patients. Most people are only loyal to themselves."

11

KATE

His breaths were deep and even from the other side of the bed as I eased my body closer, seeking his warmth in the cool morning air. I wanted to press my nose to his skin and inhale his masculine scent.

I'd already been in bed last night when Levi came in, and I'd pretended to be asleep as he slid under the blanket beside me. After all I'd revealed, I needed to get my footing back. Maybe he did too. Our *fake relationship* felt a little too real last night.

I'd meant what I said. I liked sex, orgasm or not. The caresses, the kisses, the skin-on-skin contact. But knowing it was all a means to end dulled the experience. The idea that with Levi, those things weren't a warmup, but part of the main event, had my thoughts lingering in a very not-fake-relationship place this morning.

I wanted more. I wanted him. His hands on me, his scent on my skin, and his voice in my ear. But guys like Levi, who were desirable in every way, were out of reach for most women. It wasn't happening, and letting hope run wild only led to disappointment.

My body hadn't gotten the message, though, and I scissored my legs against the familiar ache at my apex. If I were alone, I could take the edge off, no problem. My vibe and my fantasy muscles were well-honed from frequent use since college.

But I wasn't alone. Levi's presence was the source of my arousal and the block to relieving it.

I needed caffeine.

Sunlight glimmered at the edge of the blackout curtains as I slid out of bed in search of distraction.

"Good morning," Mei said, standing in her pink robe at the sweeping breakfast bar. Huge white flowers dotted the pale fabric and matched the headband in her long, dark hair. "Coffee?"

"Yes, thank you." I accepted a large cup from her.

"There's cream in the fridge. How does Levi take it?"

A tiny zing fizzed in my blood because I knew the answer. I knew how Levi Abrams took his coffee. Another thing I knew that Kimberlee Van den Bitch didn't. "Black usually, but I don't think he's awake yet."

Mei's expression was knowing. "Trouble sleeping?"

Visions of how I wanted to *not sleep* with Levi flashed and fed the sizzle in my core. I mentally gave myself a shake and poured cream into my mug.

"Probably the time difference," I said and took a sip.

"You and Levi are joining us at the beach today, right?" Mei asked. "It's on the itinerary, and Janie booked us chairs in front of the Grand Hawaiian Hotel." Apparently, all the sandy beach property here was public, even in front of four-star hotels.

"That's the plan."

"Oh, your father was out earlier and brought these

back." Mei gestured to a pastry box on the long counter. "Malasadas. They're like jelly-filled doughnuts. Try some." She smiled, and her eyes glittered with the anticipation of me discovering something new. Mei never judged me about food. Another reason I loved her.

With a plate of sweets in one hand, my coffee in the other, and an insulated tumbler of coffee for Levi shoved in the crook of my arm, I headed back to our lanai.

"Morning," he said, squinting in the sun as I approached. He wore only PJ bottoms, and seeing his bare chest on the second day was as spectacular as the first, if not more so.

He sat forward on the small outdoor sofa and rested his elbows on his spread knees as I sat. "You didn't wake me. How long have you been up?"

"Not long," I said, trying to control the flutter of my pulse. Seeing him like this, bare feet, bare chest, his voice still husky with sleep, felt intimate. Awkwardly, I motioned to the insulated tumbler and the plate of sugary pastries. "Mei sent you some treats."

His face brightened. "Oh, my favorite," he said, snagging one.

"You've had these before?"

"They're a Hawaiian tradition. Ube is the best."

"Ube?"

He smiled. "It's a yam, but before you say anything, it's sweet and surprisingly tasty. It's the purple one."

He was right. Airy dough, the crunch of sugar, and a subtle not-quite-vanilla flavor were delicious. Or eating pastries with a bare-chested Levi was delicious. It was a toss-up.

He took a sip from the tumbler and winked at me. "Thanks for the coffee. It's perfect."

Ugh, that wink would kill me … or possibly my vibrator.

"Family trip to the beach today. Are you up for it?" I asked.

"I was thinking we'd join them later this afternoon. I made other plans for us this morning."

"Other plans?"

His grin was huge. "Ziplining."

"Ziplining," I repeated.

"Have you ever done it?"

"No." Never.

"Kate, what have you been doing with your life? No snorkeling. No ziplining."

"Oh, you know, school, work, bills."

He chuckled and popped the last of his first malasada in his mouth. "Not this week. There's a great place I'd like to take you, and I made a reservation for this morning. I figured we could meet your family at the beach after. That way, it's not an entire day together, for your safety and theirs."

I rolled my lips between my teeth. "I love that part, but … I'm not great with heights."

"You're not? Would you be willing to try? Once you're up there, you'll forget about it. It's too beautiful to be scared."

"Or we could go snorkeling again. I'm a natural at that," I said, trying to keep the hope out of my tone.

"You are. But you may be a natural at this too. How will you know if you don't try it?"

I said nothing.

"It's amazing. It's like flying." He lowered his voice. "Some say it's better than sex."

I huffed. "That might not be the high bar you think it is."

A spark of laughter lit in his eyes.

"Do I have to climb something?" I asked.

He shook his head. "You start out on a hillside and go from platform to platform. It's easy. If you don't like it, we bail."

"You want to go ziplining?" Jill asked as Levi and I made for the door with our beach bag and a picnic lunch. "This is supposed to be a family day. It's on the itinerary."

"And it will be. We'll meet you at the beach."

"Snorkeling yesterday. Ziplining today. Are you planning to take part in this wedding week at all?"

"Yes, but you don't need me every minute, do you? I went shopping with you yesterday and did the dresses. We'll be there."

"I thought you would *want* to be here," she said. "This wedding is a big deal."

Right. Eyes back to Jill. "Of course it is, and I'll participate. But this is boyfriend time."

She flashed a glare at Levi, who sat lacing up his hiking boots. "You realize it's high? Like hundreds of feet in the air."

I faked my bravery. "I do, but Levi loves it, and I figured out a while ago, that with him, I can do all sorts of things." Like flying to Hawaii on a fake date with the spectacularly hot guy from work.

. . .

He was right about the no climbing, but he'd failed to mention the suspension bridge swinging across a deep ravine that had to be crossed to get to the first launch spot. Well, maybe not swinging, but still.

"I don't think I can do this." I stood on the thin strip of boards, trussed up in my gear with heavy straps cinched tight across my hips and thighs, clinging to the thick rope sides of the bridge. This was a test. If I couldn't get across, I couldn't zip.

In front of me, Levi turned. "Look at me. You're okay. Keep your focus on me, or look up at the treetops. Don't look down."

Levi wanted to do this. He wanted me to do it with him. He was here helping me. The least I could do was try.

I sucked in a deep breath as the first guide reached the other end of the terrifying deathtrap and helped the family in our group move toward the first platform. The second guide waited behind me. I hated making people wait, but I couldn't just fake an orgasm and be done this time.

With shaking legs and my heart trying to beat out of my chest, I took my first tentative step, then another and another. The bridge shimmied with my weight, and panic hit me. "Levi!"

"I've got you." He grabbed my hand. "It's a walk. We'll go slow."

"Oh, god."

He squeezed my hand tighter, and his gray-blue eyes locked with mine. "You're safe with me, Kate."

Safe with me. His low voice was a rasp I felt between my thighs.

I licked my lips and sucked in another breath. "Okay, I can do this."

"You can. Hold my hand."

I nodded, and he led me across the world's scariest bridge.

On the other side, I exhaled a deep breath and finally looked back at the deep ravine we'd crossed. The sides were steep cliffs dotted with greenery and flowering plants, beautiful but deadly.

"I can't believe I did it," I said, shaking my head.

Levi's dimple winked above his huge grin. "You were awesome. I never doubted you."

I sucked in a gulp of air and let his encouragement settle my nerves.

The first zip wasn't bad. Only about twenty feet above ground as we sailed below a thick canopy of trees. Rainbow eucalyptus, with their colorful trunks, filled the fresh morning air with scent like the best room spray ever.

Each zip got progressively higher, but I focused on the tropical landscape as I flew above rocky streams and flowered hillsides. Levi was right. It was too beautiful to be scared.

At the seventh platform, I was confident and got too close to the edge as I unclipped from the safety line. I saw the drop-off. Not only below the zipline but below the tiny platform perched high in a tree. I could fall. My vision went wavy as my stomach dropped, and I yelped, clutching at Levi.

His muscular arm wrapped around me instantly and pushed my back against the solid tree trunk. His body pressed mine firmly against the rough bark, and his sweet, earthy scent surrounded me. I closed my eyes to drink it in.

"I shouldn't have done that." My knuckles were white where I gripped his shirt.

"Take a breath," he said. "Lean into the wood behind you." I closed my eyes again and let the sensation ground me.

"I can't move," I whispered.

"You can. I'll help."

I tried to concentrate on his words and his nearness, his strength and gentleness, instead of the horror of falling, as Levi guided my hand to grip the thick carabineer I needed to clip to the next safety line. "Stand right here," he said and nudged me to shuffle closer to the launch edge.

I cracked my eyes open.

"Look at me," he said.

I nodded and took in the various shades of cool blue in his irises. Beautiful.

"Reach up and clip in," he instructed.

I held my breath, my hand shaking against his as he guided it to the new safety line. The metal clicked as the complicated latch locked into place, and I let out a deep exhale, my heart hammering in my chest.

Levi pulled me into a tight hug. I clung to him and buried my face against his chest, close enough to feel his heartbeat with mine. His embrace was firm but not painful, and his strength seeped into my bones. The knots in my stomach loosened, and my head spun with relief.

He caressed my back with sure strokes. Not quite massaging, but not light touches either.

"Sorry. I was doing so well," I said when I could speak.

"You still are." He leaned away and met my eyes. "You're amazing, Kate."

I sucked in a breath. I *was* amazing. I delivered babies by myself, for fuck's sake. I got on a plane with a man I barely knew. I was here to watch my sister marry my ex-fiancé. Hell, I could do anything.

"Breathe. You've got this."

I nodded and willed my racing pulse to calm.

The next zip crossed another deep ravine, but as I settled and prepared to launch after Levi, I heard the unmistakable sound of a waterfall. When I flew past the thick copse of trees, it came into view, and I gasped.

Water fell from a cliff at least two hundred feet above, cascading over slick black rocks, frothing, and crashing to the valley floor below. Wonder and joy replaced the fear, and I twisted in my harness to catch every glimpse before it was gone.

It was exactly how I imagined flying would be. Exhilarating. Freeing. And yes, possibly better than sex.

I landed on the platform and fell into Levi's magical arms for another tight hug. "That waterfall, Levi, holy shit."

He squeezed me tight as I melted into him. "I knew you'd love it." His voice, close to my ear, was deep and rich. His lips grazed against my temple. *I've got you. Safe.*

After a few silent beats, he pulled back, his eyes lingering on my face. Our gazes met, and I could swear he read my mind. I was in his arms on a platform high in the trees with a view of the crystal blue Pacific in the distance, and all I wanted was for him to kiss me.

12

LEVI

I ALMOST FUCKING KISSED HER RIGHT THERE IN FRONT of kids and strangers. I wanted to brush my lips across those freckles at the top of her cheeks before I lowered to taste the mouth I'd been thinking about way too much.

The pulse at the base of her throat jumped, and she arched toward me almost imperceptibly before the guides directed everyone to get locked in for the next zip.

The moment passed, and we finished the tour, with the last run taking us slowly down the mountain. I tipped and shook hands with our guides.

"I should pay," Kate said.

"Again, I asked you. I pay."

"I can pay for something, Levi."

"Just say thank you, and we're good." She did, though it sounded a bit like a huff, which made me grin as we waved goodbye to the others in our group.

She was quiet as we walked through the parking lot,

and I asked cautiously, "Are you glad you tried it? Not too bad, I hope."

A giant smile broke across her face. "So glad. It was incredible, and I never would have done it on my own. Thank you, Levi. First snorkeling and then this." She shook her head. "Thank you."

My chest swelled. "You're welcome."

That pulse point in her neck jumped as her gaze fell to my lips. She was thinking about that almost kiss as much as I was.

"I wonder what Mei packed us for lunch. I'm starving," she said and looked away to take a long drink from her reusable water bottle covered in random stickers.

"You should have had more breakfast," I said as we reached the Jeep. "Those egg sandwiches were next level. I had three."

"Three!? Where do you put it?" Her gaze roamed my body with a depressing lack of heat.

I stood taller and flexed my arm muscles, anyway. "I burn it off."

Other ways I'd like to burn calories with Kate flashed through my mind. It was time to ramp up the romance. The *real* romance. "How about a picnic? I know a great spot near here."

"Sure." She paused. "All these adventures. The hug on the platform. A picnic. If this is you on a fake date, I can't imagine you on a real one."

The perfect opening to tell her how *not* fake this was.

"What's the wildest date you've ever been on?" she asked.

I grinned, hit unlock on the key fob, then met her gaze. "This one time, I went on a first date to Hawaii."

"Levi, I don't mean fake."

I stepped close and took her hand, my thumb grazing her soft skin. "I never said this was fake."

She frowned at me. "Yes, you did."

Slowly, I shook my head. "No, I said I'd be your date to the wedding. I didn't say anything about fake."

Her eyes went round as she obviously searched her memory.

"I like you, Kate. You're beautiful and sexy, and I like flirting with you. I think you like flirting with me, too. There's no pressure, but I want you to know I'm in this for real. I was since the cold foam latte."

Her forehead scrunched like she was working a math problem. "But you're so … wonderful. And I'm just … me."

I laughed. "If you didn't know, babe, you're pretty fucking wonderful, too."

Her stomach growled, and we both laughed, but she looked at my lips for about the hundredth time today. It was a promising sign. She just needed time to get used to the idea.

"Come on. Let's get to that picnic before the monster in your stomach eats us both."

She gave me a playful shove and rolled her eyes, her tell that I'd won. I barely contained myself as I slid into the driver's seat of the Jeep.

With our windows down, all was right in the world. We reached the curvy main road that ringed the island's edge, and sunlight glinted off the endless blue water. The sky was clear, the radio was low, and the smell of the ocean combined with the hum of the road was almost meditative.

Kate was quiet, and I could feel her thinking from the passenger seat.

"Can you pull over?" she asked suddenly, with something sharp in her voice.

"Are you okay?" I glanced back and forth at her while looking for a wide spot to pull off. She looked fine, focused, not sick or upset.

"By that boulder." She pointed, and I pulled into a spot barely wide enough at the base of a giant rock that looked like it had been placed there.

Kate slid from her seat and closed the door.

I slammed the car into park and rounded the front to face her, confusion warring with concern. "Kate?"

She stood fierce, but her hands fidgeted at her side. "Will you hold me again? Squeeze me tight like you did on the platform?"

Quickly, I moved forward and pulled her in. Rather than putting her arms around me, she held them between us, and I curled my body to hers.

"Tighter," she said.

I squeezed her closer. "Kate?"

After a beat, she exhaled. "I'm okay now."

My arms loosened, and she took two steps back. "You said this wasn't fake."

I hesitated, thrown by the downshift. "No, not for me. And not for you, if you don't want it to be."

She nodded firmly, and her eyes were a little wild before she closed the distance between us and kissed me.

It took me a second to catch up, but as her arms encircled my neck and she angled her head, opening for me, I got fully on board. I held her close and touched the tip of my tongue to her lower lip. So full and sweet.

She let out the sexiest little moan, but I didn't deepen the kiss. This gentle molding of lips and mouths was too good to speed past.

Kissing a trail along her jaw to her ear, I cupped the back of her head with one hand, and her tits pressed against my chest. She felt amazing. Her coconut scent made me drunk, and her body moving against mine made me as hard as that rock by the road.

"Levi," she said breathlessly.

"Don't think. Just kiss." I covered her mouth again, and she kissed me back, harder, wetter, with more intensity and more of those faint moans my dick loved when our tongues touched.

Yeah, I liked kissing her. I could stand here and do this as long as she wanted. When I finally licked inside, she met me for every stroke and gentle suck.

"You're good at this," she said between kisses.

"Back at you."

"So, we're at the kissing level of fake dating now?" Her breath panted.

"Not fake, Kate."

"Right. Wow. Real and still as good as the fantasy. That never happens."

I chuckled against her lips. "I think so too." I brushed my now fully hard dick against her center, and the whimper she let out almost had me pulling her inside the Jeep and lowering the seats. She made the best sounds.

I don't know how long we stood there, clinging to each other, our mouths either fused or exploring the other's sensitive spots. My hands didn't move from her back where I held her tight, even though I wanted to roam lower and sink my fingers into the soft flesh of her ass. Next time.

Once again, her stomach let out a growl that wouldn't be denied.

"So seductive, that growl," I teased as I kissed my way to her ear.

She laughed and pushed against my chest. Reluctantly, I let her go but didn't hold back my enormous smile as I struggled to pull myself together. One kiss. One long, phenomenal kiss, and I was wound tight.

Breathing hard, she leaned against the passenger side of the Jeep. "That happened."

It sure as hell did. "I hope it happens again … soon."

"Just kissing?"

"At least until it gets dark." I grinned.

A flash of unease crossed her face.

"Hey, I meant it when I said no pressure. You know my history and I know yours. If kissing is all I get this week, I still want it."

"Really?"

With my heartbeat returning to normal, I could think clearer. I brushed a finger along my favorite pale freckles and lower to her jaw. "There are a lot of fun things we can do together, and most of my favorites involve kissing you … somewhere." I leered openly at her.

She bit her lip and looked at me through thick lashes as all her hesitance evaporated. "I think I'm going to like *real* with you, Levi Abrams."

"If I have anything to say about it, you definitely will."

Back on the road, we found the small turnout with a view of the ocean and a short hike down to the dark, volcanic rocks below. Water swirled beneath a huge outcropping and shot up through blowholes in the rock like a fountain with each crashing wave. The first time surprised a gasp from Kate before she laughed.

We picked a flat area near the edge, and I opened the pack Mei had insisted on sending us off with like we were kids. My mom didn't do much of that when I was young. I liked it.

Kate and I sat, eating ham sandwiches and chips, surrounded by the sound of waves and birds, with nothing else. She asked about when I'd found this place, and I told her about an extreme sports trip I took with some buddies in college. There was a fantastic spot to cliff jump farther down the trail. Her head shook with a vengeance before I'd even asked if she was up for it.

The conversation flowed, but we both gave the other an occasional suggestive glance until the food was gone, and we fell into comfortable silence. I scooted close enough for her shoulder to nestle into my side as we leaned back on our hands. The sun was bright, and the air fresh. There was no place I'd rather be.

"I guess we should meet my family soon," Kate said, like she was heading for the gallows.

"Did you bring your purple bikini?" I waggled my brows.

"You like that one?"

"Hell, yes."

She laughed. "Sorry. I brought my one-piece and a rash guard. I read something that said it was better for the beach."

I sighed. "You're right. That suit is good for a pool or … hot tub, unless you want to go skinny dipping."

Her eyes flashed, and I added *swim naked* to my list of things I wanted to do with her. I didn't want to move too fast, but we were two days into our week, and that list was growing by the minute.

We spotted her family spread out across several bright blue double lounge chairs with umbrellas among the sea of others on the white sand below the Grand Hawaiian Hotel. Phillip and Mei were in the water watching the kids along with April. Janie sat on one lounger, rooting through the bag at her feet while Jill and Troye sunbathed on another. I didn't see her mom or Sam.

"Your charger isn't in here, Steven. And I can't imagine where you'd plug it in. We're at the beach."

Steven blew out a long breath and closed his laptop.

"Hey," Kate said, and Janie's head popped up.

"Where have you been?" she asked.

"We had a picnic after the zipline." Kate looked at me with a smile I had to return.

"Well, you missed Mom and Sam. They headed to meditation class at the spa, and I'm not sure how much longer we're staying. Steven's laptop is out of juice."

"This is supposed to be a vacation." Jill squinted against the harsh sun as she peered over. "Why don't you try to have fun for once?"

"We have fun," Janie said and glanced at Steven. "We have fun."

Steven hopped up and tossed his sunglasses on the cushion. "She's right, Janie. Care to join me in the water?"

"And get sticky and salty? I don't think so."

Steven leaned over the lounger and said, "Come on, you know how much I like to get you sticky and salty." He growled low and bit her on the shoulder.

I expected him to get a punch, but Janie giggled instead before she sobered, seeming to realize others were watching.

"Let's go, baby. I wanna watch those tits bounce in the waves."

Janie rolled her eyes exactly like Kate before she stood, dropped her hat on the chair, and let her husband pull her toward the shore.

"You can sit if you want," Jill said, and Kate lowered her bag.

I leaned close and spoke low. "I don't know, babe. Steven might have the right idea."

She smirked, "You're out of luck. These tits don't bounce."

"Oh, you're wrong about that." I waggled my brow. "But you may not be watching as much as I am."

Troye stood and stretched dramatically, catching everyone's attention. "I'm getting in. It's hot as hell out here."

13

———

KATE

My boobs didn't bounce. Did they?

He leaned close to whisper, "I've seen you in that purple bikini. And when I say I've seen you, I mean I couldn't take my eyes off you. Yes, those perfect tits bounce."

Perfect tits? Not too small? A blush rose on my cheeks. Screw it. For this week, I had perfect tits, bitches.

I wanted to kiss him again. I hadn't since that one by the side of the road. It was reckless, but I was *not* sorry. That was an epic kiss I felt in my toes. Not because it was hard, but because it was soft and then hard, hungry and then sweet. He changed the tempo, nipped my lips, and trailed kisses along my neck to my nape, where I was super sensitive. I could have kissed him for hours by the side of that road. I never knew kissing could be like that.

Levi looked behind us. "Restrooms are there. Let's get changed. These boogie boards won't ride themselves." He dropped the boards he'd found in the mudroom this morning and nodded for me to follow him.

I changed quickly, shoved my dry clothes into my bag, and took a beat to check myself in the mirror. My navy one-piece suit was cut high on my hips to help elongate my legs, but there was still plenty of thigh and ass there. I tugged on the hem of the white long-sleeved rash guard, hoping it would cover a bit and help to distract the eye from my cellulite. Oh well. Couldn't do much about that now.

Levi waited for me outside the door of the women's side. I opened the big bag, and he shoved his shorts and T-shirt inside, then took the whole thing from me.

"I can carry it," I told him.

"So can I." He smiled behind his sexy aviator sunglasses and slung the bag over his shoulder, completely rockin' the boho-style quilted rainbow fabric. With his broad shoulders and muscular arms visible under the skin-tight navy rash guard, I doubt anyone actually noticed the bag.

Taking my hand, he led me back to the chairs, dropped our things, and grabbed the boogie boards.

"Let me guess. You've never done this before," he said as we stepped toward the wet sand.

"Not since I was a kid, and I think the board was more of a flotation device then."

At the water's edge, he handed me the smaller of the two boards. "It's easy. You wade out, pick a cresting wave, notch the board at your hips, and go."

"Okay."

With glittering eyes, he nodded for me to follow as he waded into the surf, his long legs making it look easy.

"I'm going to teach you something this week," I called out as I followed him.

"What?"

"You're always teaching me things. I'm going to teach you something."

He faced me as I caught up to him, his eyes hooded. "I can think of a few things I'd like you to teach me … later."

Oh, his flirt game … wait, not a game. This flirting was real. My pulse fluttered, and I returned his heady stare as I walked past, embracing the new sexy vibe between us. "Look forward to that, but for now, show me what you got, big boy."

He paused and watched, his gaze like a touch, before he followed me.

Boogie boarding wasn't hard, but it took some practice to find the right wave. I finally caught the perfect one and let the water carry me. The pull of the undertow as the wave crashed beneath me and thrust me onto the sand made me feel like a kid again.

"That's a big smile," Levi said. He strolled toward me carrying his leashed board like a natural-born surfer.

"This is fun." I panted as I bent to grab my board, leashed to my ankle, and bobbing in the tiny waves rolling ashore. "But half the beach is inside my suit."

He cleared his throat and looked out at the water. "Take a break?"

"Yes, but first let me see if I can flush out some of this sand." I walked to the deeper water, and Levi stood still, watching me intently, like me pulling at my suit underwater was a peep show.

I returned to him and smirked.

He grinned. "Turns out those tits bounce a bit in that suit, too."

I gave him a little swat and loved that he'd been watching.

We headed back to the chairs where Amelia and Carter sat, dripping ice cream and kicking their toes in the sand as Janie rubbed sunscreen on their backs.

"Can we go boarding?" Carter asked, eying us.

"Sure. You know how?" I asked.

He nodded. "Dad showed me in Jamaica."

Right. The wedding of one of Steven's clients became a family vacation last year.

"What about you, Amelia?" I grinned at my niece.

"I'll show her," April said, reaching out for the boards.

"I'll help," Steven said and hopped up to join them. "Finish your ice cream. Those boards are big, but we'll make it work."

"Where are Troye and Jill?"

Janie gestured to the hotel. "Cocktail time. Dad and Mei went too, so they can bring something back for you if you need me to text her." Her phone was already in her hand.

"I'm good." I looked at Levi.

"Me too," he said, then smoothed a hand across my low back. "How about a walk?"

"Sure," I said. "But I want to get some sun." I wrapped an arm in the hem of my rash guard and pulled it over my head.

That look in Levi's eyes after I dropped the shirt to a chair was what you called *heat*. I swallowed.

"There's a beach shower." Janie pointed toward the twisting stairs that rose to the pool deck of the hotel.

"I've been under that thing twice, and my skin is still itchy. We'll probably need to leave soon."

"We have a car, so don't wait on us," I said, grabbing Levi's hand as we walked away. I wasn't giving Janie a chance to comment or judge.

Levi shifted his hold and threaded our fingers together, pulling me away from a rogue wave. "You did that on purpose."

"What?" I asked.

"It's cool. Now I don't have to imagine you taking off your shirt. I saw the real thing."

"Oh yeah, well you had it coming. You whipping off your T-shirt on the boat yesterday is burned into my memory, thank the goddess."

With his laugh and mischievous grin, his shoulders, and those aviators, he looked like a commercial for Hawaiian tourism. All he needed was a blonde model next to him.

The sun was less intense, and I noticed families packing up sandy kids and waiters bringing cocktails to clusters of adults. At every hotel we passed, there was at least one collection of sunbathing women whose heavy eyes were on us, and the place where Levi still held my hand.

What is he *doing with* her?

"You're getting some eye fucks at two o'clock," I said.

Levi's eyes snapped to mine. "What?"

I nodded toward a group of twenty-somethings who appeared to be on a girl's trip. Their neon bikinis and colorful frozen drinks were hard to miss, and so were their blatant stares. "Those ladies are eye fucking you."

He coughed. "You can see that? They're wearing sunglasses."

"Oh, please. You see it, too."

Levi grinned and looked at me. "I can say the same about you."

"Ah, no, you can't."

"That guy in the green shorts a minute ago," he said, standing straighter.

"What about him?"

"He was checking you out … hard."

I scoffed. "No, he wasn't."

"Yeah, he was. I almost turned as he passed to give him a glare. I'm holding your hand here. He can back way the fuck off."

I chuckled. "You don't have to do that."

He frowned. "Do what?"

"You don't have to pretend like men look at me the way women look at you."

"They don't. It's worse. And I know what they're thinking. Maybe one of them will have you reconsidering this *real* thing with me."

I stopped, and Levi spun to face me. "Even if another man did hit on me or whatever, I'm here with *you*, real or not. That doesn't change until we change it. I'd never do that to someone, least of all you."

His expression was sweet, vulnerable even, and he moved closer, lowering his head. His free hand cupped my jaw. "I think we should send out some signals."

I glanced toward the neon girls still watching us.

In one move, he tugged me against him, then pressed his lips to mine.

It wasn't a porn kiss, not even any tongue. But it was slow and deliberate. His thumb brushing my cheek as his lips caressed and nipped mine. Talk about swoon. I may have moaned as I raised my free hand to his side, right above his hip bone. He broke the kiss way too soon with his signature playful wink, and I swayed a bit with all my blood rushing south. Damn, the man could kiss.

"We may need to do that every hundred feet or so to make a point," he said, smiling at me.

"Absolutely, yes," I replied, still a bit dazed.

Levi lifted our joined hands and guided my shoulder so that I twirled like we were dancing to face the way we came. "Let's head back. I'm getting hot and could use a little time in the water."

Yeah, me too.

The surf splashed cool on my heated skin as we made our way past the crests to the gentle rise and fall of the waves. Levi dove under, then broke the surface to stand chest deep in the crystal-clear water, schools of tiny fish darting by. He pushed his wet hair back and reached for me.

I moved closer, barely able to touch bottom. His strong arms encircled my middle and lifted me. I wrapped my legs around his waist like it was natural and stroked a hand through the hair at his nape. He closed his eyes on a groan.

A wave lifted us, and my chest bobbed close to Levi's face. On the next one, he pressed his lips to a spot on my sternum.

He looked at me as if asking for permission, and I pressed myself closer in response.

"This water is too clear," he said.

"What? It's beautiful. You can see all the fish."

"I want to touch you."

Sparks hit my core.

"But I don't want to shock the snorkelers." He nodded toward a group of kids on pool noodles splashing nearby.

Another wave hit, and Levi pushed off the bottom so we wouldn't be overtaken.

"Was that your plan? Get me in the water so you could grope me?" Please say yes.

"Hell, yes."

My laugh was quick, but then I added a little smolder to my eyes as I bit my lip. "*Where* do you want to touch me?" I asked.

"Everywhere." His voice was low and dark, like a secret. With one arm secured at my waist, he smoothed a hand up my side.

"I don't think that touch is too shocking."

"Yeah? What if I moved higher?" He let his hand drift to my side boob, or where my side boob would be if I had them.

I squeezed my legs around him, pressing my center to his abs at the waistband of his board shorts.

"Mmm, I like that," he said.

Emboldened, I squeezed again.

"Don't tease me when I can't do anything about it." His hands slid down to cup my ass, and I bit my lip against all the ugly voices in my head. Levi had seen my thighs. My sizable ass shouldn't surprise him.

His fingers flexed in my flesh right as a wave crashed next to us, and we tumbled.

Levi grabbed for me as I flailed for the top in the current. He stood and pulled me to the surface. With our heads above water, we both laughed and sputtered ocean water. "Sorry about that. I lost my focus," he said.

"I need more practice." He pulled me to him and returned his hands to my backside.

"You like my ass?"

"Yes, I do, Kate." His expression was as serious as if he were testifying in court.

I giggled and shimmied myself against him.

He leveled me with a look. "Are you trying to get me hard? Check that box, babe." He spun to face the oncoming waves, and I squeezed him tighter, feeling my effect on him. It felt good.

"Hey," someone shouted in our direction. I turned to find Troye practically scowling at us. "We're heading back to the house. Time's up on the rental chairs."

Levi looked at me. "Stay or go? I'm with you."

I liked the sound of that. The day had been magical, and I wasn't ready for it to end. "How about we grab dinner somewhere first?"

14

LEVI

THE FOOD TRUCK AT ONE OF MY FAVORITE BEACH PARKS had a line that wasn't too long, and standing there gave us a chance to take in the beginnings of another spectacular sunset, this time from the water's edge. The thin strip of natural sand, more tan than white, had a thin row of leafy trees separating it from the busy road to Kona.

We sat at a picnic table, eating the best vegetable tacos with fresh papaya salad, and soaking in the vibe of a place meant more for locals than tourists before we made the drive back. I held Kate's hand or stroked her exposed thigh the entire way. Now that I could touch it, I couldn't get enough of her skin.

"Mind if I shower first?" Kate asked as we entered the house.

I glanced out toward the laughter coming from the pool.

"No problem. I'll grab a beer. Let me know when you're done."

Checking the huge double fridge, I grabbed a Kona

Brewing Longboard and headed out into the evening air. Shades of bright orange and pink painted the sky, and I wanted a night to sit and watch the entire show with Kate, naked on our private lanai. That would be a memory to keep.

"Hey, I didn't ask. How was the zipline?" Phillip gestured to me with his beer as I opened mine and sat at the table with him, Mei, Jill, and Troye.

"Amazing. I picked a place that's good for beginners. It starts off slowly, but Kate's a natural."

"I knew she would be," Phillip said with obvious pride.

"I can't believe she did it," Jill said.

"She had a great time, and all it took was a little research and effort." I said the words to everyone but looked at Troye. The fucker who was too proud or too lazy to figure out how to help his fiancée come.

I was sorry Kate had to go through that, but not sorry they were done. Kate was capable of orgasms, and if she wanted to have them with a man, *I* wanted to be that man.

THE TROPICAL SCENT of her body wash lingered in the air as I turned the shower temperature to scalding. Even staring a hole through Troye hadn't kept the memory of Kate's kiss from running on a loop in my brain. My fingers sifting through her hair, her lips pressed to mine, and the velvet touch of her tongue made me want to do more, feel more, taste more.

I needed to get a handle on this fire in my veins if I planned to spend time with her family tonight. A quick session with my hand would do it.

I lowered my head under the stream and remembered the way Kate's curves felt pressed to me in the ocean, the way she squeezed her lush thighs around my waist. Damn, I loved her legs. I wanted to be up close and personal with them as soon as possible.

Blindly, I reached for the shampoo and knocked the bottles together, causing Kate's bodywash to fall on its side. I needed a hit, so I grabbed the bottle, closed my eyes, and inhaled a deep breath of her. As I replaced it, a bright pink object resting against the back of the ledge caught my eye.

A bullet vibrator. It wasn't here yesterday when I showered. Kate must have brought it in here earlier.

That little truth slammed into me, and I was rock-hard picturing it. Her perfect tits, exactly the right size to fit my palm. The low buzzing sound of the vibrator as she lowered it to her center, and those maddening soft moans low in her throat.

In my mind, her free hand caressed a breast and teased the nipple to a hard point. Her eyes were closed, water streaming down her dark hair and shoulders to her perfect round ass. I wanted to make her feel good. Would she bend over and let me tongue her sweetness from behind?

If she did, would she peek back at me, and let me see her lips part with a pleasured sigh? That little vibe would tease her clit exactly right, so I could fill one hand with her soft thigh and stroke myself with the other, all while my tongue stayed buried inside her.

Damn, that would be hot. My balls drew up tight, grabbing my attention. I gave myself a hard tug and another. The images grew brighter, her moans louder, and my rhythm picked up, my orgasm imminent in record time. It was all Kate. My legs shaking, and my eyes locked on that pink vibe on the shelf, I fucking lost it.

"Who's up for a game of horse?" Jill asked, nodding to the poolside basketball net once I returned to join the family, reasonably confident I wouldn't pop a boner any minute.

Kate's parents and their partners had retired to their rooms while April and the kids went to watch a Pixar film in the home theater on their side of the house. Which left the three *happy couples* alone on the pool deck, surrounded by tiki torches in the moonlight.

"No," Janie said firmly. "My nails." She waved her perfectly painted fingertips. "What if there isn't a decent nail spa to do a repair? It's too risky. I can't have a broken nail in your wedding pictures. Mantel photo, remember?"

"Fine. You can hot tub." Jill's face brightened, and she looked at Kate. "Wait, that's it. Let's play for which couple gets a private hot tub tonight." She waggled her brows suggestively, and I suddenly had a strong desire to win at pool basketball.

"A private hot tub sounds good," Kate sighed and gave me a sultry look. If she was on board with me holding her close, stripping her out of her purple bikini, and making out under the stars, I had to win.

Everyone went to change. Kate took our bathroom, and I quickly pulled on another set of swim trunks in the bedroom, wanting to give her some privacy but also not wanting to imagine Kate taking off her clothes only a wall away. One session with my hand cooled the fire, but it wouldn't take much to bring it back to full strength.

At the pool, Troye and Steven were shifting the basketball hoop closer to the edge. I grabbed the nearby orange ball and took a shot as I jumped in to get wet.

Steven snagged the ball while Troye stood and rested his elbows back on the tiled edge. "You know, it's weird Kate never mentioned you to her sisters."

Steven glanced over like he was listening.

"I don't know. She hasn't said much about them either. Seems we always have other things to talk about."

Like your lazy ass performance in bed.

Steven jumped out of the water and dunked the ball, nearly causing the stand to fall in.

"She's a great girl," he said, steadying the thing back at the edge.

"She is. Can't say I'm mad she and this guy didn't work out."

I grabbed the rebound and didn't watch Troye's reaction to my comment because the sight of Kate walking with her sisters toward the pool deck had me frozen in my tracks.

Her hair was off her neck in a messy pile on top of her head again, and I scanned her white lacy swim cover to the tops of her lush thighs. She held my gaze and lifted the fabric off like it was for me, revealing that fuck-hot purple bikini and all those curves in all the best places.

Steven punched my shoulder. "Put your tongue away."

I chuckled and wiped my hand across my mouth as I watched her approach. "You know how it is," I said, loud enough for her to hear. "Sometimes, she looks so good, it feels like the first time she showed you all that skin, and you knowing you got to touch it." I didn't look away from Kate. "I'm sure it's that way with you and Janie."

Steven said nothing as he moved toward his wife. And then I didn't care about Steven or Troye or anyone because Kate sat on the smooth pool edge close enough to touch.

"Hey," she said, her eyes roaming my bare shoulders and chest appreciatively. I liked that heated gleam and knowing I put it there.

"My favorite suit," I said.

"It's new." Uncertainty flashed in her eyes, even after I'd told her earlier how much I liked it. I needed to work harder to get rid of those doubts, starting now.

I stood to my full height and leaned in to speak low in her ear. "You look incredible. Sexy as hell." My hands slid to the side of each knee, my thumbs brushing against her. Without breaking eye contact, Kate shifted and slipped into the water, barely causing a ripple, putting her sweet body between my arms, the pool edge at her back. I pressed closer.

"This is the suit you packed for a fake date?" I shook my head. "Bad plan, Kate. If I hadn't already decided this date was real, seeing you walking toward me in this would have done it."

She glanced at my lips, then licked hers. Jeezus, those plump strawberry lips were pornographic this close up. People were here, I reminded myself, and didn't take it further. Later, when we were alone, I planned to take it as far as she'd let me.

She laid her palms on my chest, the tips of her fingers massaging with hesitant pressure.

"I like your hands on me. You can touch me, anywhere, anytime. Consider this my enthusiastic consent."

She grinned at the buzzwords. "No second thoughts about making this real?"

Was she kidding? "Not one." I wrapped my arms around her low back and pulled her to me. Her eyes lit with a sultry gleam as she caressed her hands along my shoulders. The movement brought her breasts to press against my chest, and I barely stifled a groan. One shower session was no match for Kate in her tiny bikini. My dick went to half-mast.

I was a touch guy all the way. Skin-to-skin could damn near take me over the edge sometimes. Kate's skin definitely would.

I let my hands roam now, and my fingertips slid up the indent of her back as I pulled her down into the water, leaving only our shoulders exposed to prying eyes. On the last downward path, I slid lower, filling my palms with each cheek of her glorious ass for the third time today.

My head fell forward and pressed against hers. "Babe, you have a great ass." I teased around the edge of the fabric at her hip as a throat cleared above us.

"Can you two horn dogs do that later?" Jill asked. "I'm ready to play."

Kate didn't release me, and I sure as hell didn't move a finger. "I guess if we win, we can pick this up later in the hot tub," she said.

Damn right. "Anytime. Anywhere, Kate."

Troye coughed, and we both turned to face him. I left an arm slung across Kate's shoulders. For a guy getting married in four days, he sure acted jealous of the man with his ex. I had some ideas forming about the cause of that jealousy, but either way, I would take every opportunity to touch her, whether he liked it or not.

Steven and Janie were already getting cozy in the hot tub when the first game started. We played teams, best two out of three, but in the end, Kate and I couldn't do it. I admit, I lost focus a few times as Kate swam close or hugged me after she'd made a shot. I needed my hands on her somewhere private, where I could take my time and enjoy every inch of her.

If we were alone right now, I'd press her against the tiled pool wall, strip off that sexy bathing suit, and explore the sweet part of her with my fingers. Or I'd lift her out and set her on the edge where she'd open her legs to me so I could use my tongue.

Sex outside was my thing. Not because I wanted to be caught, though the idea didn't freak me out. But because being naked with another person out in the open was freeing. That was the best word for it.

Most women in my past hadn't been into it, though I tried to create spaces where it was safe and private. I wasn't about making anyone do something they didn't want to do. But, despite those efforts, it didn't happen often.

Tasting Kate, touching her, wrapped up together in the warm night air, and listening to her sighs of pleasure would definitely be next level.

15

KATE

Jill wrapped her arms around Troye and giggled as they strolled to the hot tub to celebrate their victory. Janie and Steven had long since headed inside, giving each other flirty glances.

"We still need that game of one-on-one," Levi said, walking toward me in the shallow end, water droplets on his skin glistening in the shimmering pool lights. He raised both hands and pushed them through his hair, making his biceps pop.

"One-on-one … what?" I stammered.

Levi's answering grin, a little happy and a little sultry, said he knew exactly what distracted me. "What's on your mind, babe?"

Yeah, I wanted to touch him, lick a water droplet right off the bump of his collarbone. *Anytime, anywhere,* he'd said. Now and here seemed good.

With one fingertip, I traced a line from his shoulder, past one flat nipple, all the way to the edge of his trunks. His chest barely moved with his breath, and his smile faded to something serious.

"Kate?"

I didn't answer him. "Kissing," I whispered.

His eyes burned, and he smoothed his thumb along my jaw. "Yeah, me too." Taking my hand, he pulled me to the steps, and I followed him out of the pool. I grabbed a beach towel and wrapped it around me. "I need to rinse off the salt and chlorine." If I didn't, my dry skin would itch. Itching wasn't my sexiest look.

"You take the inside. I can use this one out here." He gestured to the outdoor shower tucked in the corner by the house. "Enjoy it, but not too much—" his eyes glittered "—and I'll meet you on our lanai."

There was no mistaking his intent. My belly fluttered.

As I walked to our room, I looked back and caught Levi watching me. This purple bikini had been a great purchase, and I owed Kristen, now back in my good graces and the best friend ever, for talking me into it. "Love that body, girl," she'd said when I tried it on. I was working on it.

The magical suit was rinsed and hung to dry before I stepped inside the huge shower, big enough for two. Earlier, with my vibe, I'd imagined Levi was here, pressing me against the tiles and stroking my clit until I screamed. I had to do something after waking up aching, then experiencing the mind-scramble that was his kisses.

Thank the goddess for waterproof vibes. Wait. What had I done with it? My head was in such a fog after the explosive release that I couldn't remember if I put it away. One quick glance along the ledge, and I found the hot pink toy resting there … in plain sight.

Levi had seen it. I closed my eyes with a sigh. That's why he told me to "enjoy" it.

Nothing to do about it now. I refused to be embarrassed and left my vibe there. He knew, so there was no need to hide it. I'd likely be using it again, anyway.

I stepped out of the shower and dressed in my sleep shorts and tank. The shorts were snugger than intended, but most bottoms that fit my waist were tight everywhere else, whether or not they'd been designed to be.

While I brushed my hair and smoothed on my favorite coconut lotion, I heard Levi in the bedroom. After one more pep talk, I joined him outside, where he leaned back on the comfy outdoor sofa, one arm stretched out along the cushions. He'd switched off all the lights, and the shimmering glow of Kona was bright in the distance, but the show-stealing view was Levi's bare chest above low-slung sweats.

His head turned, his gaze roaming my outfit. "How was your shower?"

I smirked at his glittering eyes and sat. "Not as good as before."

"Oh?" His smile was knowing and way too seductive.

I angled toward him with my legs tucked underneath me. "Okay, yes, I used my vibrator in the shower earlier. I'm not sorry. You kiss a woman like that, she needs some relief. I blame you."

"I couldn't stop thinking about kissing you, either. I didn't want to hang by the pool with a hard-on, so I had some shower time myself earlier." He showed me my favorite dimple. "I focused on your little pink toy the entire time."

That was … well … hot.

Resting his hand on my knee, he stroked his talented thumb absently over my skin as he held my gaze. "I pictured you using it while water streamed over all the places I wanted my hands to be."

Heat bloomed deeper, and I rolled my lips against the urge to launch myself at him.

"Other than the amazing shower, was it a good day?" he asked, sounding more like the Levi who'd held me on the zipline platform this morning. Was that really just this morning?

"You know it was great."

He said nothing while his thumb continued its teasing torture.

"What's on your mind, Levi?" I asked, repeating his earlier question.

"Ah, let's go with you. Everything you."

"What do you want to happen tonight?"

He tilted his head. "I think I'm supposed to be asking you that."

"I asked you first."

"The taking turns thing." He angled closer. "I want to touch you, hold you, and see that spark in your eyes. But no performing or faking. There's no expectation for how tonight ends. Let's just make each other feel good until we decide to stop."

"Yes," I said in a breathless voice.

He lowered his head and leaned closer. "Do you get off every time with your vibe?"

I nodded, not looking away. Embarrassment battling arousal as liquid pooled in my core.

"Anytime you want to use it, I'm good. I'm not like your ex. Anything that gets you off, I'm here for. Even more, if I can be involved."

"Involved?"

"Watching, touching, helping." He slid his hand higher on my leg, reminding me exactly what Levi touching me would be like. Could I let him watch me? Would I still be able to orgasm?

"I've never done that before. Let someone watch me. But you make me want to try." I wanted to do it all. I wanted to let him watch, and I wanted to watch him.

His grin was slow and sweet. "I'd say that makes me a very lucky man."

For the second time today, *I* kissed him. I let my hand glide across his smooth, bare chest, feeling every contour and dip. He didn't have the razor-sharp six-pack like a gym guy, but the low rise of his sweats showed me the start of that subtle V at his hips. I had to touch it.

He growled against my lips before kissing a slow path along my jaw. His hand found my waist and pulled me closer while the other slid under the fall of my hair. With the lightest touch, his fingertips danced across the spot where my shoulder met my neck.

My nipples peaked, and my pussy swelled as arousal flooded my center. "That spot. Oh, I like that sooo much."

"This one?" he asked and ghosted his lips across my skin. A full body shiver shot through me. "Yeah, that's the one," he said with a satisfied smile I could hear.

I knew a few *spots* too. I lowered my fingers to skim through the silky hair below his navel and tease around the band of his sweats.

"Come here," he said, pulling me closer, his hand diving into my hair, massaging. His touch was more intense now, like he was struggling to hold back.

I teased over his hardness, and he groaned, then claimed my mouth in a powerful kiss. His sweet nips and sips were history as he gripped my thigh and pulled it across his lap until I straddled him.

"This okay?" His voice was deep and urgent.

My heart beat fast. I didn't do cowgirl. Hands tended to roam my substantial ass, and shame killed the mood when trying to work up to an orgasm. But Levi said he liked it, and this was my week to do something reckless.

"Babe, I need the words," he said, leaving languid kisses along my collarbone.

My mind struggled to focus. "Yeah," I answered before I could over-think it, and I rolled my hips to rub my center along the solid ridge of him. We both moaned.

He gripped my waist and guided me into a rhythm. With each slide of my pussy, he rolled his hips beneath me, increasing the friction. "Good?" he asked, eyes locked with mine.

"*So* good." Great. Amazing. Better than anything had been in a long time. Maybe ever. "Good for you?"

"Fuuuck, Kate," he said, shifting me and kissing me like the world was on fire. I was burning, my thoughts trying to catch up with my body. Everything pulsed into the familiar sense of climbing.

Other lovers had turned me on, and I'd feel the tension build like a string pulling tight, but then, without warning, the sensation would slip through my fingers. I'd learned to enjoy the build before it evaporated, and I rode Levi's lap with abandon.

His hands stilled my movements, and he leaned back,

his breath sawing in and out. "Too good, Kate. You feel too good." He sucked in air before rising to hold me close and let his hand smooth over my shoulder and the thin strap of my tank. His breathing slowed as his fingers traced along my backbone, glided lower to the silky fabric of my shorts, and stroked the sides of my thighs.

Awareness lit again, and I fought the desire to pull away.

"Promised myself I'd spend some time here," he said, pressing light kisses below my ear. "You have these little dimples."

Dimples? What? Like my fat? *Sleep with the fat girl.*

I stilled.

"I need to know how far up they go." He nuzzled below my jaw as his fingertips slid along the edge of my silky sleep shorts.

"Levi, those *little dimples* are cellulite," I said, trying to hide the shock in my voice.

"They're also fucking cute," he said, continuing to nuzzle. "I want to run my hands over them while I tongue you from behind. Would you let me do that?"

I blinked. "Are you … are you making fun of me?" My voice wavered, and my stomach dropped.

He pulled back, his expression instantly concerned. "Making fun of you? No. What part of me saying I want to palm your sexy thighs while I lick you is making fun of you?"

"Levi, those bumps are ugly." I shifted away, but he held me to him.

"Who said?" His voice was gentle, but there was an air of defensiveness, too. "Did Troye say that? Or that fucker in college?"

I sighed. "They didn't have to. Every ad in the world tells me." Along with the women in my family.

"Kate. Nothing about your body is ugly. Nothing." He met my eyes and slid his hands back to massage my ass through the silky shorts, his strong fingers spread wide.

"Your body is sexy. Thick and soft and so fucking *female*." He groaned and squeezed my hips. "Makes me sound like a caveman, but there you are. I want to touch you everywhere. Let my hands roam and memorize every sweet curve. Kiss you breathless while I do."

His expression was intense and sincere. This was Levi, not some dickhead in college.

I settled on his lap again, and his eyes brightened. "You think you could sit here and be still?" He returned to the tortuous, sultry kisses on my neck.

I closed my eyes and fought the urge to squirm against his erection at the thought of him wanting me to *"be still."* Pleasing him was turning me the fuck *on*.

"You wouldn't prefer smooth skin?"

"A boring ass with nothing to explore? Nowhere to dip my tongue and trace my way higher? No thanks, babe."

I bit my lip. I wanted to believe him. But this was … he was … too much.

16

LEVI

Goddamn those ads telling women they had to look a certain way to be desired. Skinny women were beautiful, but so were lots of other shapes and sizes. I'd always been more attracted to women with curves. Someone soft where I was hard. The yin and yang. The pull of opposites.

At first, I dated women who did the same things as me, like biking and hiking. It seemed easy to connect with our shared interests. But those connections based on ease didn't turn out so well.

As a wiser man, I leaned into my pull toward women who weren't like me. Women who challenged me and let me challenge them in return. That was the real adventure of life.

The woman currently on my lap and driving me out of my damn mind was the best adventure so far. But instead of letting me worship every dip and curve, she slid off my lap to the side, taking all her warmth and softness with her. This time I let her and tried not to whine about it.

"I want to believe you, I do," she said. "But …"

"What?" I asked, keeping my tone gentle.

"This … *you* are a little unexpected. Half the nurses in the hospital want to sleep with you. You know that, right?"

Doubtful, but it didn't matter. I only wanted the sexy nurse in front of me.

"Kate, I'm attracted to *you*. Being here with you is the best idea I've ever had." I took a breath. "But I don't want to push—"

"No, I like you pushing me, with the snorkeling and the zipline and … other places." Her eyes flashed with heat.

I wanted to raise both my arms and shout victory. Instead, I said nothing. I needed to take some care. She had trusted the wrong guys in the past, and they hurt her. I wouldn't be one of them.

"I want this, but I need a minute. I woke up this morning aching, and you were so out of reach. And now, here you are. It's a lot … to take in."

"You woke up aching for me?"

"That's all you heard me say?" She chuckled.

"No. I got it all. That was just my favorite part."

"Well, it's true. Hence the vibrator."

We both laughed.

"Babe, we can take all the time you need. I meant what I said. I'm happy to kiss you … in *all* your best places or only a few." I stroked my thumb along her lips. "Can't promise I won't be hard all week, though."

She shoved my arm playfully.

"I like your body, and I like this outfit. Come back to my lap and let me show you how much."

She eyed me. "You really think my thighs are sexy?"

"Hell, yes. I've been thinking about them all day. Actually, ever since you slipped off your shorts yesterday and my dick went to half-mast."

She bit her lip and gave her head a tiny shake, deciding, like she did that first day at the coffee shop. Then, holding my gaze, she rose and settled herself over me again, her hands landing on my shoulders.

Looking up, I let myself take it all in this time. The lights in the distance. The bluish darkness making her skin glow. We were outside, in the warm air, listening to the night sounds. A fantasy come to life.

With her fingertips, Kate traced down my chest. "You shave this?"

"I don't have much hair there." I nodded to my upper body. "I've always shaved it."

"I like it," she said.

And I liked that glassy look in her eyes as she watched her fingers play with one of my nipples.

She leaned in, and I pulled her closer. This kiss was slow, tender, and a bit tentative until she opened and stroked her tongue along my lower lip. My dick, assuming we were back on track, jumped with the joy of it.

"You like that?" she asked, the smile clear in her tone.

"You know I do," I whispered, grinding up to her center. The layers of clothes between us were no match for her heat, but I wanted more. I wanted to be naked.

But she was in charge tonight. She needed to *take it in* and be in control, which was fine with me.

Her hands tunneled into my hair as she pressed her body to mine. I tuned in to her every move, reveling in the feel of her kissing down my neck with tiny bites and sucks.

I stroked along her sides to the full curves of her hips and down, filling my palms with the softness of her incredible ass. I hummed low in my throat. Now that she'd let me touch it, caress it, it was all I wanted to do. At dinner. Swimming. At the wedding. I wanted her ass in my hands at all times.

The strip of exposed skin between the band of her sleep shorts and the edge of her tank top called to me. I didn't miss her quick intake of air or the goose flesh rising when I smoothed my thumb there. Our kisses went deeper, grew hungrier with her muffled sighs, and I slid a hand under the silky fabric to tease below the swell of a single bare breast.

"Yes," she said, and I filled my palm with one mound, testing its weight, and the heady sensation between us ramped higher. I gave the full bud of her plump nipple a light pinch before rolling it between my fingers.

She responded with a subtle moan, and the grind of her hips increased. Kate liked nipple play. Good, because her nipples were a goddamn wonder. Large and strained tall, I couldn't wait to get my mouth on them.

Hell, just thinking of it had me close. "Kate," I whispered into her neck. "My dick has been on edge since you walked out here without a bra. I can't promise I won't come. Tell me now if you hate that idea."

"Mmm, if I did, it wouldn't be very nice of me to do this." She rolled her hips again, but this time her pace was slow, and she pressed hard against the ache. That alone could have gotten me there if I let it.

"No," I mumbled, desperation clear in my voice. "That wouldn't be very nice."

"And I'm a nice person." The seduction in her low voice had me unbelievably harder. Any uncertainty from earlier was gone, and a confident Kate, teasing me like this, made rational thought seem like climbing a mountain.

"Yes, you are. The nicest."

"I want to make you come, Levi." Fuck, I liked her voice. She returned to the steady rhythm and roll of her pussy. This was not my first dry hump, by a long shot, but damn if she didn't have me there already.

"That's perfect, babe. Like that. So. Good."

"Mmm," she hummed against my lips. "Can you hold me tighter? I want to be closer. I want to feel it."

Yes. Yes, to all of that. I yanked her tight to my chest and clamped my arms around her like I'd done on the zipline platform and the way she'd asked me to on the side of the road. Pressed together from hip to lip, she moaned low in her throat.

Her kiss was sweet like strawberries and dark like midnight as the pressure between us built. In my hold, her grinding became more subtle, but still powerful in a new way. Her breath panted deeper like she was desperate. Lost. Clinging tight to me and then fighting the hold to increase her movements. The push and pull of it was intense.

The telltale tingle at the base of my spine gained the strength of a hurricane. "Fuck, Kate, I'm …"

"Yes. Come for me, Daddy."

What? Oh, damn. Game over. Stars exploded behind my eyes, and I came with muffled groans against her shoulder. Shattered. Done. Possibly forever.

I loosened my grip on her, and my head fell back on the sofa.

"Oh my god," Kate whispered.

I whipped my head up at the sound of panic. "What?"

She had her hands pressed to her cheeks, almost covering her eyes. "I called you 'Daddy.' I've … never done that before. I don't have … issues. My father, who I've always had a totally normal relationship with, is sleeping like twenty feet away."

"Babe, wait. Slow down," I chuckled and stroked my hands up her forearms, gently pulling her hands away to hold them. "Calling me *Daddy* doesn't mean you have issues." I heaved in a breath, allowing blood to return to my brain. "It doesn't have to mean anything. It can just be fun or funny. Daddy memes are everywhere. It's practically mainstream."

Her eyes were a little wild. "Not for me."

"I thought it was hot because you got lost in the moment and let down some walls, didn't you, *Baby Girl?*"

She squinted at my use of the dom/sub nickname. My grin split my face. She was too damn cute, a study in duality. A badass nurse on a helicopter, but scared of heights. Hesitant one minute, then grinding me to the very edge and calling me Daddy the next. She fucking did it for me.

"Kate, this is between us. If we both like what we're doing, there's no problem. And I think we both liked it. Right?" I glanced at the damp spot on my lap, clear evidence of how much I did.

She fought a smile and nodded.

"Say it. Don't say it. Doesn't matter as long as you're real with me, here with me."

She exhaled. "I can do that."

"Good. Now, what can I do for you, beautiful? You seemed caught up as much as me. Did we miss a chance there? You want me to get your vibe?" I asked, smoothing my hands along the velvet skin of her thighs above mine.

"Oh, I already had one spectacular orgasm today, thanks to you. I'm good."

My grin was cocky and over the top, but damn, I liked she was thinking about me when she came. "Anytime you want to make that real, you let me know."

She gave me a sassy smile, one I'd seen before but didn't know the full power of until this moment.

I pulled her in for a chaste kiss, then another. I didn't want to let her move, but I had to clean up and grab a fresh pair of boxers. When I came out of the bathroom, Kate was pulling down the comforter on her side.

"I need to brush my teeth," she said and walked around the bed.

I followed her to the double-sink vanity, where we each did our thing. When she finished and turned to move away, I stopped her with one arm and pulled her close for another kiss. I wanted her ass in my hands at all times and my lips on hers too it seemed. Every time we brushed our teeth together this week, it needed to end with a kiss like that.

In the bedroom, I slid between the sheets. "Finally, some cuddle time," I said and rubbed my hands together like a plotting villain.

"I can't believe you like to cuddle," she said with a disbelieving look as she flopped back onto the pillows, making her boobs jiggle. I didn't spend enough time with them tonight. I mentally added *boobs* to my To-Do list.

"I love it." I did. Some guys acted like holding a lover was a sort of fee they had to pay for sex. Not me. "I'm a touch guy, Kate. Anything that gets me skin-on-skin, I'm here for."

Scooting next to her, I pulled her into me like a little spoon, wrapping one arm around her from underneath to rest below the swell of her breasts and her peaked nipples straining against the silky fabric of her tank. My other hand caressed down her side to rest on one luscious thigh.

"See, isn't this nice?" I placed a tender kiss on her bare shoulder.

"Mmm," she hummed and leaned back into me, skimming her fingers along my forearm. The slow drag of her short nails owned my focus.

"Can you fall asleep like this?" she asked.

I rested my head on the pillow. "Try and stop me."

17

———

KATE

THE SCENT OF SPICE AND MAN FILLED MY SENSES, AND I realized my pillow wasn't a pillow but the warm, smooth skin of Levi's chest as he breathed in a steady rhythm. Sometime in the night, we'd shifted from spooning to me using him as the world's best body pillow in a dreamy fairytale.

Here I was, wrapped around Levi, the perfect combination of strong and sensitive, held close in the middle of a cloud-like bed while birds chirped in the bright morning sunshine outside our door. I was like a fucking Disney princess except for the whole patriarchy and dead parents thing.

The real world, with its expectations and disappointments, was a far-off misty place.

The hand that rested on my shoulder as I lay lost in him moved, sliding down my arm and up at a gentle pace. I looked at his face, but nothing had changed. Was he caressing me in his sleep?

Gingerly, I pressed my mouth to his chest and watched for a reaction. He continued the slow glide of his fingers and nothing more. I kissed him again with a tiny brush of my lips and tongue. He responded with longer strokes. I loved the idea that my kisses were prompting his subconscious to touch me. Energy pooled low in my core.

Another morning, hot and hard for Levi. Except this time, I could do something about it.

I loved the feel of his arms wrapped tightly around me last night, making me feel safe. All my fears and insecurities lost their edges, and if I hadn't orgasmed earlier in the shower, I would have on his lap. Easy. Coming with a partner hadn't been easy for nearly a decade.

I refused to examine the 'daddy' thing. Maybe it was just for fun or a release to play a part. It didn't matter. I was taking *easy* however I could get it.

I kept teasing him with kisses until he rolled and pulled me close.

"Are you awake?" I asked, held tight to his chest.

"Mmm," came his response.

"Is that a yes?"

Nothing.

"Levi?"

He returned to his back and lifted his free hand to rub his eyes before he looked at me. "You're here." His smile was sleepy before he rolled back to his side and squeezed me tight again, his head resting above mine and our legs intertwined. "I thought I was dreaming."

"Sorry if I woke you."

"I'm not. Reality is way better than the dream." He slid his palm along my back, leaving a trail of tingles as he did.

I slid my leg over his hip and down again in the same delicious rhythm he was using. He didn't move, but his reaction was obvious, his cock swelling harder between us.

The simmer in my core burned in the few beats of silence that passed.

I couldn't take it anymore. Rising, I pushed him onto his back and angled above him as he blinked his eyes open with a sly grin. He brushed his hand down my side to the waistband of my sleep shorts. "Good morning. What do you need, babe?"

"Good morning," I said and rolled away from him. I kicked the covers down and pulled off my shorts, leaving only a thin cotton thong. Nothing flashy, it was comfortable, but still, a thong, and Levi's eyes widened as he came up on his elbow. His sly smile was gone as he took in the pale pink fabric with the thick, athletic waistband at my hip. "I need you to touch me."

His expression was suddenly serious, almost dark. "Turn over," he said and gently pushed me away from him to lie on my stomach. He shifted closer and skimmed his warm palm up my thigh, over the bumps he claimed to like, and over my bare ass cheek.

"Your body, Kate. You're beautiful." He placed a kiss on my neck, and the intensity of his caresses notched higher. He slid his hand between my shoulder blades, dragging my tank top with it before he trailed down the same path. He gave my ass a gentle squeeze, then soothed it as his chest heaved like he was holding back again. I didn't want him to hold back.

Rolling half toward him, I shifted to give him access to my side and the other ass cheek. He pressed more warm kisses along my shoulder to that spot on my neck, and when he set his teeth there, my pussy squeezed so hard my stomach jerked.

"Levi," I said, or possibly whimpered, and scissored my legs together as liquid pooled in my swollen sex.

"Are you aching again?" he asked in a low growl.

"Yes," I said, my eyes shut tight, immersed in sensation.

"I've got you." Sliding an arm underneath me again, he pulled me closer with my back to his front in the little spoon spot. His fingers massaged my hip with more of that intensity before roaming across my stomach. It wasn't where I wanted him, needed him like my next breath.

I placed my hand atop his and moved it lower, all the way down.

He hummed in my ear and cupped me over the fabric of my panties. "These are soaked, babe. You need this. I need it too. Touching you where you're soft."

He nipped at my neck, and my pussy squeezed harder this time. He must have sensed it because he growled low, and his arm banded tighter at my breasts. His biceps bulged, the strength in his hold a contrast to the tenderness of his touch.

Too turned on to stop myself, I wantonly draped one leg back over his, opening and angling to recline against him like he was the world's sexiest chaise. I arched my hips to pull him in and reached up behind me, threading my fingers through his hair. "Levi, please."

He quickly made use of the new room and slid his hand into the waistband of my panties. "Yes," I said as he slid lower until there was nothing between him and the place I needed him most.

He dipped a finger at my opening. "Later, I'm going to taste you here. Strip off that hot fucking thong, spread your lush thighs wide, and eat you up."

"Yes," I said, panting hard, nearly gasping. He slid a single digit through my folds and lower, collecting the wetness there and bringing it to circle my clit. Then a second finger joined the first, and he massaged the outer edges of my entrance, collecting more wetness to circle my clit again. Again and again, he repeated the motion like a sexy figure eight.

I was climbing. I made some unintelligible noise, like a cry or plea. Words escaped me, lost in the rising tide of his touch and my need for release. My hips jerked against him as my core spasmed once. This could happen.

"You're close, babe." His breath danced across my ear, and he set to work in earnest.

"I don't … want to promise."

"No expectations," he said, taking me higher with those two magical fingers stroking my opening while the heel of his hand pressed into my clit.

I gripped his hair and arched into his touch. "Oh, yes. Just like that." It was building. It was happening.

Bang. "Hey, guys! You up?" As if from a distance, Jill's sharp voice echoed into the room and the door opened halfway.

Levi's hand froze, his fingers pressed to my opening so tight I felt myself pulsing. So close.

"Jill," I gasped and blinked back from the brink. "Get out." I reached to pull the comforter up before she peered in for an eyeful.

"Sorry to interrupt your—morning," she said from behind the door. "But we have an issue." Her tone was pure exasperation.

"Is … is everything okay?"

"No! My bachelorette party has gone to shit, literally. So, family meeting. Oh, and breakfast is ready if that's a better motivator."

I heaved a breath. What in the ever-loving-hell? "Give us a minute."

"Give him the O and let's go," Jill barked.

Levi looked at me as if asking for permission. "Actually, I'm focused on Kate right now. So, if you could close the door …"

Jill huffed and muttered, "That'll take a while," but at least she left.

That did not just happen. My sister did not practically let herself into the room I shared with my fake … real *boyfriend*, as if she had the right.

Levi removed his fingers from my panties with a slow drag through my drenched center, gave them a quick suck, and dried them on his chest.

I blinked, returning to the moment and the fact Levi had me on the edge of coming.

He shifted out from under me to settle on top of me instead, his hard cock nestled at my hip. "You were almost there. I felt it."

"I was." I groaned.

"Let's turn this into a good thing. A little edging, and we try again later," he soothed. "Something to look forward to."

I huffed. "I can't believe my sister. Is nothing sacred to her?"

"She seems to be in *stressed bride* mode today." He pulled a face.

"She almost walked in on us." That would be a fun story to tell at the dinner table.

"Nah. I was prepared to pull you to my other side,

block her view with my back if that door opened any wider. No big deal."

"No big deal? Have you had that happen often?" I teased.

"Not often, but I've been interrupted." His shrug was casual, too casual.

I frowned. "Really? Why?"

He hesitated. It was Levi-speak for telling me something he was worried about sharing. "I like to have sex outside. Always have."

I raised my brows.

"I was young and stupid in my early days, but I've learned a few things since then."

"You like to have sex in public?" My heart sank. That was a deal breaker for me.

"No, I don't want to be watched. Well, except maybe in a mirror, so I get to watch too. I like the freedom of it. That's the only way I can explain it. I'm a nature guy. I'm most alive outdoors. It could be in the woods, in a field, camping somewhere in a tent, or on a patio like the lanai out there." He grinned.

"I like it in a bed, too," he said quickly. "It's not like it has to be outside." His expression was guarded, vulnerable.

I bit my lip. Last night on the lanai was amazing. He was doing so much for me. I liked the idea of giving him what he liked. With a sultry lift of my chin, I asked, "Is that on your list of adventures for us this week?"

"It is now." His eyes sparked with heat.

I laughed. "Okay. As long as it's private."

He grinned and pulled me close. "I've got you."

18

LEVI

Ten minutes later, Kate and I were dressed and headed into the kitchen, but my mind was still back in bed. Kate's body tensing and her pleasure building, and me, feeling how close she was. I may have wanted it as much as she did.

I couldn't deny the caveman in me was thumping his chest that I was the guy with her, but even more, I wanted Kate to feel good.

Troye sat at the breakfast bar, and Jill practically vibrated behind him, clutching her phone while Janie typed away on her computer at the nearby table where Steven, Phillip, Mei, and the kids were finishing their breakfasts. Bright morning sunshine streamed in through the open wall, contradicting the somber mood.

I noted that Sam and Cher were missing and wondered how they managed to avoid being summoned. Must be an early yoga class or something.

"Finally," Jill grumbled, gripping the back of Troye's chair as he shifted and scowled at his plate like a jealous asshole.

"So, what's the problem?" Kate asked, examining the remaining slices of vegetable quiche. She looked at me. "You can have the bigger one."

"If you want it, take it. Keep your strength up." I smiled and stroked my hand down her hair, pulled back in a ponytail. "Take care of you, Kate, or I will," I whispered against her temple.

With a knowing look and a hip check for me, she added the bigger piece to her plate along with a pile of freshly cut papaya and lime.

"That's my girl," I said with a wink.

"The problem"—Jill announced, commanding our attention— "is that King Luau had a water spill, or something."

"A sewer pipe burst in the kitchen," Janie stated in a bland tone, clicking her mouse and focusing on her screen.

"Oh no," Kate said.

"Right?" Jill replied, like this was a personal attack. "And because the plumber can't install a new sink or whatever until Friday, they won't be able to open until the weekend. They canceled the luau experience we planned for my bachelorette party Thursday. I mean, they couldn't find another plumber? Why is my party now at the leisure of a *plumber*?" She spat the word and threw up her arms in exasperation.

"We all live at the leisure of plumbers," Kate said. "They kinda make the world go around. I wouldn't want to live without one."

Jill stared at her sister like she'd spoken in another language. "Plumbers make the world go around? I think that's the gravitational pull of the moon."

"Actually, you have the backward," Steven added, oblivious to the tension filling the room.

"Ugh! I don't care. What are we going to do about my party?"

"What are the options?" Kate asked. "Another luau? Most of the big hotels have them."

"The one on the historic point in Kona still has availability," Janie said. "It has great reviews, but I doubt there's time to accommodate any requests like a signature cocktail or exclusive performance from the fire dancers."

"It will be like any other luau," Jill whined, and I half expected her to stomp her feet. "Troye's sister is coming, and his cousins from New York City. They're expecting an event with special perks for *my* party at the premier luau in Hawaii. I doubt any *hotel luau* will impress them." Frustration and entitlement seeped from every pore.

"Babe," Troye said and glanced at Kate. "We'll explain. It'll be fine. My family loves you."

Something flashed between Troye and Kate with that glance. Had he called her 'babe'? Hell. I was *not* calling her that again. Why didn't she tell me?

"You don't understand. This is important. This is *my* day," Jill said. "One I've dreamed about for years and planned for what feels like that long, and now it's ruined."

"I thought the *wedding* was your day. How many days do you get?" Kate asked calmly and added cream to her coffee.

Jill glared. "I don't expect you to understand, Kate. All you care about is your career."

Like a record scratch, the room fell silent. This was

more than Bridezilla. This was personal. I shifted closer to Kate and kept my expression blank as I looked hard at her sister. If no one else defended Kate, I sure as hell would.

Kate audibly inhaled and set her plate down. "I know you're disappointed, Jill, but let's just take a look at what Janie found." Her voice was calm, soothing like a therapist or … a doctor delivering bad news, but I caught the edge to it.

She gestured for Jill to join her behind Janie's chair. The woman looked like a bear caught in a trap, but she did as Kate asked, and together, they looked over Janie's shoulder at the photos of the other luau. "This one looks great. Don't you think? It's in a park, and they do a historic reenactment. King's didn't have that."

Kate put her hand on Jill's shoulder. "If this is all that goes wrong with a destination wedding, I'd say you're winning. It'll still be your day."

"You really think so?" Jill asked, her voice smaller now.

"I do," Kate said in a tone light as air, and the tension in the room ebbed. "Now, what's in this quiche? It looks delicious."

Kate smiled at me as she grabbed her plate and coffee and gestured toward the table.

What the fuck? I had whiplash.

"Shall I make the reservation?" Janie asked, raising her eyebrows.

Jill exhaled a deep sigh. "Yes. Thank you, Janie. I'm sorry for yelling. There's a lot of moving parts, and I'm extremely stressed right now, but I appreciate everything you're doing."

"Um, Kate just—" I started.

Kate reached across the table, rested her hand on my forearm, and gave her head a small shake.

Jill looked at me. "Kate just wants you to be happy." It surprised me that I didn't crack a tooth grinding out those words.

We would talk about this later. Kate took a verbal punch, then diffused the bomb that was her sister, and no one fucking noticed?

I barely tasted my quiche as I chewed. I needed to get her away from here … and me too, before I told Jill exactly where she could shove her *extreme stress*.

"Let's go to Volcanoes National Park this afternoon," I said, leaning close and keeping my voice controlled. "It's not too far from the black sand beach we're headed to already. We can stick to the morning plans with your family, then go for a hike around the crater, just the two of us."

Janie's head perked up. "Oh, let's all go," she declared, deciding for everyone. "A national park trip will be good for the kids, educational."

My eyes shot to Kate's.

"Sounds good." Her expression was resolute.

Shit.

"That was not the plan," I whispered as the conversation switched to logistics.

"It's fine. It's a day. We'll get through it."

I didn't want to *get through it*. Getting through it wasn't good enough. And this probably delicious quiche still tasted like chalk.

Mei rose and collected empty plates, placing her hand on Kate's shoulder as she passed. That was something. Phillip grabbed empty glasses and took them to the counter by the sink.

"Kate and I will load the dishwasher," I said, taking the dishes from Mei. I couldn't sit still any longer. "You've done it almost every time. It's our turn."

"Oh, thank you," Mei said.

Phillip brought the coffee carafe and filled Mei's mug. "Join me on the lanai this morning, Mrs. Wells?"

"I'd be delighted," she said, like all was well.

Again. What the fuck?

"You scrape. I'll load," I told Kate once we were on the other side of the breakfast bar. My tone was gruffer than I intended.

She eyed me and reached for a plate.

"What just happened?" I asked.

"I know what you're thinking, but it's for the best."

"How can you taking one on the chin be for the best?" I loaded the dish into the nearly full dishwasher.

"The situation was getting intense. It's what I do." She scraped another plate.

"This is typical? She says something horrible, and you take it?"

"If I'm around, yes."

"If not?"

Kate sighed. "I guess she yells at someone else. I don't know. I'm not here."

"Kate, come on."

She emptied the coffee server and added a drop of dish soap as it filled with hot water. "It's always been like this. It's why I usually stay for a maximum of three days. Notice we're on day four here?"

"Why you and not Janie?"

Kate shrugged a shoulder. "Maybe because she and Jill are closer. They get each other. I'm the fat sister who can't keep a man and values her career too much."

"What the fuck, Kate?" Stunned anger rose like bile.

"It doesn't matter. The best approach is to ignore her and not let what she says impact who I am. I left Arizona for grad school. I made my life. She made hers. There was a time I may have wanted all three of us to be close, but that's not our family. This is our family."

"I'm not sure I can ignore it. And your body is perfect."

She huffed a smile. "Levi, I'm fine. I like my body most of the time."

"I like it all the time. I wouldn't change one fucking dimple."

Her expression softened. "Thank you."

"You don't believe me," I stated the fact, my tone still gruff as I set the dishwasher to run.

She reached for a dishcloth to wipe down the now-empty counter. "I do … I did. I'm complicated."

"No, you're not. You need someone to have your back once in a while."

"I do have those people. They're just not my sisters. I'm okay. There are worse lives to lead. I have friends, and I *love* my work. How many people can say that?"

I could. But I knew it was rare. "I like how you love your work. It's the same for me."

Her shoulders relaxed as she rinsed the dishrag. "I tell my sisters my career keeps me away because it's an easy excuse to escape when I've reached my limit. I never argue about it because that would blow my cover. And I *do* love my job."

She draped the dishcloth over the faucet to dry and rested her hip against the counter. "I have a patient, Mrs. K. She's in her seventies and lives on an apple farm on Sauk Island. Her son and his family work the trees now, but she's alone in that big old farmhouse filled with the most beautiful plants and flowers you could imagine. I swear, when she talks about them, the blooms turn toward her like they're listening." Her voice was tender, her expression distant.

"Her husband died, and she refuses to leave their home of fifty years. I've seen her at least once a month since I took this job, monitoring some heart issues and bringing her a medication that has to be compounded at the pharmacy in Perry Harbor. She always has a casserole or cookies or pie *just out of the oven*." She changed her voice on the last words to sound like an elderly woman.

"She feels like family, and sometimes my visits with her and others run late. It was the thing boyfriends complained about the most, because what kind of asshole complains about my lack of orgasm?" She pulled a face. "But I didn't start limiting my time with them. I couldn't."

I moved in and wrapped Kate in my arms. "Your patients care about you, and you're good to the people who care about you."

She exhaled, and her body relaxed into mine. "Exactly."

19

KATE

NOT LONG AFTER BREAKFAST, THE FLORIST CALLED WITH changes to the flower arrangements due to supply issues, and Jill and Janie drove to the shop to deal with it in person. Wedding stress mode was here to stay, and our "fun family day" which included a trip to the coffee plantation to pick out favors for the wedding guests, a stop at the black sand beach, and a subsequent journey to the national park, had to be delayed a bit.

At least the rest of us could enjoy some drama-free time. Levi left for a run, and I headed to the bedroom for some space and a chance to check on Kristen, hopefully living her best life in Yellowstone.

Me: Hey!! Thinking about you. Proof of life, please.

Kgirl: Hey!

A photo of Kristen smiling into the camera, with her watch face visible, showing today's date, popped up. A wooded campsite was in the background with a guy hunched over the fire holding a spatula.

Me: So, you aren't trapped in the woods with a serial killer?

Kgirl: No!! Chris is amazing.

Me: How's the trip?

Kgirl: So good. I repelled down a rock face yesterday. Repelled! I'm a badass.

Me: I knew this.

Kgirl: [heart emoji]

Me: And Chris is good?

Kgirl: The best. The man knows his shit about camping. Cooks full meals over an open fire. No beef jerky here.

Kgirl: And don't get me started on the wood chopping. Shirtless capability porn x 10.

Kgirl: He does what he says he'll do. He talks! If he likes something about me, he says it. And his eyes are this incredible shade of green.

Me: [kissy face emoji]

Kgirl: I keep thinking it's not real. He's married or doesn't do commitment.

Kgirl: But it feels real. I think I'm happy. I think I'm in love.

Love? It had been days. Could you fall in love in days?

I hadn't seen Levi chop wood, but I could imagine it, and it was spectacular. He did what he said. He blurted out the things he liked about me.

But love would be so inconvenient.

Kgirl: How's your trip? Have you stabbed a sister yet?

I chuckled.

Me: Not yet. A few close calls though.

Me: I've had some adventures too. Went ziplining yesterday.

Kgirl: Wow! With your sisters?

Me: No. Could break a nail. Funny story …

Kgirl: Pins and needles.

Me: Levi Abrams took me.

Kgirl: Hot guy from the hospital?

Me: Yep.

Kgirl: OMG! [shocked emoji] He's there? Details.

Me: Not sure if Chris told you, but he was supposed to go on that trip with one of his friends. Levi.

Kgirl: This trip?

Me: Yes. And since Levi got dumped for you and I got dumped for Chris, Levi came with me.

Kgirl: !!! How???

Me: He was sitting next to me when we both got our breakup texts.

Kgirl: Seriously!

Me: I needed a date. He was free. It was supposed to be fake. Turns out, it's not so fake.

Kgirl: [celebration emoji]

Kgirl: This is fate. You guys are perfect for each other.

Me: Um, how?

Kgirl: Chris is perfect for me. It only makes sense that our best friends would fall in love. It's meant to be.

Me: This isn't a Hallmark movie. And who said anything about love?

Kgirl: He got you to go ziplining. I'm not sure you'd do that for me, and I know you love me. So, what else has he gotten you to do? [eggplant emoji]

Kristen knew my recent history with men, but she didn't know the specifics about Troye. Getting dumped more than once for not being good in bed was humiliating enough. A broken engagement was too much.

Me: He's gotten me thinking he could help me do a lot of things. [winky face emoji]

Kgirl: Woot Woot.

Kgirl: You meet the guy on Friday. Fly to Hawaii on Saturday. And by Tuesday, he's got you heading to O town. That's some fast-moving boyfriend.

Me: It's a vacation fling. [smiley face emoji]

Kgirl: You never know. [thinking emoji] Gotta go. Talk later.

Levi was the best vacation fling imaginable.

Snuggling back into the nest of rumpled bedding, I stared out at the view beyond our lanai and thought of him on his run, shirtless in the sun. His very capable … *so capable* … fingers holding his water bottle. His firm leg muscles flexing with exertion. His lips parting with his labored breathing.

I pictured his hands on my body, touching and teasing. His perfect kissable mouth there, too. His dark hair and darker smile peeking up from between my thighs, his lips shiny with my arousal.

My nerve endings buzzed as blood rushed lower. I'd been in a state of perpetual horniness since Levi and I were interrupted earlier. In the quiet alone of the bedroom, my body was jumping ahead.

I pressed the heel of my hand below my pubic bone, closed my eyes, and gave myself over to the visions in my head while my other hand teased a nipple through my thin tank top and sheer bra.

Take care of you, Levi said, and I intended to. Then, when he returned from his run, I'd take care of him too. His cock was hard as stone earlier, pressed into my low back while his fingers took me higher. He'd been as unsatisfied as I was, and I could help with that. But my body wouldn't wait.

I shoved my shorts down to the foot of the bed along with my panties and pulled my shirt off, draping the fabric over my eyes to block out the bright sunlight. The visions in my mind, a mash-up of last night and this morning, now merged into a fantasy of us naked on the lanai in the dim glow of the evening.

He liked sex outside. I let my imagination run wild as my excitement grew. A blanket on the grass or a lonely picnic table at a quiet campground. He'd be surprised as he looked up in the moonlight to see me pulling off an oversized sweatshirt, leaving me in only panties.

Fire would ignite in his eyes, and his breath would catch as he pulled me to him. He'd hold me tight and whisper about how much he liked my body, how much he wanted me. I'd squirm from the pleasure pooling in my core.

My pussy swelled against my busy fingers.

He'd be hard, like he was this morning, except this time, there wouldn't be any interruptions. Slowly, with intention, he'd slide my panties free, learn what I needed, then use his hands and mouth to give it to me in the quiet night.

He'd be gentle and then not. He'd shift to cover me, let me feel him close but still too far, then kiss me until I was begging, and kiss me some more. Finally, he'd sink into me, and his dick, not too big, would touch the inside place and stretch my opening just enough to ignite fire in the nerve endings there. I'd be free and lost, and as he moved, the pressure would build until I couldn't hold back. I'd go off like a rocket, like I did when I was younger, and Levi would too.

Then he'd do it all again.

I bent my legs and let my knees fall wide, slipping my hand lower. My sex was slick and pulsing, my arousal at full force. I attempted the same figure eight pattern Levi used, teasing and stroking with perfect pressure right where I needed it.

My nipples were hard. My blood was warm, and my face flushed.

"Levi." His name sounded right as I rocked my hips, recalling his slow rhythm from earlier. In my mind, his eyes flashed when I called his name, and he growled low, as if fighting the urge to consume me.

It was his hand there now, and the telltale contractions hit my inner walls in subtle bursts. I was climbing. I was going to soar.

Everything felt real. His firm body behind me instead of pillows, his gentle fingers between my legs, his cardamom and leather scent mixed with the smell of the outdoors.

My breath panted. "Levi … please … Hold me tight. I need it." My voice sounded distant as in a tunnel, my climax growing closer. I gripped the sheet with my free hand, and sensations overtook me like a freight train. There was only this excitement, the sound of my rapid breaths, and the images of Levi driving me higher.

My finger was his finger skating across my hard nipple in my haze. The thin mesh of my bra added to the sensation, and I arched into his warm palm there now, gently massaging and stroking in a new way. So hot. I clenched the sheet tighter in my free hand.

Wait. My breath caught, and I reached for the shirt covering my eyes.

"Don't." Levi's voice was tender but clear as he held the material in place while his other hand pressed over mine where it had stilled against my center.

"Don't stop, Kate. Almost there."

"Levi … what?" I was a little lightheaded, and with my makeshift blindfold, I wasn't sure if he was real or the result of *extremely* well-honed fantasy muscles.

"You said please. You asked me to hold you. I'm here to do that." His voice was low and pleading. "I'll go if you want, but I want to stay. You are so fucking sexy, Kate. Let me stay."

Oh, my god. Levi wanted to watch me. He'd basically said as much yesterday, but I hadn't given any more thought to letting him.

"I brought you something," he said and placed a cool object on my belly.

My vibrator.

"Give yourself what you need, and I'll hold you like you asked me to."

My mind raced with the dirty thrill of it, pushing my doubts to the distant edge. I licked my dry lips. "Okay."

"Lean up," he directed, still gently pressing the shirt over my eyes as he nudged my shoulder forward. His warm body slid onto the bed behind me, and he cradled my back to his front. My head fell against his solid, bare chest. The surrounding air sizzled with *him*. His warmth. His scent. His rapid breaths.

He wrapped his arm around my middle, under my breasts. "The view from here, Kate, I can't look away." He pulled my hair to one side and placed gentle kisses along my neck, finding that special spot with the lightest brush of his lips.

A full-body shudder slammed into me, and my inner walls contracted reflexively. I groaned with it.

"It's okay," he said while he guided my hand holding the vibrator back to my center. "Make yourself feel good."

Without my permission, my fingers switched on the toy and set it to just the right level from sheer muscle memory. The vibe buzzed, and I slid it over my clit.

Levi did growl then. "This is the hottest thing. *You* are the hottest fucking woman ever."

I let the moment take me back to that fantasy campsite, the night sky bright with stars and Levi's lust barely leashed. There, I *was* the hottest fucking woman ever.

20

LEVI

Holy shit, she was doing it. She arched against me as my favorite pink vibe rested against her center, and her hips pulsed with tiny movements.

My dick was hard as a rock the second I walked through the wide-open wall of our room after my run. I'd finally talked him all the way down after being interrupted this morning. Running with a boner was not the move. But he was full strength now, especially when she said my name.

She'd been touching herself, the petal-soft pink of her, and thinking of me. There was no way I didn't get hard.

When she let out a frustrated little moan, like she needed more, I damn near *ran* to the shower for her vibrator. Back by the bed, I heard her say please, and that was it.

Her pretty pink nipples stood firm and tall, pressing into the pale pink mesh of her bra, begging to be touched. So, I did, smoothing lightly over one peak. And when it strained higher, seeking more, I'd filled my palm with her softness.

Now, with the woman in my arms, I was unshakable. The world could burn down, and I wouldn't leave this bed. My eyes locked on the movements of her hand while mine found that tender bud again.

She squirmed as I massaged, pinched, and teased her nipple before filling my palm with the softest flesh imaginable, over and over while I bit and kissed anywhere my lips could reach.

"So damn sexy, Kate."

"Levi." It was a moan and a plea.

"I'm here, wishing those fingers were mine, wanting to stroke and pet, and know those moans are for me."

"They *are* for you. You get me so hot."

My dick swelled thicker, and I had to suck a breath through my nose to calm my shit down.

Her movements increased in tandem with her breathing. She scissored her legs and fisted the sheet. She was getting close.

"Tease those plump lips," I said. "It's my mouth there, hungry for your taste." I bit that magic spot on her neck, and she gasped as I licked and sucked her skin. "I'm doing it, and you taste amazing."

"Levi," she panted. "I'm … oh god … I'm." Her voice broke as her bent legs trembled and her middle curled and contracted with spasm after spasm. She let out a hushed, keening cry, then rolled to her side with the vibe still humming at her center.

She didn't move, except to switch off the toy. I smoothed her hair off of her face and ran my fingertips over the ball of her shoulder, down her arm then back again while she breathed, and I waited. "Kate?"

Like a cat stretching, she arched and flashed a smile

before rolling to face me. It was a three-sixty view of all those curves. "I came with a partner," she said, her eyes glittering. "I came with you."

"Yeah, I saw." I let the truth settle. "Thank you for letting me stay."

"Mmm, my pleasure, obviously." She pulled herself up and kissed me. Our lips locked together, and I slid lower on the bed to pull her body over mine. She still wore only her bra, and her tits pressed against my chest. I held her center to my hard dick, aching to break out of my running shorts.

"You have something in your pants," she said between kisses.

I chuckled. "You noticed? I might have to do with the hottest woman ever touching herself and moaning my name. That'll do it every time."

"So, it's my fault?" She teased and nipped my lower lip. My dick jumped.

"A hundred percent you."

She broke the kiss. "Then I better take care of it. Shower?"

My grin was so big it hurt my face. "I thought you'd never ask."

She shifted away, and I followed like we were tied together.

I'd pulled off my shoes, socks, and sweaty shirt before I climbed on the bed earlier. Shoving off my remaining clothes hardly caused me to miss a step walking behind those swaying hips. She twisted an arm around to unclasp her bra before it fell at my feet, and she reached to turn on the water.

With a glance back at me, she stepped inside the

stone tile walls. No hesitation or shy regret. Just a sultry smile I would follow anywhere.

She'd let me watch her come hard, her body rocking with it, out of control. Amazing. *She* was a volcano.

"Kate," I said and pulled her to me, my hands cupping her face on both sides. I needed to kiss her, get my hands on her, and this time, it wasn't sweet or slow. It was hard and fast, our tongues tangling, our arms wrapped around each other in the warming spray.

She broke the kiss and leaned away, watching as a finger slid over my collarbone and lower. She looked up and licked her lips.

Damn those lips. They *were* the same pink color as her plump nipples, standing at attention. I'd never unsee it. "Kate—"

"Shh. I'm busy," she said as the water pulsed against my back, and she leaned in to suck a droplet from my skin.

"Ba—" I stopped myself. "You'll get cold."

"I'm not cold." Her hands continued down my torso until a single finger brushed across the head of my dick. It jumped, straining for contact. "I'd say I'm getting warm, hot even."

She met my eyes again, this time with an evil gleam in hers, and repeated the touch. She did it again and again, circling and stroking but never going lower than the crown, never squeezing the way I needed, pure torturing pleasure.

I groaned and let my head fall back into the spray. "You are bad, and I don't give one fuck."

With the teasing mask still in place, she turned to face the back wall and canted forward, pushing her ass toward me. "Do I need a spanking, Daddy?"

I froze at the image of her incredible backside stained pink and tingling as I caressed and kissed each bump and valley.

She spun with a giggle, and I pressed her to the wall with a merciless kiss.

"Not a funny joke, Kate," I warned. "Don't tease me about your ass. It's like waving a red cape in front of a bull. I've never been anyone's Daddy Dom, but you and all that body of yours make me want to try."

I shifted closer, notching my painfully hard dick at her hip, and she squirmed.

"You're right. That wasn't nice," she said, breathless. "And you were so nice to me. Let me do better."

Her eyes were bright, and she pushed me away to reach for my body wash, squeezed some into her hand, and breathed deeply. "I love the way you smell."

I gripped her hips. "Same. I don't think I'll ever be able to eat coconut again and not get a boner."

Her soft laugh bounced off the walls, and I had to laugh too.

With intention and a washcloth, she soaped my chest and moved to my back. A little hum escaped as she stepped into the spray behind me.

"I knew you were cold," I said and shifted to turn, ready to do my part in touching Kate.

"I'm fine," she said, stopping me and continuing her efforts, washing my legs and over my ass before moving to face me again.

"Now you," I said and reached for her body wash.

"Not yet. One more spot." Her focus moved down my body. She smoothed the cloth over my hips and upper thighs, coming closer to my dick each time, but never close enough.

"Thought you were being nice," I said, tucking my finger under her chin and raising her gaze to mine. "You're killing me here, ba—um, Kate."

"What happened to 'babe'?" She looked at me with something like playful hurt in her eyes before she kissed my throat.

I swallowed. "He called you that."

She brought her hands to my chest, her easy expression unchanged. "Now he calls Jill that. And *you* call me 'babe.'"

"I don't want to call you what he did. I don't want you to remember one thing about being with him."

"But that's it. Every time you say it, it erases one time he did. His voice is fading while yours is getting louder, stronger, sexier." She glanced at my lips. "I want *you* to say it."

"You're sure?"

"Yes."

"You wouldn't prefer Baby Girl," I said and winked.

She lightly pinched my nipple and gave me a smirk.

"Or Sweet Tits. That could be my favorite. Let's see." I bent my head and sucked one of the swollen tips, long and full, into my mouth. So. Good. I rolled my tongue around it with teasing sucks before I eased back to skim my lips over the pursed flesh. She was definitely sweet.

I glanced up, and her eyes were closed, her mouth open.

"No saucy come back?" I asked, bending to give her other nipple the same treatment. I needed to spend more time with my mouth on her perfect tits.

"Why would I do anything to make you stop when you're doing just what I like?"

"You like my mouth on you, *babe*?" I asked, with emphasis on the last word.

"So much."

"Yeah, me too."

I liked a helluva lot more. I liked her. She could be demanding, and playful, and vulnerable, all at the same time. How did she manage it? I'd never met anyone like her.

Surrounded by her signature scent, I washed her body, concentrating on certain spots and watching her breathing change as I did. Clean, she stepped into the water to rinse off, and my eyes followed the sudsy bubbles down the shallow valley between her tits and over her soft belly to the thick patch of curls at her center.

"I want my lips on every curve and dip, babe."

"Not this time," she said and returned to me. Her warm fingers wrapped around my dick and stroked.

"How do you like it?" she asked. "Will you show me? I showed you mine."

I covered her hand with my palm and guided her. "Yes, you did. And I plan to use that information responsibly. I hope you do, too."

Kate was a quick study, taking control and slowly making me lose my mind.

My dick swelled as I watched her, and her pace quickened. "Feels good," I grunted. My blood was hot, and pleasure pulsed. "I'm … close." Talking in complete sentences while nearing the point of no return was a struggle.

Her voice was low and sounded like a smile. "I want you to come hard, Levi. Can you do that like this, or do you need my mouth?"

"Oh, fuck," I nearly shouted. Just thinking about her wet tongue on me got me there. I covered her hand with mine, and she squeezed as pleasure shot straight from my spine through my balls. I exploded, hard. As instructed.

For a minute, I stood there, my dick pulsing as the warm water fell over us. She stroked me gently once and released me. I steadied myself with a hand on the wall as the spots in my vision cleared and I opened my eyes to see her satisfied expression, the evidence of my release on her hand and my stomach.

"Here," I said and shifted us both to clean up before I held her against me. I needed to feel her, all of her, skin to skin. "That was incredible, Kate." I kissed her hard, then soft.

Her face was almost innocent as she looked at me. "It was. Maybe we can do it again later."

Hell, yes.

We eventually left the enormous shower space and helped each other dry off with the fluffy white towels.

"You were right," Kate announced as she finished dressing in bright green shorts that looked like a skirt. My sister called them skorts. Whatever, they were sexy as hell, showing off her tempting thighs.

"I like hearing you say that. So, what exactly was I right about?"

She strolled over as I pulled my Kona Brewing T-shirt over my head.

"There are lots of ways to make each other feel good."

I grabbed that fine ass of hers and yanked her against me. "And we haven't even done my *favorite* kissing ones yet."

21

KATE

HAVING AVERTED A FLOWER CRISIS, JILL AND JANIE returned, and everyone gathered in the kitchen, where Sam and Mom announced they wouldn't be joining us for *family day*. They were meeting with a realtor instead.

None of us were surprised that Mom flaked on the day, but … moving to Hawaii? Together? That was out of left field even for her. Who was this woman?

I made eye contact with Janie, the question clear on my face, and nodded at Dad, who again seemed nonplused. Janie's expression of surprise mirrored my own, but we both said nothing as the happy couple made their way to the door.

Once it closed, I looked at Dad. "You knew about this?"

He shrugged. "I knew they were thinking about it. They mentioned it the last time we had dinner."

Janie shook her head. "Start at the beginning. You have dinner with them?"

Dad looked at Mei as if checking the facts. "We've

met a couple of times, yes. Your mother and I *were* married for over twenty years, you know. There's history there, and it wasn't all bad."

"She cheated. She hurt you." My voice was nearly a whisper.

He nodded. "She did, and I hurt her back. But you can't stay in that place forever, Katie-girl. You could miss out on some pretty great things." He smiled at Jill. "There was a family wedding coming up. It made sense for the four of us to get to know each other, if only for that reason."

He gave us his signature head nod, like when we were kids and moved to press a kiss to Mei's temple. She gazed up at him, her smile full of love, and went back to packing a cooler with snacks and drinks as the room filled with silence. I needed a minute to process. Maybe we all did.

"I'll drive the big rig," Steven said, changing the subject. "Who's with me?"

Levi jumped in. "Kate and I will take the Jeep so we can stay later. The hikes we picked at the park could be hard for the kids."

"You're a genius," I said as we rolled down the road a few minutes later in our own peace and quiet. "And thanks for driving."

"I'm right, *and* I'm a genius." He winked at me. "I assumed you could use the space."

"Right again."

My parents were friends. Or at least friendly after cheating, lawyers, money battles, and not one shared holiday for years. Huh.

Levi reached over, took my hand, and brought it to

his lips for a small kiss, then threaded our fingers together. He did it all with his eyes focused ahead, familiar, like he'd done it a hundred times. My heart thumped.

The stop at the small coffee plantation was quick. After a brief tour of the processing house and roaster, nestled above the slope of trees that resembled bushes more than anything else, Jill selected beans for the white decorator bags she planned to give away at the ceremony.

"There's a food truck round-up not too far from here. We could stop for lunch," Levi suggested to my family as we made the short walk back to the parking lot. "Should be something for everyone."

"I doubt there's organic," Janie said with a sigh. "But, when in Rome."

I raised my brows at Levi, and we both chuckled at the relaxed version of her today. That hot tub time with Steven last night may have worked a miracle.

We all placed our orders at various trucks. Levi and I chose the Hawaiian spicy shredded pork with steamed rice and macaroni salad, then grabbed a bag of malasadas for later.

We were the first to settle at one of the picnic tables in the center of the space, bordered by the sweet and savory smells. I took a bite of the saucy meat and fanned my mouth. "This is spicier than I expected."

Levi eyed me with a gleam. "Too hot, Baby Girl?" he asked, leaning close.

"If it was, what would Daddy do about it?" I sassed as Janie and Jill rounded the table from behind.

"Don't let us interrupt," Janie said, raising a single brow.

"No interruption," I replied, returning to my meal and my normal voice as the rest of my family joined us. The sound of munching and chatter cut off any other remarks, thankfully. I didn't talk about sex with either of my sisters, real or fantasy. At least, not since our high school crush days.

Back on the road to Punalu'u Black Sand Beach, the breathtaking coastline stretched for miles. I glanced at Levi in profile. The sharp edge of his jaw contrasted with the silkiness of his lips. I watched the way his forearms flexed when he gripped the steering wheel.

I *liked* his arms. And the feeling of them tight around me. Strong. Gentle. A *real* man's arms. No other had taken such care to make me feel safe and sexy, two things I'd struggled with for a long time. And this morning, I'd not only climaxed with a partner, I did it with him watching. Levi made it happen.

I wanted to do something for him. A quick Google search revealed the perfect option. I navigated to the site, made a reservation online for tonight, and pocketed my phone.

The famous black sand beach, known for its wildlife, wasn't crowded. Several signs warned of strong currents, keeping most swimmers away. Instead, a few families were here with kids flying kites or examining the nearby tide pools, while others stood watching a couple of sea turtles playing in the surf.

Amelia and Carter ran heedlessly across the pocked black rock to the side of the shore in search of unknown sea creatures like any other seven-year-old and five-year-old while the rest of us wandered the glittering sand like powdered onyx.

"Careful, kids," Mei called from up the beach as she walked toward the surf. "The tide is coming in."

At that moment, a wave swamped the kids' feet and legs, causing them to squeal and wobble.

"I've got them," Levi shouted. He was closer than anyone else. Wearing his beloved hiking boots, he hopped across the expanse of pointy rocks and scooped up a kid under each arm. They squirmed with laughter as he carried them to a spot farther away from the water's edge.

I wouldn't say my ovaries exploded, but there was a twinge somewhere in their vicinity.

Setting down my niece and nephew, he pointed at something in one pool, and the kids peered into the swirling water.

"So," Janie said, sidling up to me as Steven joined Levi. "Baby Girl? Daddy?"

"It's a joke."

"I'm not judging. A little submission can be fun." She waggled her brows.

"You?"

She lifted her sunglasses and winked at me.

"And Steven's into it?" It had to be him doing the submitting. Janie would never.

"Of course he is. Not too complicated, my husband. He's bossy, sure, but it's hot, and he's more than tender after, which is even better."

I blinked under my baseball cap keeping the sun off my face. "You're the sub?"

"Are you shocked?"

"Actually, yes."

Janie chuckled. "Don't be. Who we are in the world isn't always who we are in the bedroom."

Well, that was for sure. Confident nurse by day, not-so-confident lover by night.

"It's good to explore who you are and what you like, if there's trust. Steven and I have been together for a long time. We know each other better than anyone. Trust each other more than anyone. If what we do works for us, who cares?"

I gave my head a tiny shake. "I … never would have guessed."

She let out an exaggerated sigh. "I have layers, Kate."

"So it would seem," I said, and we both chuckled.

"What's funny?" Jill asked, joining us, her eyes landing first on Janie, then me through her designer sunglasses.

"Nothing," I said with emphasis as Janie said, "A little sex chat."

I shot a glare at her. I may talk to Janie about this stuff, but not my ex's fiancée, sister, or not.

"Any questions before your honeymoon?" she teased, having not seen my look.

"Ah, no, I think I've got it. But don't let me stop you and Kate." Jill smiled sweetly.

"Actually, I'm good." I held up a hand and returned my focus to the two giant turtles rolling in the frothy waves.

"Really?" Jill sounded surprised.

I looked at her. "Yes, really."

"Oh, well, if that's true, great."

"Why wouldn't it be true?"

"I'm sure it is. But if not … you can talk to us." She hesitated. "Sex, good sex, is important. Janie and I both have very satisfying sex. We're your sisters. If you can't ask us for help, who can you ask?"

I turned to face her. "Help? What makes you think I need help?"

She gave me a pitying look.

"What?" Then it hit me. "Troye."

"He said you can't orgasm. He said it was a problem."

My eyes went wide. "He told you that? Under what circumstances exactly did he need to tell you anything about my orgasms?"

"Is this the time for this conversation?" Janie asked, lowering her voice.

"He thought I already knew," Jill said, ignoring Janie.

"Or he was comparing sisters," I said, disgust clear in my voice. "Talk about the ick."

"He wasn't comparing," she insisted, her tone a mix of exasperated and defensive. "He was talking about what wasn't, what *didn't* work with you. We were talking about us, how we *did* work."

Janie's hand brushed against my forearm, but there was no backing down this time.

"Jill, I'm aware it was a problem. Sussed that out all on my own with the breakup. But orgasms alone don't guarantee good sex. Maybe *he* was the problem."

"Kate, be serious. We both know it wasn't Troye."

"Right, because you fucked him, too. You and I are *not* comparing. Don't you think this week is awkward enough? Let's just get through it." I looked out at the surf, seeing nothing.

"But that's it. I don't want it to be awkward," Jill said. "I want to put it all behind us, finally. Maybe what happened with you and Troye wasn't anyone's fault. You two weren't compatible. We are. That's all."

"Wonderful. Then he's marrying the right sister." I turned to walk away.

"Wait," she said, her eyes pained. "I'm sorry. I want you to be *compatible* with someone too. I want to help. That's all. I didn't mean to pick a scab."

"There's no scab," I nearly shouted. "The past *is* behind us. It's done, and we don't need to talk about it. You've got him, and believe it or not, I don't want him back."

"That's good to hear," Levi said, surprising me with a playful grin as he put his arm around my shoulders, breaking the tension like he didn't know about it. But this was Levi. Ten bucks said he knew exactly what he was interrupting.

"I wasn't too concerned though," he added, a casual lilt in his voice. "She tried that on and was over it years ago. It's still good to have it spelled out. Thanks, Baby Girl," he whispered the nickname close like it was a dirty secret, but loud enough for my sisters to hear.

Janie smirked at me while Jill gaped.

"The sun won't be high forever, babe," Levi said with a sigh. "If we're going to hike at the park, we should get moving."

"What was that back there?" Levi asked when we were in the Jeep and on our way to the park.

"Troye told Jill I can't orgasm."

He glanced over at me.

"No worries, though. Jill assured me he wasn't comparing notes, but of course he was. And found me lacking. Probably wondered if it was genetic and fucked Jill the first time for science."

There was a beat of silence, then the Jeep slowed and pulled to the side of the road. Levi threw it in park and left the motor running.

I sighed and stared out the windshield. "That was bad. I didn't mean it. But there's this … tension between us. Like they think I still want him, or I'm hurt, or something."

Levi turned to me, draping his left arm over the steering wheel.

"Kate, look at me. First, you are not lacking anything. I'm not saying that because I'm here with you, or I want to get laid, or whatever women tell themselves when a man says nice things. I'm saying it because it's true. Second, I think there *is* something unfinished between you and Troye, something related to sex, and Jill's noticed it, too."

"Levi, I don't want to have sex with Troye."

"I know," he said. "I'm not sure that he doesn't want to have sex with you."

I stared, then shook my head. "There's no way. He didn't want to have sex with me when we were together. Those last months, I wanted it, wanted to keep trying to find my long-lost orgasm. He didn't. He's the one who gave up."

"You want to hear my theory?" he asked.

"Sure." Why not?

"Okay, this is him, not me." Levi raised his brows. "I think he's worried he was the one lacking. I think he couldn't figure out how to make you come and couldn't handle it."

"Troye did *not* take responsibility for my lack of orgasm."

"Okay, but I can say for me and for a lot of men, it's fucking fantastic to make a woman come. And when we can't, it's like *we* fail. We're just supposed to know how to do it with no further information. It was like being expected to pass a test without having gone to class, and all the girls had to do was give us a grade. A-plus for an orgasm. F-minus if not. We were doomed. Women don't always know their bodies, yet we're supposed to, and most of us were never told what to do with a clit, or even how to find it with a flashlight and a map."

I covered my grin with my hand. "You certainly found mine. Were you always such a natural?"

He chuckled. "No. I spent a lot of time huddled in the Sexual Health section of the public library, stealthily reading. Then, when I finally got a partner, it was a lot of trial and error, but I was willing to listen and learn."

Thank the goddess for that.

Levi's voice softened to a sexy rumble. "I think Troye sees us together, the way I look at you, and he doesn't like it."

"How do you look at me?"

"Like getting between your legs is next to heaven. He thinks we've fucked, and I've made you come, often. He hates I might know something he doesn't, aced a test he failed. He's jealous."

"But he's with Jill. She's probably coming all over him nightly. Why would he care about me anymore?"

Levi's expression was serious. "Maybe he wants another shot at that test."

"No."

"I said this was him, not me. Some guys let their pride cause them to do stupid shit."

"Like try to re-fuck a sister when engaged to the next one?"

Levi shrugged a single shoulder. "Stupid shit, Kate. Either way, you're on his mind. That's a fact."

I huffed. "That's it? That's your theory?"

"That's it."

22

LEVI

Kate eyed me. Whether or not she believed me, Troye *was* jealous. A small part of me felt bad for the guy. A tiny part. But expectations for most men to perform were high since about puberty. I wasn't always confident telling my friends about my number or my choice *not* to stick my dick in a girl just because I could. I didn't want to be mocked by my boys.

The road to being an adult was long, and for some guys, even longer.

"That can't be true." She stared out the windshield.

"What I *know* is true, Kate, is there is nothing lacking about you. Whatever the issue, it was as much him as it was you. That's how it works. It takes both partners to make it good."

She sighed and looked at me with a smile that finally hit her eyes. "Thank you, Levi. Where would I be without you this week? I don't even want to think about it."

I shifted the Jeep back into gear and checked my mirrors. "Me neither," I said, but I felt that way for a different reason. If I hadn't been here this week, I may not have known Kate. I may have lived my life without knowing her smile, her strength, her taste.

Sure, I could have met someone else, but it wouldn't have been like this. There weren't many Kates out there. I'd looked. I'd been looking.

At the park, we rejoined her family and made a quick stop at the Visitor's Center for maps and eruption information. We drove through vent fields, where clouds of steam rose from holes in the ground, on our way to the best viewpoint, miles away from the cone and its orange glow.

It would have been cool to get a closer view, but the only way to do that was via helicopter, and I'd heard too many puking stories about helicopter rides to attempt it. There were plenty of other non-vomit inducing adventures to be had.

The enormous crater was edged by a paved path on this side, and the short walk gave everyone a last chance to stretch their legs before the long drive back to Kona. There weren't any more comments from Jill, so I didn't have to swoop in and rescue Kate again. Though, I enjoyed rescuing her. Possibly to an alarming degree.

"Here's where we break off for *our* hike down to the lava field," I told everyone and took Kate's hand. "Have a safe trip."

"Will you be late?" Mei asked. "When should I worry?"

I looked at Kate. "We'll grab dinner after it gets dark—"

"Don't worry," Kate said. "We'll be fine."

Mei nodded, and Phillip stepped forward to give

Kate a hug and a quick kiss, like he might not see her again.

"We're coming back," I said with a grin. "The hike is steep, but we can do it."

"I know," he said, looking directly at me. "But she's my Katie-girl. Take good care of her."

There was something serious in his voice as he straightened.

I stood straighter too. "Yes, Sir. I will."

He nodded and joined the rest of his family on the walk back to the parking lot.

I didn't move.

"What?" Kate asked from a few feet ahead on the trail.

"Nothing."

But it wasn't nothing. If I didn't know better, I'd think Kate's father gave me his blessing. His approval to be with his beautiful, kind, generous daughter. The same one with the spectacular body teasing me in the shower this morning. Damn, I was in trouble. Or my pieced-together, formerly shredded heart was.

The organ in question thumped as if reminding me of the pain and the risk, and demanding protection. But Kate wasn't like other women. Maybe my heart didn't need protection this time.

"The difference is so stark," Kate observed as she glanced between the lush green forest around us and the barren gray lava field to our right. Taking the fork, we scrambled through a narrow section of the path until it opened up close to the top edge of the blown-out earth.

Plumes of smoke rose in the distance as we walked, and the light shifted with the sun. Kate checked her watch and hustled her steps.

"Need to be somewhere?" My tone was laced with smartass.

"Actually—" she rolled her lips between her teeth "—I have a surprise for you, but it's timed, and I don't want to miss it."

Oh. I grinned. "A private tour?"

She shook her head. "Not exactly."

"Dinner reservations in Hilo?"

Another head shake. "I said it's a surprise."

"Okay, when do we need to be there?"

"Six," she said.

I checked my watch. "How far away is this surprise?"

"Twenty minutes outside the park."

I grinned. "Okay, if we step up the pace, we can still hike part of the lava floor loop. Let's go, Wells." I grabbed her hand, and we hustled down the steep trail to the bottom of the old crater.

Scorched decades ago, the earth was still packed dust like a desert except for the dark snakes of more recent flows twisting over places where new life had finally grown. A struggle to recover, next to another setback or do-over, depending on how you looked at it.

We'd gotten some good pics this week and snapped a few more selfies as we hiked, then made the return climb to the cooler forest.

"You better drive since you know where we're going," I said, tossing the keys to Kate when we reached the Jeep. We both guzzled water from our refilled bottles and hopped in.

"Let's have those malasadas," she said as we pulled out of the lot. "Before my stomach starts howling."

"Would you like me to feed you, Baby Girl?" I glanced over at her, giving her my sexiest grin.

She eyed me, and I chuckled, handing her an ube one.

"That's not where we're going," I said, looking at the brightly painted helicopter in front of us. Its bold stripes looked like a birthday party. Others were here, one larger and one smaller, but Kate was heading toward the colorful one.

"That's where we're going," she said, and my stomach dropped as she pulled into a parking spot. "Have you ever been in one before?"

"No … aren't you scared of heights, though?"

"This, I'm used to. It's an hour's flight above the crater at twilight. We can see the lava better."

Fuck. I was mister capable-adventure-man, and I didn't want to blow it, literally. Not in front of Kate. My two malasadas churned in my stomach.

Climbing out of the Jeep, I sucked in a couple of deep breaths, and we greeted the woman who introduced herself as the pilot. She showed us to a small waiting area, where we filled out forms. Another couple was there too, newlyweds on their honeymoon.

"Good to meet you," I said and settled with Kate on a bench to await takeoff. There was coffee, tea, and other refreshments on a side table.

"Need a coffee?" Kate asked.

I shook my head.

"Are you nervous?" she whispered.

I cleared my throat. "What? No." Yes.

Kate beamed. "Wow. Finally, something I can help

you with. How about I hold you tight and whisper, 'I've got you'? Seems to work for me."

That sounded good. "I wouldn't say no to that."

In the end, I only *needed* her comfort for the first few moments. Take-off was … interesting, but once we were in the air, I was hooked. I didn't tell Kate, though, because I liked her squeezing my hand when the chopper dipped and turned to take another pass around the crater.

Red-orange and yellow lava bubbled so hot we felt the heat hundreds of feet in the air. "Forming new earth," the pilot said as a thin line of red stretched to the sea, where it hardened in a puff of white smoke, making the island a little bigger with each passing minute.

On the ground and high from the experience, I pulled Kate's body to mine in the shadows of the parking lot. "Thank you. That was unbelievable," I said, my blood pumping. "And now that's two incredible experiences you've given me today." I winked, thinking of our morning.

Her knowing smile was the best one yet. "I'm just giving back a little of what you've given me."

"Oh, I'm not done giving, Kate. Not even close." I pressed my lips to hers, and when she opened, I dove in, hungry for more of her. Right now. She moaned low, and my urgency notched higher.

This time, it was *my* stomach that broke through the lust-haze of lips and bodies molding together. Kate laughed against my mouth.

"Ignore it," I said and recommitted to the kiss.

She pulled away with a laugh. "It's getting late. Come on, let's eat. We need to keep our strength up … for later."

I pointed at her. "That's a promise, babe."

"WE COULD STOP at the Grand Hawaiian," I said, gesturing to the four-star hotel on the left. Dinner at a table on the sand and a moonlight walk would set the mood.

Kate brushed dust from her shins. "Not sure I'm dressed for that, and I could use another shower."

"I like showers." My grin emphasized the innuendo in my tone.

"*Plus* … the rehearsal dinner tomorrow will be fancy," she continued. "I don't think I can do fancy two nights in a row."

"Why is the rehearsal tomorrow night instead of the night before the wedding?" I asked because I'd been in a wedding or two.

"Some guys Troye wanted at the bachelor party couldn't make it until Thursday, so they decided to have the rehearsal tomorrow and the bachelor party the night before the big day."

"I'm surprised Jill was okay with that."

"As long as she gets to be the center of attention, I'm not sure she cares about the order of events," Kate said, giving me the side-eye.

Instead of the Grand Hawaiian, we stopped for teriyaki at a restaurant Kate found with excellent reviews. She even tried my sushi.

"I still don't like fish, but if I did, that would be my favorite." She smiled, and time got away from me. The house was silent and dark when we walked through the door later.

"What are the chances we have the place to

ourselves?" I asked, too many ideas popping into my head.

"Hmmm, hot tub?" She waggled her brows.

That was one of them. "Absolutely."

On the pool deck, Kate whipped off her T-shirt in the quiet night. I did the same and watched as she shimmied out of her shorts and dusty socks. She stepped into the outdoor shower in a shimmery lavender bra and matching thong. Fucking thongs. Like a picture frame, all they did was accent a masterpiece. It wasn't *naked*, but it was close. My dick was hard in a second.

I stripped down to my boxer briefs and joined her to rinse the day from our bodies.

Dripping, and following Kate's nearly bare ass, I entered the hot water and flipped the switch for the bubbles but left the lights off. "It's easier to see the stars this way," I explained.

"Or is it easier to talk me into losing my undies?"

I faked my surprise. "I hadn't thought of that. What a great idea. Do you want to go first or …"

Her laugh was low, and her eyes bright as she floated over to me and settled her knees on either side of my thighs, which was more than fine with me. My hands found a home on her hips. I loved those curves.

"How about we start topless, since you already are?"

"Are you asking me? Because yeah, yes, please."

Her grin was sly as she popped the gold clasp between her breasts, and the bra fell away.

I helped finish the job, pushing the straps off her shoulders as my eyes feasted on pale swells and plump nipples in the fizzing water. It took me a minute to register her bra was floating away.

I snagged it and tossed it onto the tile, then reached

for her. With her body pressed to mine, as it should be, I kissed her, and not too gently. My hands roamed her bare back, and her hard nipples teased against my chest.

"Damn, you feel good," I said and lifted her so I could kiss down her neck to her collarbone.

"I like your hands on me," she whispered.

"I like my hands on you, too. Touching your skin."

She sighed, closed her eyes, and threw her head back, giving me more of her to explore and kiss.

Alternate plan. I gently shifted her to face away from me, then pulled her to rest against my chest.

"You like this view," she said with a subdued laugh and arched so her tight nipples poked out of the water.

"I do. But this isn't only about my view. You can look at the stars while you float, and I do some more of that touching."

23

KATE

HIS STRONG HANDS WERE GENTLE IN THE WARM WATER, and it lit me up inside. His palms smoothed over my shoulders, my arms, and lower at a drugging pace. All the passion he ignited with his kisses settled into a nice, relaxing hum, accompanied by the low rumble of the hot tub and the blue-tinted darkness.

"We're outside," I mumbled. "You like outside."

"I do," he said. "I'm exactly where I want to be. And, ah," he said as his fingertips trailed from my hips to the crease where my legs met my ass. "Here are those sexy thighs I can't stop thinking about. I need to take a little time here."

And he did. For long moments, Levi massaged and caressed me there, up my sides, over my breasts, and back down to start the circuit again. I was nearly boneless when a light flicked on by the pool, and Steven strolled out.

Levi flipped me and shoved me behind him in two seconds. More alert, I clung to him and hid my face in his neck like Steven wouldn't know it was me.

"Oh shit. Sorry. Janie thought she left her watch out here." His eyes darted around, stopping briefly on my discarded bra and the nearby pile of our clothes before searching the table closest to us. "Got it," he said, waving the item at us. "As you were," he said and jogged back the way he came, slapping the light off as he went.

I closed my eyes and giggled into Levi's back.

"Are you okay? I didn't push you into the tile?" he asked, twisting to face me.

"No, I'm fine." I laughed harder. "What is it with interruptions today?"

"I don't know, but that has to be the last one," he said and pulled me against him, his eyes fixed on my lips.

I rested my hand on his chest. "Maybe it's a sign. Live to try another day."

He looked longingly at my breasts, then bent his head in defeat. "You may be right. Stay there. I'll get you a towel."

Once we'd washed off the chlorine and salt in the outdoor shower, we headed inside. Wrapped in towels, we brushed our teeth, and as I stepped away, Levi said, "Ah, wait, kiss."

This one wasn't the hot promise of more to come. It was sweet, comfortable, and a little like coming home. I wanted to hold onto that feeling, wrap it up tight, and keep it close while I could.

Levi returned to the bedroom, and I slipped on a clean thong from my bag by the walk-in closet. I didn't bother with my PJs.

In the bedroom, Levi had switched off the lamp, and darkness settled. The blackout curtains were closed against the bright morning sun that would soon rise.

I slid under the covers and reached for him, the exhaustion of the emotional day catching up with me. He pulled my back to his front, his arm engulfing me as he curled around my body. The cotton of his boxer briefs brushed against the bare skin of my thighs and butt.

"You're topless again," he said, his dick twitching against me.

"Seems I like skin-to-skin, too."

"Mmm," he hummed and smoothed a palm along my thigh, over the band of my panties to my hip.

"Levi?"

He hummed again in response as his hands continued to caress.

"Are you trying to turn me on?"

"Maybe. Is it working?" His voice was low and sexy as hell.

I chuckled. "Of course it is, it's you." I rolled to my stomach and propped up on my elbows to face him. "I love your hands on my body. I want your lips there too. Everywhere." His eyes glittered in the darkness. "And I want to be fully alive when it happens. But this day …"

"Hey, I get it." He smiled and leaned in for a chaste kiss. "This day has edged the shit out of me. But I get it. Can I still touch your skin? Hold you while we fall asleep?"

The sincerity in his eyes nearly had me changing my mind. *This man.* "I'd really like that."

He nudged me back to my spoon position, settling me in his arms with a warm palm cupping a breast. Holding me tight, he brushed a light kiss on my shoulder. "Good night, babe."

. . .

"WHAT ARE WE DOING TODAY?" I asked Levi over a breakfast of yogurt, granola, and fresh mango. I'd woken to his hands roaming my skin, *edging the shit out of me* this time as I made plans in my head for later tonight when there would be no roaming family, no itinerary to accommodate, and no interruptions.

"What time do we need to be back?" he asked.

"We have to be dressed for dinner by five."

He nodded. "My favorite ATV tour is close to Hilo, too far away for today. But there's a new one on this side of the island I haven't tried. It could be touristy, but it gets positive reviews. It has historical village reproductions and cultural stuff at all the stops."

"I'm game," I said.

When we told the others our plans, the kids looked interested. Janie, Jill, and Mom needed to stay here to manage the rental deliveries and demanded Troye, Steven, and Sam stay too. So, Mei and Dad offered to bring Amelia and Carter along.

I looked at Levi, unsure of how he felt about the change, but I shouldn't have worried. With his easy charm, he said, "This one looks perfect for kids. Give me a minute to update the reservation."

Waivers signed, safety talk finished, and helmets on, we set out with the tour group a couple hours later. It took a minute to get the feel of my ATV, but I soon settled into the ride through trees and broadleaf plants in the most vibrant shades of green along the brown, rutted path. I followed Levi, and Dad, Mei, and the kids followed us in a four-seat UTV, the bell-like sounds of the kids' laughter and my father's deep chuckle wafting out.

The various cultural stops were entertaining. The

first one highlighted Fijian culture, and we had the chance to throw a traditional spear.

"Ah, the feats of strength," Levi said. "Shall I impress you with my skills?" His voice was confident, with a slightly British flourish, and I laughed out loud along with Amelia and Carter. He wasn't too bad, of course. My toss was less impressive, but Levi gave me a congratulatory hug, anyway.

"Auntie Kate," Carter shouted from where he and Amelia stood with Levi, watching what looked like the Hawaiian version of a piñata game. "Come smash a pineapple. You get to use a real warrior's club and everything."

"I've never done that before. You'll have to show me how," I said, walking closer.

"Levi did it on the first try." Carter sounded somber, and I understood why. Levi was a lot to measure up to, being the outdoorsy man that he was.

"He's wonderful," Mei said, watching Levi and Dad help the kids swing the mallets to play the huge Tongan drums at the next stop. Olympic swimming wasn't in the kids' future, nor was a music career, but they were having a good time, and that's what mattered. Those kids were pros at creating fun.

"Dad or Levi?" I elbowed her.

"Both," Mei said and looked at me expectantly. "Will we be back here soon for another wedding?"

I ignored the zing that came with those words, and said, "We're new still. Not sure it will last. Lots of new-relationship-energy right now."

"Can't be too new. He's here. And the way he looks at you, I don't think it matters if it started last year or last week. He's pretty far gone. And that's the business.

Some people take a while to fall, but once the deed is done, time doesn't matter much anymore."

I blushed and looked at my shoes. My sturdy trainers, so clean and boring before this trip, now smudged and dusty and changed in only a matter of days from my adventures with Levi. Not unlike me, maybe. Changed.

Was it too much to hope for falling? For more? I usually kept hope locked up tight, because hope was risky. But, this time, I wanted to hope. I really wanted to.

"I see how you look at him too," Mei continued. "It's good to see you happy, Kate. You give so much. I like seeing you receive a little too."

If she only knew receiving was all I'd been doing with Levi. Receiving his touch, his kisses, his consideration and rescue. All of it delivered with those arms of his and a swoon-worthy smile.

Another zing landed. This time in my chest, dangerously close to my heart.

"This isn't working," I told Levi at the next stop. "If we had to survive in the wild, I'd be no help."

Levi grinned and took the stick I was rubbing against the larger one, which had a tiny fringe of coconut husk inside. "Let me try," he said.

"The husk could be wet."

"Nah, just needs a little muscle."

I squinted at him.

He glanced at Dad and whispered, "I want to do this in front of your father. Be manly. Show him I can be helpful to you."

"Oh, you've been very helpful to me in the best of *manly* ways." I winked.

"I'm not sure it will impress your father, but I'm

willing to give it my all, babe." He flashed his dimple because he knew what it did to me.

On cue, my panties went up in flames, and I realized he'd had a point with the edging thing. Sex was never far from my mind, and it seemed I was ready to go in an instant.

Was this what was missing before? Time to let things simmer and build? Knowing I'd be safe with him and that there was no set finish line? Just pleasure until we decided to stop.

It must have been the muscles or the intensity of his laser eyes, but the husk soon smoked, and Levi puffed his chest. The guide came over with a larger pile of husk, and Levi scraped the tiny smoking fringe onto it, then blew lightly to spark the flames. "There, I saved you. Looks like we'd survive after all," he announced loud enough for Dad to hear.

I rolled my eyes, but inside, a hundred butterflies took flight.

By the end of the tour, we were all smiles and laughter, if not a bit dirty. The day had been easy, and Levi fit seamlessly. I chose not to think about that too much.

"Should we stop for a shave ice on the way home?" Mei asked.

"I'm in," Levi said without hesitation.

"You know I'm in," I said. Janie had already called out my long-standing sweet tooth. No sense in denying it now.

"What's shave ice?" Carter asked, Amelia listening beside him.

"It's like a snow cone," Mei explained. "Except better. They have lots of different flavors, and for the extra special ones, they put sweetened condensed milk on top. Very tasty on shave ice if you like sweet."

"I like sweet," Carter said.

"Then it's decided." Dad nodded at Mei, and she tapped on her phone, pulling up directions to one of her favorite spots.

Ten minutes later, we sat in the shade of a tree across from another stunning public beach. The picnic table showed faint, colorful stains in spots from the treats that had come before us.

"Try not to get it on your face, Carter, or your mom will have to scrub your skin off tonight. She needs perfection … for the sake of the mantel picture." I brushed my hand across my forehead dramatically, and Carter gave me a toothy grin.

"More like Aunt Jill," Amelia said, scooping up a crunchy bite of purple and green from her bowl. "No juice on the sofa. Don't leave books out."

"Don't bounce the super ball over the fence," Carter added, planning his next taste from the orange and red mound before him. "And *don't* play with the Star Wars Legos. That's a big one." He nodded, eyes wide in emphasis.

Ah, those would be Troye's. He spent big money on the giant ones with thousands of bricks.

"I touched one, and it crashed," Carter said. "I didn't mean to. It was an accident."

"They look like they'd be fun to play with," Levi said, shaking his head. "But they're too fragile. I'd rather have something that wouldn't break just because I touched it."

Carter and Levi knocked their spoons together like swords.

"Janie told me their last visit was a bit rough," Mei said, looking chagrined.

"It's not like Gran and Grandpa's house where there are fun things to do outside," Amelia said, and Mei smoothed an ageless hand over my niece's head with a secret smile.

"We went to the museum but couldn't touch *anything*," Carter piled on.

"Portland Glass Museum," Mei explained. "Not the best choice for young ones. They aren't babies in strollers anymore. And they were out of their element. Amelia had trouble sleeping, and Carter had an overnight accident," Mei whispered, intentionally not using the words *wet the bed*. "Jill didn't handle any of it well. Call the mood tense, I think. It's probably better for Troye and Jill to visit them now. Keeping everything in its place is hard with two kids running around."

Amelia took another bite, leaving her own drippy marks on the table. "That's what Mom says. That's why our house has the fancy room, and we can't go in it. Mom's the only one allowed."

Carter turned from his frozen dessert as if making a decree. "I don't care because all my toys are in the other rooms. I don't like that room."

"But it's sooooooo pretty," Amelia said with a sigh. "There are flowers and a white fluffy rug and pink pillows and shiny boxes with mirrors. When I'm bigger, Mom says it will be *our* special room. Just for girls."

I hadn't been to Janie and Steven's most recent house in the Hollywood Hills, but I could picture it. This room in particular. Pristine and photo-shoot-ready at all times.

Carter shrugged, unaffected by the future unavailability of the white fluffy rug, and scooped up another bite for himself.

When we returned, the house was transformed. At least ten round tables filled the main living area where the large sofas had been, and several high-tops lined one edge of the pool deck. How many people were attending this thing? I thought one benefit of a destination wedding was keeping it small. Jill had refused a wedding party, after all. I thought simple was the goal. But this didn't look simple.

Stands for flower arrangements fanned out from the gazebo, bordering the rows of pristine white chairs. Bolts of white tulle and ribbon, along with a giant shrink-wrapped bundle of white linens, sat next to an inner wall, waiting for the decorator and florist to use in a couple of days. Definitely no juice around those.

"Finally, you're back," Mom said, greeting us with a bright expression that didn't match the critical words.

"We said we'd be back by four and we are."

"You know Jill," she said like *duh*. "She was worried an hour wouldn't be enough time."

"We don't leave for dinner until five-thirty," I said and glanced at my watch.

"Yes, but the rehearsal starts at five."

I frowned. "We're not in the wedding. Why do we need to be at the rehearsal?"

Mom waved her hand. "Jill wants everyone there."

And so Jill would have it.

I sucked my teeth and gave Levi an apologetic glance. "Fine."

24

LEVI

"It's fine," I said, and neatly rolled the sleeves of the light gray button-up shirt I'd paired with beige, tailored linen pants. "Compared with yesterday's Bridezilla, she's better today. Plus, I know how this goes. I've been to a few rehearsals. We sit, don't talk, and try not to sigh. The upside is, here, we can at least sneak a drink while we do it."

"You're a saint, Levi," Kate called from the bathroom, where she was doing her makeup, based on the conversation pauses and the snap and click of tiny bottles and cases hitting the marble counter.

She didn't need makeup, with her high cheekbones and deep brown eyes. The cupid's bow mouth didn't need to be highlighted. I barely resisted kissing her as it was. Tonight would be an exercise in restraint, at least until I had her alone. I was no saint.

Actually, being alone with her would be an exercise in restraint too. I had plans. It wasn't about finishing too soon. I'd gotten that issue mostly under control years ago, though Kate was pushing my limits. It was about not letting my dick call the shots.

I'd imagined how it would feel to be inside her, her soft thighs squeezing my hips. To settle into her snug fit and kiss her breathless while I did. I was dangerously close to falling dick-first into feelings. Big ones. For the first time in a long time.

Was I ready for big feelings? The anatomy in question twitched, but he didn't get a vote. I needed to focus on something else, like all the spots I planned to kiss tonight.

Kate walked into the bedroom, startling me from my thoughts, only to be lost again at the sight of her. The dress was deep blue, and it made her skin glow. The top was lace from the thin straps at her shoulders to below her breasts, the frayed edges drawing attention to bare skin exposed from the shallow V to nearly her waist. No way she was wearing a bra.

The floaty fabric below her waist flared out in delicate folds down to her slim ankles. A pair of silver, heeled sandals dangled from her fingers, and small silver hoops shone from her ears against the backdrop of long dark hair.

"Taking my breath away, babe." I let my eyes roam her figure again.

She blushed. "You're not so bad yourself." She turned and winked at me, but I almost missed it because, below the crisscrossed straps at her shoulder blades, the dress was cut low, revealing all the skin at her waist available for caressing. My thumb itched to do it.

"Very rude of you, though. I don't think you're supposed to be more beautiful than the bride."

Kate bit her lip. "That's at the wedding. But thank you."

I stepped close and ran my palms down her arms, soft where I was hard. "You may not see it, Kate, but I do. You are absolutely more beautiful."

The pulse at the base of her neck jumped, and she smiled.

I wanted to kiss her silky lipstick right off, but I knew enough about women not to do it. So, I kissed the row of freckles on her cheek and inhaled my favorite scent, her.

And we got that drink. The caterer had brought tastings for last-minute decisions on some food earlier, and I snagged one of the open wine bottles along with two glasses when we headed out to the lawn.

I paid little attention to the ins and outs happening on the steps of the gazebo but sipped from my glass and openly stared at Kate seated next to me in a row of white chairs. Jill asked her opinion a few times and frowned at my distracting her, but I didn't care. This wedding got me here with Kate. So, for me, its job was done.

Troye's parents rented a private room at an ocean-side restaurant to host the formal dinner. From the outside, it looked like a grand beach house, with a large, open layout and tropical touches, such as white Bahama-style shutters and high ceilings with wicker fans turning lazily above tables set close together. Patrons relaxing on comfy outdoor sofas filled the spacious lanai stretching to the edge of the craggy volcanic rocks at the shore. In a corner, a small band tuned their instruments.

Our space was upstairs and lit entirely by string lights and paper lanterns hanging around a large, covered deck that offered a view of the sunset so close you could almost touch it. A perfectly set table, which would have impressed even my mother, was the focal point, and waiters passed champagne and small bites as the guests gathered. I placed my hand on that stretch of skin at Kate's low back and guided her outside for a quiet moment.

"Nice place," she said, downplaying the surrounding beauty.

I laughed. "It'll do." Then I kissed her because … the sunset, the swish of the surf in the distance, that cupid's bow lip, her easy energy, and about a million other things that made Kate, Kate.

A few toasts were made, and Janie called Kate over for a sisters-only photo with the bright orange sunset behind them.

"Champagne flutes in your left hands, ladies, and raise them up together to catch the light," the photographer directed. The diamonds on Janie's and Jill's fingers glittered, highlighting the lack of said sparkle on Kate's. Did she want a ring? Did she want to share a life with someone?

A hand on my shoulder stopped that train of thought.

"Thanks for taking the kids today," Steven said, flashing a grin. "With Janie and Jill running the show, I mostly tried to stay out of the way. It was no hardship relaxing by a pool all day, especially with a sunbathing April." He waggled his brows.

Troye shifted his weight and huffed.

"Settle down," Steven said. "She's a pretty girl. I'm a man. Sue me."

"She works for you," Troye said, his voice low.

"I'm aware. She lives in my house with me too. If I wanted in, I'd have already tried. I don't. But I'm not blind. I won't pretend to be."

"There are HR rules."

"We don't have an HR department at the house."

Troye shook his head. "It's guys like you that cause problems we all pay for. There're rules about everything because assholes like you can't keep it in your pants."

Steven faced Troye directly and smirked, "Whether or not I keep it in my pants is between me and Janie. You make it sound personal." He paused. "What rules are we talking about? Rules against swimming in the hotel pool after hours, or HR rules around interoffice dating?"

Troye said nothing.

"You know, it's been my experience that rules only piss people off when they stand in the way of them getting what they want. Had a little trouble bypassing some rules to openly date Jill, did you?"

"You don't know what you're talking about." Troye looked away to sip his beer.

Steven took another beat, his assessing gaze still locked on Troye. "Some of those sports teams have pretty strict policies meant to discourage fraternizing with players." His voice was less smug tease and more cross-examining counselor now. "Rules where one party has to quit if the relationship continues, and everyone knows it won't be the player. It keeps the money players free of romantic complications, but the entire organization has to follow them. Kinda sucks."

Troye glared. "You're not a sports attorney. Stay in your lane."

"There *is* usually a way around it, though," Steven

continued, ignoring Troye. "Like if you were already together when they hired the second romantic partner. Then openly dating someone you work with is fine."

Troye's eyes flashed, his jaw clenching.

"But you have to disclose the relationship." Steven paused, his eyes still assessing. "If you don't, and you keep dating, one of you might lose your dream job. That's a big risk. Those rules could lead to some tough conversations if you had a reason to keep a romance quiet. I assume Portland doesn't have that rule, since you and Jill don't seem to be hiding anything. I bet I could find out for certain, though."

Troye glanced at me, then scowled at Steven. "You're not as smart as you think you are."

Steven huffed, "Oh, I think I'm exactly that smart."

Something was off. I thought Kate said Troye got Jill the interview as a favor to her, before their breakup, and that Jill and Troye didn't start dating until later. Months after she started her job. But if Portland had that rule, that wouldn't work. One of them would have had to quit.

Troye ran a hand through his hair and spared another glance for me. "You're way off. I have a sister. I care about women. You're being a dick … to April. Quit being a dick."

He stormed away as Steven mumbled, "Right, *I'm* the dick."

My brain buzzed like it was working a puzzle. I remembered the way Troye said sex with Jill *was* easier, like the comparison was more real-time. Remembered Jill's *years* of waiting and dreaming, and it all clicked into place along with the truth about Kate's sister and Kate's ex-fiancé. Motherfuckers.

. . .

Kate escaped the photographer, and I motioned for her to meet me at the bar, where I ordered a whiskey neat and shot it.

"Whoa," Kate said and ordered a glass of wine. "You okay?"

I cleared my throat and asked for a beer. "Yeah, I'm good." I grinned.

"You were talking to Troye and Steven, and it didn't look fun. I guess I'd need a shot after that too." She chuckled.

What did I say? Did I tell her? Did I not? I didn't have proof her ex and her sister were lying, cheating assholes. Maybe Steven was wrong.

He wasn't.

I needed time to think. Telling the truth was usually the best way, but why hurt Kate if it wasn't necessary? What would be *best* for Kate?

I stretched to my full height and pulled her in for a kiss. This was better. Her soft lips and warm embrace leveled out my blood pressure.

The surrounding bustle grew, and they announced dinner was served. If I told her, it wouldn't be tonight. She was smiling and beautiful, and that was my focus.

My favorite, poké, was the first course, and it was some of the best ahi tuna I'd tasted. I leaned close and whispered, "I can eat yours if you want."

Heat flashed behind her eyes, and I realized how that sounded. "I can do that too," I said with a smirk.

Toasts became speeches between courses. Troye and Jill were dedicated professionals, smart, and committed to each other. Yeah, yeah. They were *perfect*. Kate stiffened at that one, and I wrapped my arm around her shoulder, pulling her close to brush a kiss across her cheek. "I'm glad she's perfect for him, and you aren't. So *fucking* glad."

She looked at me from beneath those long, dark lashes, a tiny grin curving the edges of lips I couldn't wait to kiss again. "Me too."

After dinner, I led Kate out to the deck for a little space and quiet. We sipped the last of our drinks and listened as the notes of old Hawaiian classics drifted up to us from the band below. My hand rested low as she angled toward me, my thumb working to memorize the feel of her skin and the dip at her backbone.

"What are they doing over there?" Kate pointed to a group of swimmers gathered around a surfboard above a bright light shining in the water.

"Swimming with the manta rays."

Kate's eyes widened. "Really? Have you done it?"

"Sure. It's like swimming with the turtles the other day. You stay still, floating in the light, which attracts plankton. The rays come close to feed, often very close."

"Let's go," she said with a new light in her eyes. "Another adventure."

"Too late for tonight, but I like your energy. Are you turning into an adventurer?"

"I think so."

"Want to know one of the best things about going on an adventure? Coming home, getting clean after all that adrenalin and effort, and sliding into bed with someone warm to cuddle."

"You and cuddling," she said with a sassy smile.

"Especially naked cuddling. I'd do that every night."

"Just cuddle?"

I shrugged a shoulder. "Some nights. Others, I may like a little something more before or after."

She quieted and focused on one of her fingers playing with the top button of my shirt. "I'm glad that seat was the last one in the coffee shop."

I looked into her eyes, so earnest and good. This was a truth I could share. "I lied."

"What?"

"It wasn't the last seat."

She licked her perfect lips, bare of any lipstick now, and the same color of the nipples pressing into the fabric of her dress in the cool evening air.

"A table cleared on the other side of the café as I walked by. I angled my approach specifically so you wouldn't see."

She grinned.

"I meant what I said to your family on the first day. I saw you and wanted to know you."

"And now you're here," she said with a flirty gleam.

"And now I'm here."

25

KATE

I couldn't get out of there fast enough. First, the toasts and his parents talking about how happy they were Troye found *true love* was just plain insulting. I got it. I wasn't the one.

Steven ran a hand down his face, saying, "This is awkward as balls," and I laughed. I suppose it would be awkward as balls if I cared. Jill and Troye were good together. He and I weren't. Great. Moving on.

Second, Levi. His shoulders in the button-up shirt and the casual, confident way he carried himself when meeting new people. It was the cologne model, and I needed my hands on him ASAP.

The dinner party shifted to join with the crowd at the restaurant bar for more drinks and dancing. Levi and I had one dance, swaying together as he held me firmly yet gently, leaving sweet kisses at my temple while his hand rested above the curve of my ass and his finger-tips caressed the exposed skin below my waist. There was no mistaking where his hands would be later, and the fact everyone knew it gave me a little thrill. Troye chose Jill, but this incredible man chose me.

In the Jeep, he settled that palm on my leg and didn't move it other than to caress his thumb along the side of my thigh through the thin fabric of my dress. That small touch alone had heat pooling low. My sex drive was roaring back to life with him.

I smoothed a finger over the back of his hand, tracing the raised veins there.

He glanced at me and shifted to thread our fingers together. I lifted our joined hands and kissed the back of his thumb before placing a tender kiss at the tip with my lips slightly parted.

His jaw clenched in the streetlight filtering in, and he clicked on the indicator to shift lanes for a turn. "Babe, I'm trying not to speed, but you have me calculating the probability of a cop on this road right now."

"So, it would be bad if I did this?" I slid the tip of my tongue along the pad before giving it a little suck.

He cleared his throat. "Define bad."

I giggled and lowered our joined hands to my lap. Crashing the rental car would completely kill the mood.

Instead, I asked, "How did you get this?" I ran a fingertip across the recently healed cut starting to scar on the back of his hand.

"Uh … what?"

"This cut." I gave the new pink skin another tender stroke.

"Ah, that." His voice was the slightest bit unsteady as he shifted in his seat. "Mountain biking. I banged it on a tree, taking a turn too close. It happens."

"Does it still hurt?" I asked in a husky tease, channeling my naughty nurse.

He glanced at me again. "No. All healed up, but …"

"But you have some other spots that need to be checked by a professional like me?"

"Yeah, a professional exactly like you."

The next intersection was deserted, and Levi faced me when he stopped, his eyes turning darker. "You're good at this, too good. I still have like five more minutes of driving, and if you keep it up, we won't make it. I'll be pulling over by another rock, and it won't be one kiss on the lips." He raised his brows in warning.

I grinned. "Yes, Daddy."

He closed his eyes and blew out a long sigh. "Oh, Baby Girl."

We'd been the first of my family to leave the dinner. So, the only lights on at the house now were the ones glowing in the front lawn. Out of the Jeep, Levi grabbed my hand, pulled me to the door, entered the code, and we were in. He pressed me against the heavy wood as it shut, and I felt the effect of my actions notch at my stomach.

He loomed over me, all broad chest and heat, and I got wetter. "I want to be sweet and go slow, but you, the dress, all that teasing." His voice was a low growl. "Maybe I need to show you what a tongue can really do." The mixed threat and promise weakened my knees.

Hastily, his hands worked to pull up my dress on both sides as he kissed my lips hard, demanding entrance. My body burned, and I gripped his shoulders to stay steady as his mouth did all the wicked things to mine. This was happening fast, and I loved it.

"I need this, Kate, need you," he said and dropped to his knees.

Oh god. Right here against the door?

"Just a taste. A start. Hold your dress for me." He shoved the balled-up fabric into my hand and pressed his nose to my center. "Damn, you smell good. Let me do this and hear the sounds you make when I do." He breathed against the place I wanted his tongue.

I groaned. "Yes … and I'm good … clean bill of health."

He peered up at me. "Me too. I'll leave these on for now," he said, pulling my panties to the side with a hooked finger. "Too pretty to miss. Lace?"

"Yes. I wanted to show you."

"You will … after this."

The hand not holding my panties caressed my thigh and then lifted my leg over his shoulder.

"Hold on, babe. I've got you."

I moaned, gripped his other shoulder, and threw my head back against the door.

Bit by bit, his mouth moved along the tender skin of my upper thigh, finally reaching the point where my leg met my center. He pressed a wet, open-mouthed kiss there, and the blaze in my blood sparked higher.

"Good?"

"You know it is." I panted.

"Give me the words. I want the words."

I moaned again. "Yes. Good, but I need more. Please, Levi. I need … your mouth, your tongue."

And he was there, sucking and licking and taking me higher to where I floated, lost in the sensation and the light brush of his short beard. No pressure. Only pleasure.

"Oh, yes, so good." I sighed. "Please …"

With one last deep kiss, he tongued my entrance, then stood. He wiped his hand across his face and grinned at what I knew was a clear look of disappointment on mine. "Yeah, I need more of that, too," he said. "Let's get you naked."

My heels clicked on the tile floor as he led me through the house. He slowed only to grab bottles of water from the fridge and after closing the door to our room, had me in his arms, walking me toward the bed. "You can tell me to stop, and I will. You can tell me you don't like something, and we'll change it. Tell me what you like, and we'll do more. The goal is feeling good, whatever that looks like."

"Wait," I said, and he stilled. My heart skipped at how quickly he'd done it. He would stop if I asked. He'd respond exactly as he promised. The same sense of safety washed over me, like when we were ziplining, and he held me tight in his arms.

"All of that sounds great, but I think I know how to make it even better." My voice hinted at wicked things as I broke from his hold and strolled through the dark room toward the open wall. I slipped off my sandals and shrugged off the thin straps of my dress on the way. At the door, I lowered the side zipper and pushed the lacy top down over my hips, letting it fall with the rest of the filmy fabric to puddle on the floor.

The moon was full and rising above the mountain behind us, casting light on the far edge of the pool deck and the sweeping lawn below. Our lanai, with its comfortable sofa, was still in shadow.

I looked over my shoulder, and Levi hadn't moved. I gestured with a single curved finger. "Come outside with me."

Suddenly, he was all movement, unbuttoning his shirt, loosening his belt, and kicking off his shoes. When he pressed his front to my back next to the sofa, he wore only boxer briefs and me in the lacy undies. I arched into him and reached back to caress the sides of his thighs.

He palmed my breasts and stroked my aching nipples while his mouth sucked the spot that was a direct line to my clit.

"My favorite place," Levi said.

"Outside, I know."

"No, here. This spot on your neck. I want to find all the spots that make your legs shake."

Oh … "Yes … but first …"

I pulled out of his grasp, grabbed one of the pool towels drying nearby, and spread it out on the sofa. "Sit down."

He complied, his grin dirty and suggestive. His eyes focused on my chest. I stepped between his bent knees, dropped a pillow on the stamped concrete, and kneeled, pushing away the coffee table behind me as I did.

"Yes?" I asked, sliding my hands along the insides of his thighs, enjoying the roughness of hair there and nudging them wider.

"Yes," Levi said, settling back against the sofa. His eyes held me along with that dirty grin. He was so comfortable in his skin. So comfortable doing this. I envied him. But if anyone could make this easy, it would be him.

Holding his gaze, I let my hand stroke over the soft cotton at his hips, coming closer to his erection straining the black fabric.

I pressed my lips to the inside of his thigh, near the place he wanted me most, and inhaled the musky scent mixed with his usual leather and spice. He liked my femaleness. I liked his maleness. I shifted to give the other thigh the same treatment, humming my approval.

His dick jumped.

With another wicked grin, I placed a tender kiss at the root. "This could be my favorite place."

"You're not sure?"

"I need to explore more."

"Again, enthusiastic consent, Kate." His dimple popped.

"Can we take these off?" I asked, tugging at the waistband.

He lifted his hips in answer and kicked the garment off to the side. I'd seen him in the shower, touched him, but never this close. He was steely and warm, with silky skin. Thankfully, not too big. I wanted to take him deep and for a long time. His size was perfect.

I teased him first, nuzzling and leaving wet, open-mouthed kisses along the shaft as my hands massaged his groin and pelvis. His noises of pleasure in the night were the sexiest soundtrack, and my drenched pussy pulsed.

Knowing my effect on him, was a high like no other. And knowing how much Levi liked sex outside, added an extra thrill. Out here in the moonlight, I wanted to take him all the way.

"Tell me what you like," I said, meeting his hooded gaze while his hands gripped the cushion edge by his knees.

"I like this view. I like your lips. I like your mouth."

"My mouth pleases you?" I asked and licked his crown.

"Fuck, Kate." His stomach muscles flexed, and his stare was severe, almost dangerous.

I shuddered at it.

"You're waving that red cape again." His voice was low. "Yes, your mouth pleases me. I want inside. I want those full lips wrapped around me. I want to watch you do it. I want warm and wet. Feeling it and seeing it."

I grinned, and taking him in hand, I caressed and licked, then gave him what he wanted. I brought him inside, deep and then shallow, to tease my tongue around the head before sucking him down in the rhythm he guided me to, with his fingers threaded lightly in my hair.

He groaned a curse, his breathing ragged. "Keep that up and I'll come."

"Good," I said with a sultry gleam. "I like you on edge." I returned briefly to the caresses and kisses I'd started with.

He growled and let his head fall back on the sofa.

"And I like pushing you over that edge." I drew him in deep for a slow suck.

His eyes met mine. "Damn, Kate. I like you so much."

26

LEVI

Goddamn, she pleased me. The caveman in me roared with it.

Gone were her teasing licks and kisses. She had my rhythm down and added a little hum to her sweet torture that vibrated in my dick. There was no stopping the assault of pleasure when I came moments later.

She took it all, even sucked lightly one last time, to be sure.

I ran a hand through my hair and pulled in gulps of air before sitting forward and cupping her cheeks with both hands. "So fucking good, Kate. But now it's your turn," I said, desperate to get to her and knowing I needed to slow down. "My turn too, because I've been thinking about this all night. That bit at the door was only the beginning."

The pulse point on her neck throbbed.

"Stand up and let me see these undies." It wasn't a request.

Silvery lace with tiny strips of satin stretched across

her hips. My hands followed their path around to find more bare skin.

"What do you think?" She cocked her hip and bent her leg.

"I think you brought these on a fake date because you're evil."

She chuckled. "No. They're new. I bought them the day of the dress fitting."

I looked at her, surprised. "You bought sexy undies on our second day here?"

She bit her lip.

"*You* should have said something sooner, Baby Girl." I gripped her ass, making my point.

"And miss this big unveiling out here in the night air?" She smoothed her palms along her belly and hips to her thighs.

"You're right. It's like Christmas, and I'm getting everything I want. Turn around."

She did, and my dick swelled, already coming back to life at the sight of her rounded ass with those faint dimples accented by the silky thong.

"That's it. That's so nice, babe."

In an effort to stop my heart, she looked at me from over her shoulder and hinged forward to rest her hands on the coffee table. "You want me like this? Tongue me from behind, right?"

Fuuuck. Her feigned innocence was another duality when compared to the siren who pulled me out here with the flick of a finger.

This. Woman. My fantasy. I was gone for her. All the way lost … completely.

Ready or not, big feelings, here I come.

Slowly, I ran my fingers from the backs of her knees to the full globes of her ass and those cute as fuck dimples. I stroked back down with equal slowness and did it all again, caressing every contour, coming close to her center, but not all the way.

Panting, she hung her head between her arms. "Levi, please."

"I've got you."

Leaning close, I caught the scent of her, and my mouth watered. That sweet part of her was right there for me to see and touch and taste out here in the open. My dick thickened, but I ignored it. My hands were where I wanted them to be.

"So sexy, Kate, but I need you naked." I pulled at the strip of satin, and when it slid away, another surge of caveman rushed through me at the sight of her bent forward with her legs spread. All that glistening, warm pink. *Mine. Mine. Mine.*

I wanted inside. Instead, I grabbed her hips and held her as I bit one cheek before soothing the mark with my kisses.

She gasped, then moaned, but didn't pull away. I set to work, tracing every dip on each thigh with my tongue. Then it was my hands there, because my mouth was on her pussy, nipping and licking her swollen lips. She was hot and so incredibly wet. Every time I dipped my tongue inside her, a new flood of sweetness was there.

My dick was hard and leaking. I was losing the plot. I needed to make her feel good. I grabbed myself and squeezed at the base for a little relief.

"Oh," she moaned. "I want to touch you. But I can't reach."

She was watching me from between her legs? Damn, that was hot.

I wanted her gone like I was, needy and panting, and under a spell. No more teasing. I stood and pulled Kate to stand against me, her back to my front, my hands at her middle, my mouth at her ear. "On the sofa. Now," I growled, then added "Please," at the end before sucking in a steadying breath.

She stepped around me and lay on the cushions, her neck and face flushed, eyes wide, all that skin catching the pale light. I hooked one of her legs over the top of the sofa, then pulled the other wide to rest her foot on the ground. She was as open to me as she could be, and her breasts heaved.

Those beautiful tits, her nipples puckered tight and standing tall in the cooling air. There were too many places I wanted my mouth at the same time. I growled in frustration.

"A quick taste," I said and lunged toward her, sucking on one perfect mound. I nipped the pink bud, and she gasped but didn't move. "Next time, there will be more of that. I promise. Now, I'm gonna do this, do all the things I've been thinking about doing to this pussy." I loomed over her, anticipation making my heart race. "If something is working for you, tell me. If it doesn't work, we'll try something else or stop, whatever you need. If you get there, great. If you don't, just enjoy it. I know I will. But no faking."

She nodded.

"Words."

"Yes. No faking."

I fell to my knees and ate her up like a man starved. My face was slick with her in minutes, and her heady scent filled my nose. I licked in patterns and slid my fingers along her folds, her opening, or gently inside, listening for what she liked. "Oh, there," she said, and I sucked at her swollen clit while I pressed my thumb to the tender spot below. "Oh, yeah. Like that." Her hips bucked, rocking her hot center against me as her legs trembled. I pressed harder, sucked softer. She was close.

"Oh … Levi … touch yourself … I want … you to come too."

With my free hand, I grabbed my dick in a rough grip and stroked. A deep groan escaped my throat and blew across her mound. I was right on the edge with her.

I put my mouth on her again and massaged the spot she liked.

"Levi," she called, and then a keening cry, her stomach muscles lurching, her core spasming against my lips while she came. While we both did.

MY HAND WAS on her belly, my cheek resting on her thigh. Her taste on my tongue and the scent of her still thick around me in the open night air. No fantasy compared to this.

Grabbing the other towel to clean myself up, I asked, "Are you okay?"

Kate had one arm flung over her eyes, and the other gripped a sofa cushion. She sniffed. "I'm good. I'm really, really good."

I didn't like the sniff. "Babe? Let me see your face."

"I'm not crying, because that would be ridiculous."

"Sweetheart?" I shifted closer.

She lifted on an elbow, and there was a sheen in

those deep brown eyes, but her smile was pure joy. Relief washed over me.

"I'm good, Levi."

"Yeah, you are." I bit the inside of her thigh and growled loudly this time. "Delicious, I'd say." I bit her belly, then a breast, as I slid my body on top of hers.

She smiled. "You have a little *sexy beast* in you when we're outside."

"That's you, babe. You bring it out." The way I wanted her was intense. I felt like a beast.

"Good. I like it."

"Shifting back to a regular man, now, though," I said and kissed her tenderly. "Hope you like him too."

"Mmm. I like him, but there's nothing regular about him."

Warmth bloomed in my chest. I moved my kissing assault to her neck and shoulders and shifted us both so we lay together on the sofa. Our kisses became languid, our hands caressing, as we soaked in the feel of each other with nothing between us. Time passed in the quiet hum of the night, and it was everything I loved about sex outside.

A light flicked on around the corner by the pool. Her family was home. "Come on. Let's go to bed."

"No," she said. "I like it out here."

A vision flashed in my mind. A house with an open sleeping porch complete with a big bed and plush pillows cradling a naked Kate. Yep … I wanted that.

"Another night. Come cuddle with me. We'll leave the curtain open for a while so we can see the sky."

She mumbled a curse with her whimper and stood, then bent to grab the two pool towels.

"Ah, no, I got it," I said, grabbing the one I'd used

for cleaning up along with the other. "I'll add them to my laundry pile. Something to do tomorrow."

She gave me a sweet kiss, still a little drunk from her release, and her hips swayed as she walked inside.

"I need to brush my teeth," she said.

"I'm going wherever those hips are going."

She looked back at me with a grin. Then, dressed in the house-provided robes, we handled our business, and after the required minty-fresh kiss, I leaned against the wall and watched her take off her makeup.

"You were beautiful tonight, but I think I like you this way best."

"Wearing nothing but a robe?"

"Well, yes, but I meant no makeup. Your hair behind your shoulders. Your body relaxed, and that robe giving me a tantalizing peek at a breast."

She looked down and pulled the gap closed, like it was a habit.

I stepped behind her, wrapping my arms around her middle. "I said I liked it. Why did you take it away?"

She screwed the lid onto the jar of cream she'd smoothed on her face and caught my eye in the mirror. Something passed between us there in the low light of the bathroom then she loosened the tie at her waist. She rolled her shoulder so the side that had gaped fell open again, wider this time, until it slid down her arm, and she let the rest of the robe fall with it to the floor.

"Another unveiling," she said.

I shed my robe too, then caressed my hands over her shoulders and arms. I pulled her against me and left kisses on her temple and the side of her hair. My dick already had ideas, but twice was enough for tonight. I wanted to hold Kate now more than anything else.

"Come to bed, Sweetheart."

Snuggled under the sheets and blankets in my favorite spoon position, my hand cupping a soft breast, this moment was all I ever wanted. *She* was all I ever wanted. I'd known her for six days. Not nearly enough time to fall in love, but there I was. And I called her Sweetheart. I hadn't done that with anyone in a very long time.

"Let's never leave this room," Kate said, reading my thoughts. "I want to sleep, wake up, and do all that lanai business again."

Same page. I smiled against her shoulder.

"We came together," she said in a quiet voice, a bit awed.

"We did. There was no way I couldn't. God, you're beautiful when you come." I squeezed her tight. "No pressure, but I'll be trying every trick I know, researching new ones, and using every toy on the market to make that happen as much as possible."

She laughed into the pillow. "No pressure?"

"None for you. Plenty for me, but I'll take it. I can handle it. You are the sexiest puzzle ever."

"I like puzzles," she said with something extra in her voice. "I think I could do a *puzzle* all day and all night."

"Me too, babe. Believe me, me too … but your presence is required at the bachelorette party tomorrow."

She twisted around, nudged me to my back, and rose on her elbow to face me. Her bare breasts pressed to my side, and one of her legs hitched over mine. "You should go with Steven to Troye's."

"I don't know about that."

"You're going to hang here with my parents? Play bingo?"

"I highly doubt your mom and Sam have ever played bingo."

She thought for a moment. "You may be right. Strip bingo, but that could get awkward."

I huffed a laugh.

"If Steven asked, would you go?"

"He already did. He said we should stick together in case Troye goes off the rails with his buddies. I guess they're college friends who like to get rowdy."

"Really … a sports bar, beer, burgers, and darts. What could go wrong?"

I laughed. "Don't jinx it."

"I think we're meeting you guys there after the Luau. I'll need some *Levi time* by then. Come on. Help a girl out." She batted her eyes.

"What will you give me?"

"What do you want?" she asked in her sultry voice.

"Even satisfied from two phenomenal orgasms, my mind is reeling with ideas."

"Pick your favorite and tell me tomorrow."

I already knew my favorite. Inside her. "Just like that?" I asked.

"Yes."

"Fine. I'll go."

"Wait." She eyed me. "You already told Steven you'd go, didn't you?"

I rolled to put her on her back under me and attacked her mouth. "You're getting what you want. I'm getting what I want. Hell, Steven is getting what he wants. Everybody wins."

"Mmm," she said and wriggled under me, reaching for my dick. "I can think of something else I want."

"You're insatiable. I like it." I loved it.

Her hand moved to my back. "You said it feels good to make a woman come. It's the same for me."

"Ah, Kate, you are perfect, you know that? And yes, to doing everything we just did again tomorrow. But first, sleep. I'm not going anywhere." Not now, not at the end of this week, and if she'd have me, not ever.

27

KATE

Unfortunately, the lie-in doing *puzzles* all day was not to be. At least Jill didn't barge in again. Instead, her screams from outside were harsher than the late-morning sun pouring in at the edges of the thick curtains. We both woke up with a start and by the time Levi and I had scrambled to put on clothes, everyone was gathered by the pool.

Troye had his arm around a sobbing Jill.

"What happened?"

"Sunburn. Jill slept out here and didn't have sunscreen on." Janie's tone was flat, but she leveled a glare at Troye. "One side of her is definitely a different color than the other."

"I look like Two-Face from *Batman*," Jill shouted, her head buried in Troye's chest. "I'm sure that will make a lovely mantel photo, Janie."

Janie rolled her lips between her teeth, fighting anger or laughter. *I* wanted to suggest she take all the photos from the left. If it was reasonable for me to stand all day in a dress that didn't fit, surely Jill could turn to the right all day.

"The spa will have a solution," Mom said, referring to the one known for its therapeutic treatments, where she and Sam had spent a lot of time this week. Traditionally, people believed the Big Island to be a healing island, lucky for Jill.

"I'll call ahead," Mom offered. "You can't be the first bride to get a sunburn the day before her wedding."

Mom led Jill inside, and Janie turned to Troye. "Why was she sleeping out here?"

"I don't know," Troye said. "We had an argument. She was still a little drunk from the party and said she needed space, so I went to bed."

"What did you argue about?" Janie put a hand on her hip.

"Nothing." He shot a look at Steven. "Couples argue."

Steven put his arm around Janie and pulled her to his side. "Baby, relax. His marriage isn't our business, like ours isn't his."

Janie sucked in a breath and said, "Fine, but I'm watching you, Troye."

The man held up his hands in defense. "Everything is fine, Janie. Chill."

"Who's hungry?" Mei asked with a clap and a bright smile. "There's still some breakfast in the warming oven if anyone's interested."

Crisis over, I started inside, but Mei stopped me. "Perhaps you want to get dressed first." Her expression was sweet as she whispered, "Your sleep shorts are inside out."

I glanced at Levi, who fought a grin.

"It's how I wear them?" I squinted one eye.

"Oh, okay." Mei winked.

AFTER THAT, everyone needed a little spa time. Levi joined a yoga class with Sam and Mom because, as he said, "why not." I had a massage, then met Janie in the mud bath for a soak. Was it really a *bath* if you ended up covered in mud?

"How's Jill?" I asked.

"She's getting some anti-toxin treatment and something else. It's supposed to decrease the redness so it's less noticeable. We'll see."

The devil on my shoulder nudged me. "She *could* take all of her photos from the left."

Janie giggled and then let out a deep sigh. "This wedding is too much."

I looked at my sister.

"What?" she asked.

"I thought you liked *too much*."

"Not always. Layers, Kate. Layers."

I chuckled. "Layers. Maybe you got them from Mom. I can't believe she and Sam are moving in together and doing it here. After the way she was about Dad, saying she felt trapped, I never thought I'd see her commit to one man again, one man *on an island*."

"Maybe Sam has a magic dick." She grinned.

"Janie! He's not that much older than us. I don't need to think about his dick."

She chuckled. "Or they could be poly."

I blinked as something like a light turned on in my brain. "Oh god, I bet they are. It would explain a lot." I sighed. "Whatever they are, they must be happy. Mom has hardly criticized my weight all week."

Janie shifted in the thick goop and turned to me. "Hey … sorry about what I said at dinner, about you and dessert. It was bitchy." She sucked in a breath. "I do like sweets. It's not *impossible* that I could be … a tiny bit … jealous."

Shocked, I huffed a laugh. "Why?"

"No one eats dessert in public in LA. Order it sure, but never eat it. It's a travesty."

"So, keep a stash a home."

She gave me a side-eye.

"You already do! You sneak desserts in the pantry while the kids are at school."

She smirked and relaxed back in her tub with her eyes closed. "It's possible being a size four *doesn't* feel as good as ice cream tastes."

"Janie, stop. You're blowing my mind here. How many layers do you have?"

"Lots." She smiled, and a sense of loss hit me. I missed my sister. Missed knowing about her life these last few years when she'd developed all those *layers* because she didn't have them growing up.

"It probably depends on the ice cream," I said. "Remember Potter's Parlor across from our grade school?"

"Don't remind me."

"The pistachio chocolate chunk. Or the mango fizz flavor with those mini pieces of candied ginger. So good."

"Why are you being cruel right now?" Janie lifted her head and shot me an exaggerated glare. "I'm rich.

I'm used to getting what I want. Why would you make me want something I can't have?"

I grinned. "Actually, they ship it overnight anywhere in the US."

"You've ordered it?" she asked with what sounded like excitement, not judgment.

"No, but I've thought about it. Call it … often."

Janie slid lower in the tub, closed her eyes again, and laughed. "I hated that you got a cone, like every week. I hit puberty, and one lick of ice cream showed up on my thighs the next day."

I looked at her, confused. "Janie, you and Jill are like Mom. Effortlessly beautiful and fit. Even now, after two kids, you have great legs and a flat stomach. Surely you could have indulged a little."

Janie cracked one eye and examined me before lolling back on the tub's edge. "Strive for perfection, and when you don't make it, at least you'll be close. Close is enough."

I let her words sink in. *When* you don't make it. Not *if*. Maybe Janie didn't have to have perfection. She just pushed hard. A swimmer who almost made the Olympic team was still an excellent swimmer. A mom with busy kids could have one room that was pristine. And a mantel picture with matching dresses could look perfect even if the people in it weren't.

"There's my dirty girl," Levi said as I sat next to him in the spa's seaside garden. He leaned over and smacked a kiss on my lips. "How was it?"

"Interesting."

"Need me to check any spots for mud?" He waggled his brows. "I can be very thorough."

"Oh, I know you can." I flashed him a flirty smile.

"I got this for you. Flavored water is the house wine here." Levi handed me a tall slim glass with a floating slice of cucumber and looked out at an ocean view that could only be described as serene. Or gorgeous.

Levi Abrams was gorgeous, leaning back, wearing those sunglasses, a little sheen of massage oil glistening on his shoulders.

How was he here with me? How was he not taken? He was sexy and fun and good. Why had it been so long since he had a girlfriend?

I realized Levi hadn't said much about his past, his romantic past, only that he'd had serious feelings for four women, and it had been a while since the last one. Did things end badly? Or did he not want serious? "How are you still single?" I blurted.

His gaze snapped to mine, and I repeated the question.

"I'm not," he said, taking my hand. "My girlfriend is sitting right here."

"Levi, any woman would be lucky to have you, to … love you. Men like you are never single. Do you not want to be married?"

"Are you proposing?" He tilted his head at me.

"Levi."

His expression sobered, and he sucked in a breath. "I want to be married … to the right person." He absently bumped our joined hands on the arm of my chair. "A long time ago, I thought I found her. I was wrong. I'm more careful now."

A bad ending. I let the silence linger for a beat. "Do

you want to tell me what happened? You don't have to if it still hurts."

"It doesn't hurt," he said, smiling at me. "Not how you think."

That made me happy. I didn't want Levi to be hung up on a woman who wasn't good enough for him. He deserved to have every bit of his love returned. It wasn't because I expected to be the woman who had it and returned it. I didn't.

But I was here now, and I could return everything he gave me. Passion. Pleasure. Unquestioning support. For the next three days.

He cleared his throat. "A few years ago, I was involved in a criminal investigation."

I frowned.

"Computer fraud." He chewed the edge of his bottom lip.

"*You*? Why?"

He released my hand. "I knew the two people being investigated." His expression was … feigned nonchalance. Guarded.

"The friends you did the golf course thing with."

He nodded. "I hadn't talked to them since college. They … went in a different direction. But people in the Comp Sci department knew about the things we did in high school, and when the cops came around asking questions, digging into their past, my name came up."

"Like you were involved?"

"Like it was possible. It was all part of a larger FBI investigation. Two weeks later, I was charged."

I sat forward and faced him. "That must have been terrible."

"My girlfriend couldn't handle it." His tone was flat. "I wasn't involved in the crime."

"Of course you weren't." I shook my head. "You're not that person. You were facing a firing squad, and *she* couldn't handle it?"

He stared at me, then shifted in his seat. "We'd been together a long time. She was sick for a couple of months in the early days, in the hospital with an infection, and I'd done everything for her. I was happy to do it, but when I needed her, she left to 'give me space' until things settled down." He sighed. "She blindsided me. I'd been wandering into jewelry stores wearing a big dumb grin, but if she didn't believe in me, there was no point. When the charges were dropped, and it was finally over, I didn't want her back."

My heart cracked a little. "Levi, I'm sorry."

"I had to turn in two of my oldest friends. Yes, they were doing something illegal, and I had to tell the truth, but fuck I felt like shit. I mean … guys, we just don't do that to each other. It's like an unspoken rule. Guy code or something. I wasn't sure if I was the bad friend for getting them caught or if they were the bad ones for putting me in that position."

"Them. They were the bad ones," I said with no hesitation. "And her too."

He looked at me. "Or I trusted the wrong people."

So, he held himself back, at least physically.

"Aaannnd … that's why I'm not married," he said in a light tone like it was a joke or the end of a tall tale.

"Was she your last girlfriend?"

He shook his head. "No, there's been someone since then, but it didn't work out." He shrugged. "She cheated. Return-of-a-first-love type deal. Destiny or something."

I made a face. Who were these women? Had they never heard of decency? Loyalty? This was Levi. A *great white whale* of a man. One who'd just shared two deeply wounding experiences. I wanted to hold him and protect him from anyone who couldn't see how truly special he was. I didn't expect it, but I wanted it. God, I wanted it.

"It's okay. I cared about her, but I'm not sure we would have gone the distance."

"You deserve better."

He held my gaze. "I know."

Those butterflies again.

"And you deserve better too."

AFTER ALL JILL'S FUSSING, the luau Janie booked for the bachelorette party was a blast. So, there wasn't a signature drink. Who cared? The Mai Tais were excellent, and no one was complaining. Even Troye's sister, a quiet woman I'd only met twice before, had a good time after that first awkward greeting.

And when they pulled Jill on stage for a special performance by the warrior dancers, which Janie had been able to arrange after all, she got to be up close with all that brown chest and arm and the whorls and angles of blue tribal tattoos. No bride-to-be would complain about that.

"Are there really men in the world who look like them?" asked Susie, one of Troye's glamorous cousins from New York, who was actually quite nice. "Rugged and … just … so damn capable."

"Kate's boyfriend looks like them," Janie added, and

I turned to her in surprise. "What? He's hot as hell. I'm married, but my vision is fine." She nodded toward a dancer. "See that guy there? Levi looks like him."

I found the guy she meant. Lean and strong, with soft eyes. Bedroom eyes. Levi had bedroom eyes.

"His skin is lighter, and he doesn't have the tribal tattoo, of course, but the body is him," I agreed.

A chorus of Oohs rang out around the table. "Let's see some pictures," Susie demanded.

Oh. Thank the goddess, I had a few from the week. I grabbed my phone and played it cool. "Here are a couple of recent ones." I pulled up a photo of Levi and me on the zipline platform, several from snorkeling and one of him hugging me from behind on our volcano hike.

"Damn, he *is* hot, and *into* you," Susie said as my phone traveled around the table, the others flipping through the pictures. "Where did you find him, and can I have the agency number?"

I laughed.

"They work together," Janie said.

"He's in IT security at the hospital."

"Another office romance," Susie's sister, Cameron added. Her pout did nothing to mar the easy beauty in her symmetrical features. "Janie, if you tell me you and Steven worked together before you were married, I'm changing jobs." She worked for a women's athletic clothing line that boasted nearly all female employees.

"We didn't realize we worked together until our first date." True. "We met outside the hospital, and it didn't come up." Also, true.

"Too many other things to do rather than talk?" Susie winked above the rim of another cocktail.

I grinned and said nothing, and the table rang out with a round of sighs and "Get it, girl."

"He looks like that, he has a job, and he came to a family wedding with you. Hang on to him," Jill's college roommate said. "Or, I will."

I laughed. "Hands off my man," I said, faking a glare.

"Oh, the way he's looking at you in this pic—" Cameron held up my phone with a photo of Levi and me on the boat "—I don't think anyone else has a chance. He's a smitten kitten."

This was a first. Women fawning over *my* boyfriend, not one of my sisters'. I bit my lip and soaked in the sensation until I saw Jill shooting eye daggers straight at me.

What the hell? I'd come on this trip. I'd played nice. All week, I'd calmed her down, taken her shit, and gone along with the orange dress and interrupted orgasm. She was the one marrying my ex but acted like *I* was the problem.

This time, I didn't give a fuck about her daggers. I'd gone above and beyond and was fresh out of said fucks at this point. I grinned and raised my glass. "Isn't this great, Jill? I knew it would all work out."

28

LEVI

I MISSED MY GIRL. BEING WITH ALL THESE LOUD BROS around a dart board wasn't helping. You know it's bad when the guy you most connect with at a party is a sometimes douchy entertainment lawyer from LA.

"Another beer?" Steven asked. "The best man, Kevvie, is buying. So, I say go for something good. Is it me, or is that guy kinda a dick?"

"It's not you," I said. "But I'm good. Kate should be here soon, and I'm not sure how long she'll want to stay."

"She says jump, and you jump?"

"That's about the size of it. Is it a problem?"

"Nah, no problem. Kate's great. Has her head on straight. Puts up with some shit with a ton of tolerance. And if you don't mind me saying it, she has a very pretty face."

"She's pretty everywhere, man, but you can take my word for it. Keep your eyes on your wife." I nodded like it was a threat. It was a joke. Mostly.

He smiled and patted me on the shoulder. *Message received. No worries.*

A roar came from the large table in the back by the dartboard.

"Who thought it was a good idea to get a bunch of bros together and give them beer and sharp objects to throw?" Steven asked.

I huffed. "That's why I'm sitting at the bar, keeping a safe distance."

"Smart," he said and sat next to me. He nodded to the bartender. "What's the oldest scotch you have?"

I WAS DRINKING eighteen-year-old Glenlivet when my girl finally walked in. The entire group was smiling and laughing and had clearly had a few at the luau or in the limo. I swiveled on my stool and spread my knees, inviting her to slot in where she belonged. Kate did not disappoint.

"Hellooo," she cooed and pressed her mouth to mine.

"Hello back," I said and licked my lips. "Mmm, rum. Having fun?"

She wrapped her arms around my neck and threw her head back. "Yesss. It's been a while since I let loose. How'm I doin'?"

"Good, now that I've got you." I chuckled. "How many did you have?"

"Enough to ignore the daggers shooting out of Jill's eyes. I'd say she's a weeeee bit pissssssed at me?" She squinted and gestured with her thumb and forefinger about an inch apart.

Interesting. "What did you do?"

"Got a hot boyfriend. That's you, B-T-Dubs." She winked.

I barked a laugh. Kate did not say B-T-Dubs. Ever. I'd bet on it.

"Okay, so why is Jill pissed about you having a hot boyfriend, me that is?"

She sighed. "Who knows why Jill gets pissed about anything?" She slipped from my arms and sat on the stool Steven vacated when he went to greet Janie. "She's having her dream wedding, and everyone is kissing her ass. I'm over it. So, what are *you* drinking?"

I chuckled at the quick topic change. "Expensive scotch compliments of the best man. Can I get you something, maybe a sandwich?" I grinned. "I like tipsy Kate, but I have plans to keep you awake later."

"Ooohh." She shimmied in her seat, and her small tits jiggled in the tight white tank top she wore. Without a bra. Perfect. Her face was bare of makeup. Also, perfect.

Before leaving for the luau, she'd said, "Not trying to impress anyone but you, and by the time we're together tonight, it will have all worn off, anyway. No sense wasting good makeup."

"You may not be trying to impress, but those tight little pants will get noticed," I'd responded and gave her ass a tiny smack that made her squeal.

She was still wearing the pants with blue geometric shapes, the tank, and flip-flops, with toes freshly polished in a deep coral, not orange, color. Vacation sexy all the way.

"You and Steven bonded, then?" she asked.

I sipped my glass. "I wouldn't say *bonded*, but he's not too bad. Better than Troye and his bros."

"How was dinner?"

"Good. My steak was great. We talked *a lot* about sports. Troye's friends told stories."

Kate smirked. "I'm sure."

"I guess you've met some of those guys …"

Kate glanced at the crew as they emptied another pitcher of beer among them. "A couple, but I think most are from his undergrad days."

"I hope they're better at darts sober."

"Stinking it up, are they?" She laughed.

I watched one guy turn his back on the target and throw over his shoulder. "More like a danger to themselves and others."

"It can't be that bad. Should we play next?" Her eyes glittered.

"Are you any good?"

"Me? I'm great at drunk darts. That was *my* Olympic sport."

Yeah, I liked tipsy Kate.

"Bring your drink." She grabbed my hand and pulled me toward the action in the back.

We were better at darts than pool basketball. It may have had to do with the fact that Kate wasn't wearing her tempting purple bikini. And we were mostly sober, well I was. We lost the first game but won the next three, making us the champs of that round.

"You two make a good team," Steven said and slapped me on the back as we sat at a nearby table with our celebratory waters. On another night, in Perry Harbor, at The Boathouse bar, when they had live music, I'd buy the expensive scotch. Revel in my girl letting loose, but I wanted us both clearheaded tonight.

We had two nights left in our week, and we needed to talk.

Steven nodded at Janie. "We may need to get in there, wifey. Show them what *we* can do."

Janie grinned. "I think we're good right where we are. Especially if you order some pretzel bites for me."

"They won't be organic," Steven warned.

"Oh well, my diet is screwed anyway. Hope you like a bloated wife because that's what you've got."

"I have a sexy wife," Steven growled and kissed her neck.

"Do you need us here for this?" I asked, gesturing at the two of them wrapped around each other.

"Like you aren't all over Kate," Janie said.

She was right, so I said nothing and pulled Kate in for a quick kiss on her temple. If you can't beat 'em, join 'em.

Steven gave us both another one of his assessing looks. "So you know, I looked into you."

I furrowed my brow.

"I did a background check. Troye had some questions."

Kate huffed from the seat beside me.

"*And,*" Steven emphasized. "Kate's my wife's sister. If you think I'm letting some guy sweep her off her feet and not check him out, you'd be wrong."

I nodded. "Protective. I can't argue with that. So, what did you find?"

I already knew what was out there. I'd had to explain a few things when the hospital hired me. The police had mostly wiped my record in the computer fraud case due to what I'd done. I'd told the cops how to set a trap to catch my former friends and the people they worked for, and they kept that part of my involvement out of it. I was brought in on charges and released, and the charges were dropped a few days later. That was it.

"Nothing really, as I'm sure you're aware," Steven said. "A couple of speeding tickets, one in a school zone." He tsked. "A bogus computer fraud charge."

"You didn't need to run a background check," Kate said. "I could have told you he wasn't involved in anything illegal. Not Levi." She smiled at me with a soft gleam in her eyes that I felt in my chest. "He's a good man. All you have to do is spend time with him to know it."

She overwhelmed me. The worst thing in my life, and Kate believed in me after only a few days, when my ex hadn't after two years.

"How did you know the charges were bogus?" I asked Steven.

He smirked. "I'm a … fairly experienced attorney in one of the wealthiest, most public industries in the world. I can spot bogus claims anywhere."

"A good man to know, then." I tipped my glass at him.

He held my gaze with a small grin. "Kinda like a skilled computer hacker with a soul."

I casually nodded my agreement and said nothing.

Steven glanced at his watch. "We should wrap this up. Big day tomorrow."

"Thank you," I said to Kate on the ride home after we, along with Janie and Steven, poured everyone else into a series of Ubers. Jill and Troye were fine, but the bros, and possibly some of Jill's friends and Troye's New

York cousins, would all be wearing sunglasses at the ceremony.

"Thank you for what?" she asked.

"Believing in me."

"Of course. *Anyone* who comes for my hot boyfriend has to go through me." She waved her hand with a flourish, and there was no way I couldn't love her.

"Same, babe." I felt exactly the same.

29

KATE

Levi headed to the bedroom while I went to the kitchen for a late-night snack. Getting everyone into safe rides at the end of the night took some effort. Levi and I both deserved a sweet reward, and I'd seen a plate of chocolate-dipped fruit in the fridge earlier. There wasn't a sexier snack than that.

"Eating at this hour? Is that a good idea?" Jill appeared and leaned against the wall with her arms crossed, giving my body a once-over. "You have a dress to wear tomorrow."

Ah, yes, the orange one. I couldn't wait. I set more of the delicate treats on my plate, because screw her. "It's always a good idea to eat chocolate off my hot boyfriend's abs, but thanks for your concern."

Jill smirked.

"What is your problem tonight? You shot daggers at me at the luau and again when Levi and I won at darts. I know you like attention but come on."

"You think this is about darts," she huffed. "This was a big night for me. *I'm* joining Troye's family tomorrow.

Not you. But you're the one laughing with his cousins about how your boyfriend is *sooo in* to you, chatting up his friends from college, and making an impression. You couldn't give me one night."

My eyes went wide. "What are you talking about? I'm here giving you an entire week of nights."

"Oh, yes. Thank you for the sacrifice of your precious time. You with your important job, doing everything by yourself, not needing help from anyone. You barely see your family. Then, you show up with a man none of us have ever heard of and monopolize everyone's attention at *my* wedding."

"Oh my god. So, I have a boyfriend. You are marrying my ex, who dumped me, by the way."

Jill scoffed and raised her chin. "You have a *fake* boyfriend."

I froze.

"That's right." Her voice was low. "I know this whole thing with you and Levi is fake. I saw your text to Kristen when you were passing around those photos earlier. You met him a week ago. He was never your boyfriend."

"Kate?" Levi asked, strolling into the room in nothing but PJ pants.

I wanted to answer him, but the red mist at the edge of my vision was like a magnet holding my focus. "You read my text from Kristen? So, you searched on my phone? What gave you the right?"

"You don't deny it then?"

"Answer the damn question, Jill."

Troye joined the party, followed by Janie and Steven. Troye stood close to Jill. Her rock. *Her* support. Fine. I could stand on my own. Same shit, different day.

Jill straightened. "Troye was … *we* were worried. I had an opportunity. I took it. Steven ran a background check and found out he has a criminal past."

"Hold on—" Steven started.

"I can't believe you." I squinted at Jill.

"We were trying to protect you. You clearly need it."

"He's *not* a criminal," I ground out. "And you wanted to protect me? From Levi? The only one who has treated me with respect this week? The stranger who's been more considerate to me than my sister? *That* Levi? That's who you wanted to protect me from?"

"He may not be guilty of computer fraud." Jill shrugged. "But he can't be completely aboveboard. You're having sex, and it's *illegal* to pay for it."

What the? "You think I paid him? You think the fat sister can't get a man unless she pays him?"

"Jill," Janie barked.

"Susie said it earlier, and I thought, *that explains it*," Jill said, ignoring Janie once again.

"She was joking—"

"No one is paying anyone," Levi growled from where he stood beside me. "And you're wrong about my relationship with Kate."

"Then why did you lie about being together? You met her a week ago." Jill glared at him.

"Nothing about me and Kate is fake. It never was," he said, his voice dangerously calm, a storm vibrating beneath the surface. "I met an incredible woman in a coffee shop. I asked to see her again, and it happened to be a date for your wedding. We did lie about the timing. But … you know what that's like … lying about timing."

"No, I don't," Jill snapped.

"Jill," Troye said with a sigh and a nervous look at Levi.

Her glare shifted to her fiancé, and she shook her head. "No, Troye. Not the night before our wedding. We talked about this yesterday! I wanted to clear the air months ago and plan a great big event with sports stars and WAGs on the guest list. Press coverage. But no, you were too worried about it hurting *Kate*."

"Hurting me? How?" It was like a record scratch in the charged room. "Hurting me how, Jill?"

Silence stretched, and my mind whirred. "How would *clearing the air* hurt me?" I shouted.

"Knowing I cheated," Troye said calmly, pushing his shoulders back.

I blinked. "On Jill?"

"No. I cheated on you … *with* Jill."

My brow furrowed, then my head spun as the features of the room blurred. Was I fainting? Having a stroke? "I'm sorry, what?"

"When Jill and I first … you and I were still engaged."

"But you said …" Light dawned. "You dick! You absolute piece-of-shit dick! You lied. I blamed myself for our breakup. And you let me. I have punished myself and doubted myself ever since. And it was *you*." I turned to Jill. "And you. You're my sister, and you fucked my fiancé?"

"It wasn't like that," Jill protested, a shadow of panic rising in her expression.

"Yes," I said, my eyes wide open now. "It was. What the hell is wrong with you? I defended you. When you and Troye said you were dating, I got the eye from everyone, but I said, 'No way, my sister wouldn't do that to me.' Not the sister I took care of when Mom and Dad were fighting. I missed that awards dinner at graduation to help you study for the SAT. I smooth out all your shit, and this is what I get. Want to know why I don't come home? It's not because of my job. It's because I'm sick of being your punching bag one day and your pity party the next."

Jill's face fell.

"Kate," Troye said. "If you need to blame someone, blame me, but neither of us planned it. There was … attraction when she came for the job interview. We had dinner. It just happened."

"Oh, was it an accident … like you slipped and landed with your dick in my sister?"

"*We* were already falling apart. You know that."

"Right. Because I can't orgasm. Only, turns out, with the right man, a *better* man, I can. Easy. So, you know what? I'm glad you fucked my sister and dumped me. You saved me from a lifetime of bad sex." I waved him off. "You can have him, Jill. Enjoy. And as for your wedding tomorrow, cancel it. Go have that big fab event you dreamed about. It won't hurt me because I won't be there either way."

"Kate, what in the world?" Mei entered the kitchen in her robe, Dad behind her, his expression nothing but concern.

"Ask Jill. I'm leaving."

"Pack what you need for tonight," Levi told me, throwing his worn carry-on satchel on the bed. "I'll come back tomorrow and get everything else." He'd changed into jeans and a plain white T-shirt that stretched across his shoulders and chest.

I would not cry. *I would not.* Instead, I grabbed my backpack and shoved a few clothes and toiletries inside.

Levi zipped his bag and took my hand in his. "Come on. We're getting out of here."

I barely saw the stunned faces of everyone as we silently walked through the house and out the front door. The world was quiet and dark in the Jeep, like it was last night when I'd teased and flirted with Levi, like a woman who was enough. A woman who hadn't trusted the wrong people.

My sister thought I had to pay Levi to be with me. Did everyone?

I bet if you lost some weight, you'd have a boyfriend.

Is that why you work so hard? Because you can't keep a man?

Bright lights caught my attention, and I shoved the voices in my head back into the box where they lived. Levi stopped the Jeep in front of the tall, stark white columns lit from the ground that marked the entrance to the relaxed elegance of the Grand Hawaiian Hotel.

"Here?" I asked.

"Here," Levi said and gestured to the valet. He was out of the car in a second, had both our bags in one hand and my hand in the other.

The temple of trees and tropical plants with colorful blooms, blurred along with the sparkling mosaic turtle designs swimming across the marble floor. The smack of my flip-flops echoed in the late-night quiet.

"Aloha, how can I help?" the woman at the reception desk asked. She wore a trim-cut dress with floral designs in subtle hues, and the white plumeria blossom behind her ear was pristine. At midnight.

"I don't have a reservation, but I saw online you have availability in your spa rooms."

Her smile was bright as she took in our disheveled appearance. "We do. The rate is thirteen hundred per night with a three-night minimum."

"We'll take it," he said and set his card on the high stone counter. "The most secluded one available."

My brain finally engaged, calculating the price, which included one night we wouldn't even be here. "Levi, no."

"Kate, it's fine. I have the money. And this isn't my first time in this hotel. I've always wanted to try the spa rooms. Let me do this for you."

"You're returning then—" the woman checked her screen "—Mr. Abrams."

"I am."

"Mahalo. Welcome back." Her tone was more genuine now. "We have one available on the edge of the property. It's a walk, but very private."

"Perfect," he said.

"Do you need help with any bags?" she asked, tapping buttons on a screen and handing Levi his card.

"Tomorrow. Tonight, we want to get to our room. What about room service?"

"Complimentary room service is available to the spa rooms twenty-four hours a day."

"Great. Thanks, ah, Mahalo." Levi grinned.

She handed a key card packet to an older woman who appeared next to her. "Leilani will show you to your room."

"It better be fucking fantastic for four grand," I whispered to Levi.

"Trust me," he said.

He was right. It was fucking fantastic. The spa rooms were situated in a wooded area to the side, separate from the main hotel. "These are the originals," the woman said as she led us along the lighted footpath. "When the hotel was built, these huts were made into exclusive spaces, set aside for quiet relaxation in nature with all the Grand Hawaiian services and conveniences only steps away."

"They nailed it," I blurted as I took in the thatched-roof huts, each nestled into the flowering trees only feet from the rocky shore and set at angles for privacy.

Ours was the last one. Leilani keyed us in and flipped on a low lamp in the corner before heading to the bedroom for a few beats. "Here you are. I set up the outdoor space for you, and the amenities menu is there on the coffee table. Enjoy your stay." She gave Levi the key, pressed her hands together, and closed the door behind her with a quiet, "Aloha."

The room glowed with light wood floors, pale walls, and rich fabrics. I barely noticed as the revelations of the evening consumed my thoughts once again.

Levi strolled to the bedroom in the back and opened a wall of sliding doors, letting the dull roar of the ocean fill the space.

"Kate," he said, returning to me. "Take a breath. Take a bath. There's a soaking tub out there. I'll order some food, and we can talk or sleep. Whatever you need." He rubbed the pad of his thumb across my lips and kissed them gently. Worry filled his expression.

"Will you hold me?"

"Of course," he said with a sigh. "I'm sorry I didn't do it sooner." He pulled me in, my arms pressed to his chest, and squeezed me tight against him, the way I liked. The way I loved. And the tension seeped from me.

"Are you okay?"

I exhaled a weighted breath and took stock. Was I okay? I was angry… and embarrassed. I felt betrayed, but did anything hurt? Did my heart hurt?

Levi's strong arms held me secure until I could breathe again. No, my heart wasn't hurt. My heart was safe right here in his hands. I was in love with him. And I had two more days to give him all of it.

"I'm okay," I said and didn't cry.

30

LEVI

Kate said she was okay. That was all that mattered.

I released her and rubbed my hands along her arms. She'd been too quiet, possibly fighting tears, and all I wanted to do was make it better.

"Come on, Sweetheart. A bath under the stars can cure a lot." I led her out back to the private view of the vast Pacific. A huge, gleaming white, oval soaking tub sat next to one of the thatched side walls of the lanai, and I turned the knobs to start the water. A small bin held thick towels, soaps, and assorted jars of salts. I picked the prettiest jar, and the night air filled with the scent of eucalyptus as I shook the contents into the tub.

"May I take this off?" I asked, lifting the hem of her shirt. Her answer was to raise her arms above her head. Next were her pants and her thong. Her skin glowed in the night. "Goddamn, you're beautiful."

She rolled her lips, definitely fighting tears.

I held her hand, and she stepped in as steam rose around her. She was a goddess, and this was my chance to worship. "Lie back and let me take care of you." I waggled my brows as she sat and finally smiled. I placed a small towel behind her head and then went to order some snacks, including a decent bottle of red wine.

I unpacked a few things for both of us and noticed she'd brought her vibrator.

I wanted to make love to her. And I wanted to fuck her so hard and long that she would never doubt this was real. What her sister and Troye did cut deep, and I wanted to burn down the world, starting with their half.

More than that, though, I wanted to burn up the sheets with Kate. Make her forget everything in the past and look forward to a future with me. We definitely needed to talk, but now wasn't the time. My plans would have to wait.

I left the vibe where it was, pulled down the comforter on the bed, answered room service's knock, and checked on my girl with a glass of red wine in hand.

The stars were midnight bright, but Kate stared out at the dark sea. She turned to face me as I knelt by the tub. Milky water rippled with her movements. The scent of floral soap mixed with the eucalyptus from the salts.

"Here," I said and handed her the glass.

"Thank you." She took it with slippery fingers.

"Feeling better?"

She smiled, but it didn't quite meet her eyes. I had more work to do.

"Um … there's room in here for two," she said, and a shy gleam sparked. I could work on her smile in the tub.

"There is," I said and stood to whip off my T-shirt, jeans, and boxers as fast as possible. Kate scooted forward, and I slid in behind her, bracketing her thighs with mine. Warm water sloshed over the low edge in the middle. "Good thing this is outside."

She chuckled and lay back against my chest. I had the perfect view again. The night sky, the ocean, and Kate's naked curves. The world righted on its axis.

I smoothed my hands along her shoulders and pressed a kiss to her temple. Together, we sat in the quiet, and I let my heart love her.

"You knew," she said moments later, breaking the silence.

"I suspected."

"How?"

"Last night at the rehearsal dinner, I was there when Steven was talking to Troye and figured it out. Troye admitted nothing, but it was clear they were together when Jill started the job in Portland, and I knew that was before you and Troye ended. I was working out how to tell you. Maybe it was selfish, but I didn't want to hurt you."

She shook her head. "No. I understand." She exhaled. "I'm angry, but then not. I'm sad, but then not. I don't want Troye. I'm glad we broke up. I wish it wasn't because *my sister* fucked him so well, but I'm glad we're done, or … I wouldn't have met you."

Not meeting her? I couldn't imagine it now. I pulled her close and kissed the spot on her neck we both loved. "We have something, don't we?"

She nodded.

"I want to keep seeing you, Kate." It was the wrong time, but I said it anyway.

A long pause stretched.

"I live on Coho Island, a two-hour ferry ride from Perry Harbor that's more like a two-hour plane ride, with the planning and weather delays and waiting in line. I failed at long-distance too many times. I don't think I could bear failing with you."

I kissed her temple and bent my head to her ear. "I may not know the answer right now, but I know I want to figure it out … and I know I want to make love to you." She stilled. "Not tonight. You've had enough for one day—"

"What if I want it tonight? Would you?"

My hard dick pressed against her low back, and she swiveled to catch my eye. The hesitant gleam was still there in hers.

"Anytime, anyplace, Kate. You know that. But today has already been a lot for you."

She shifted in the water to meet my eyes. "I don't think anyone has ever *made love* to me."

That right there pierced my heart. "I can, and I will, if you let me."

Her hands on the edges of the tub, she pushed herself to stand but didn't climb out. I stayed seated for a beat. All that body, her round ass and thick thighs, were right there. Perfumed and soft and pink from the warm water.

Her smile down at me was all the invitation I needed. I caressed my fingertips up her calves, then lingered on the backs of her knees before going higher. I made the journey again, using increased pressure and massaging along the way.

I pressed my thumbs to the crease where her thighs met the globes of her ass, and she sighed. "I love your ass, Kate. Your legs. Your hips. Your breasts. Your eyes. All of you." I swallowed at the truth of my confession.

She said nothing. Right now, she didn't need to. It

was there on her face and the way she trusted me to see her. I wasn't alone in this. My love wasn't misplaced here, like it had been with others. Kate needed time to trust what I already knew.

She reached for a towel and stepped out of the tub. I did the same and followed her into the bedroom, where she crawled to the pillows on her hands and knees, naked. The only light was from the main room and the moonlight reflecting off the water nearby, but I could make out her shape, and the dark shadow of her center waiting for me. I wanted to do this right, better than I ever had.

I stroked a hand along her hip and side as I paused to switch on the small lamp by the bed. "Okay? It's just the ocean and us here, and I need to see you."

She blinked away the wariness that flashed in her eyes and rose to kneeling on the bed. "I want you to see. And I trust you."

Those were her words of love.

"You're beautiful, Kate. Your skin, your smile—" I shook my head. "I want you more than I can say."

She lowered her palms back to the bed and reached back to caress her hand over a hip. No more hesitation. Only sexy confidence. "Then touch me, Levi. Show me what you want, because I want to give it to you."

Stepping behind her, I forced myself to go slow. Kate deserved slow. We both did.

Instead of flipping her and pushing inside with one hard stroke, I kissed up the inside of one thigh until I licked the edge of her swollen sex, and then did it again on the other side. With each lick against her wet heat, her hips rocked back, seeking more.

"Levi, please …"

"Want to go slow, babe." I kissed one perfect ass cheek, and then the other. "We only get one first time."

She whimpered, and I smiled to myself. Yeah, my dick was screaming at me too, but this was everything I'd imagined. I couldn't rush.

Crawling over her, I let my body weight push her to the bed before I slid to the side and kissed my way up her spine. "I love this part of you, too. This curve of your waist above your hips and how it all comes together in this single column. So pretty and feminine. It calls to my inner caveman."

"The sexy beast," Kate whispered.

"Yeah," I shifted away, the beast in me rising now that she'd called it out. "Turn over."

She did, and when she lifted her arms, inviting me to her, I shook my head. "Not done going slow. Put those arms above your head and leave them there. I need some time here." I teased the tip of one full nipple, then the other.

Kate's eyes darkened, and she gripped the pillows behind her.

I caressed the creamy swell of her breast before I bent to nip and suck until her hips were writhing.

"Are you ready for me?" I asked, knowing she was. Knowing if I cupped her pussy, I'd find her dripping. Her body made no secret of how much Kate liked sex.

"Yes," she pleaded, her breath panting.

I went to my bag for a condom.

"When did you get those?" Her voice was a little sex dazed and perfect.

"A week ago," I said, setting the packet on the nightstand.

"Really?" She gave me a coy smile, then rose to her

elbows with one knee bent in the universal pose of sex goddesses everywhere. I had to swallow to make my tongue work.

"Let's say I had an abundance of hope after meeting you at the coffee shop." I returned to her side.

She laughed and shook her head. "I'm not sure if I should be insulted or complimented."

"Complimented. A hundred percent. I'm good at reading people, and I knew you were special the minute I heard you turn down my buddy, Pete."

"Then I feel complimented. Why don't you make me feel something else?" Her eyes glittered in challenge, and she pulled my mouth to hers.

I broke our kiss, remembering the depth of that challenge. "No faking, Kate. Just be with me here, and we'll figure everything else out as we go."

With a sultry smile, she nodded. "No faking."

31

———

KATE

I couldn't imagine faking it. Levi had me teetering on the edge back when I was on my hands and knees. Then, I thought I'd come from his nipple play alone, which would have been a first. I wanted him, especially the sexy beast. The sharp bite of lust was taking over, pushing all my insecurity and anger to a far-off place.

I met his kiss and stroked a knee up his side, angling to get him closer to where I needed him. He rolled away to reach for the condom, and when he was ready, he settled between my open legs. His arms slid under my shoulders as mine encircled his back, and he kissed along my jaw as he finally filled me in the best way.

Connected, the intensity of the moment was overwhelming. This was a big deal. For Levi and for me. I was now one of a very elite club of women he'd allowed to know him like this. It was supposed to be a vacation fling. Not big feelings and making love. But here I was, heart and body completely, irrevocably, open to his.

Fully seated, he dropped his head to my shoulder.

"Don't move," he whispered. "I want to feel this a minute. Plus, I may come if you do."

I chuckled, and he did too, which made his hips and cock move. Which made us both groan.

I brought my knees up to cradle him. He was hard and stretched me fully, but not too much. He fit like he was made for me.

He lifted his head and met my eyes. There was heat but also joy and tenderness in those gray-blue depths. Slowly, he rocked into me, pleasure rising like the tide as he increased his pace and pushed deeper. My blood hummed, and I climbed higher. My breath panted, and I tried to let him know with my entire body how much I wanted him, wanted this. But then, without warning, the sensation ebbed, my body betraying me once again.

No. Not now! Not with him!

Levi stilled, his gaze locked with mine. "Okay?"

"Yes, no, I … I may have lost it. I don't know what happened. I'm sorry. But you asked me not to fake it." I tried to make light of the humiliation. How much was I supposed to bear today?

"Whoa, hey. No apologies. This is about what feels good. That's all. Whatever else is in your head, expectations or doubts, get rid of them."

I swallowed as his hands came up to caress my cheeks, and he pressed soft kisses to my face.

"Be *here* with me, Kate. That's all I need."

I nodded, and when he moved again, it was full of gentleness. "How does that feel?"

I closed my eyes and breathed, letting the sensations wash over me. "Good."

He kept moving, and I met him each time, soaking in the connection and clearing my mind of anything other than Levi, this moment, and being this close to him. A gift to savor.

"Keep breathing deep," he said. His chest lifted, and then his mouth was on my nipple, laving and teasing like before. My eyes popped open with surprise, and he flashed a wry grin. He propped himself on one hand, his other arm still wrapped under my shoulder on the other side, and when he moved his hips this time, the angle was different. Instead of grazing my clit, he pressed into it.

Reflexively, my hips ground up to his.

"Better?" he asked, his voice low.

"Yes," I said, meeting each grind with my own.

He shifted his weight fully to one elbow and curled his athletic body to keep thrusting while he held my breast with one hand like an offering for his warm mouth. Tingles became sparks, and I arched, seeking more contact with his mouth and with his hips.

"Bring your knees in, wrap your legs around the backs of mine."

I did, and when he thrust, the connection was more intense, deeper. Sensation radiated through my clit. I gasped, and those sparks ignited into flames. I needed more.

He settled over me, and my hips took control, moving instinctively with his to the sound of our mingled breaths. He ground out a curse, and I sighed out my pleas, our movements more and more frantic, until I was there, all the way over the edge and falling, my middle jerking against his with each round of spasms in my center. No way to fake that.

Levi stilled and swelled inside me, letting release take him too.

I was boneless, and we stayed connected until I surprised myself with a giggle.

He furrowed his brow above a grin. "I'm not sure I like the laughing."

I shook my head and laughed harder before getting myself under control. "I'm not laughing. It's just been a while since I did that. I forgot how it felt."

"And how did it feel?"

Euphoric. I sighed and stroked his back. "Really good."

He grinned and dropped a kiss on my mouth. "Hang on." He pushed all the way up, grabbing the base of the condom, then pulled away and strolled to the bathroom.

I was exhausted. I was exhilarated. I wasn't broken. Not emotionally by my sister and Troye. And not physically by the asshole from college and the ones who came after. "I love you," I said with a barely audible sigh and let the truth settle. We'd made love. Not because I orgasmed with him but because I was hopelessly in love with him.

The mattress dipped as Levi returned and slipped beneath the blankets to wrap me in his arms from behind. "You okay?"

"I'm happy."

He pressed a kiss to my shoulder. "Me too. Sleep now, Sweetheart."

The feel of his lips, his whispered words in my ear, and his spicy, clean scent were the only things on my mind as I drifted off.

. . .

Early morning sun filtered through the open doors, and I woke to the familiar sensation of Levi's heavy arm around my middle, his hand gently cupping my right breast in his sleep. Our last full day in Hawaii.

I wasn't ready to face it, so I rolled toward him and snuggled deeper into his chest to block the light. The hand that had been holding my breast caressed my shoulder blade while his breathing stayed soft and even.

When I woke next, the sun was much higher, and the sound of ocean waves mixed with distant laughter. Levi was on his back, and like the mornings before, I kissed my favorite spots on his chest.

Aware I hadn't brushed my teeth last night, I pushed away, but as usual, Levi's arm resisted. He cracked his eyes in the bright room, smiled, and lifted his head before it plopped on the pillow. "Where are you going?"

"Bathroom. Toothbrush. Shower."

He loosened his grip and let me go. "I like showers," he called to my retreating back, and I giggled.

I did my business and started the water warming. Levi appeared then, naked, with his toothbrush in hand. He moved to the sink to brush his teeth and do whatever else before joining me and setting a foil packet on the ledge along with my vibe.

I couldn't stop my grin. Or the buzz starting in my core.

His hands came around my middle from behind and pulled me against his hardness while his mouth clamped onto that spot at my nape. My pussy spasmed, as usual, and I reached to steady myself on the wall in front of me, panting. "How do you know just how to do that?"

"Paying attention and practice." His hand cupped a breast and teased my nipple with the gentle brush of his fingertips, sending sparks to my clit as if he were touching me there. And then he was, pressing and stroking exactly the way I liked.

He hummed in my ear. "So responsive. Are you sore?"

I shook my head. "No, thank god. I need you."

He slid a finger inside where I was slick and ready, and I ground myself against his palm. "So good. I … don't want to … lose it again."

"If you do, we'll find it again." His hand plucked my nipple, and my inner muscles gripped his talented fingers.

He knew I was close, and his rigid cock pressed harder into my back. I lifted on my toes to rub him between my ass cheeks, and he groaned.

"Last night was slow. Today, I want fast." I turned out of his hold to face him, and his lips were on mine, kissing with an urgency that only drove my need higher. "I want the beast."

He grabbed the condom and rolled it on, leveling me with his eyes. "Get those thighs around my waist."

"I'm heavy," I said.

"No. You're sexy as fuck." He pushed my back to the tile. "Soft and sweet where I'm not. Own it, Kate. Because I want to see that."

I took a deep breath, and with my best alluring gaze, I lifted my knee to rest at his hip.

"That's it, babe." He pulled my other leg up, moved me against the wall until he was right where I needed him, and then he made me need him more.

We didn't use the vibe.

Two condoms down, finally sated, and lying across the bed naked, we were quiet until Levi said, "Since we have the room until Sunday, let's change our tickets. Stay another day." He turned his head to face me with a gleam in his eyes. "My treat."

An extra night of Levi? My joy was automatic, and I went with just being here, in this moment, and not thinking about anything else. "Okay."

He growled and rolled over me, peppering every inch of my neck with ticklish kisses until hunger, our old nemesis, interrupted us. After we decimated the cheese board and snacks he'd ordered last night and a beautiful room service breakfast, we dressed, and Levi left to collect the rest of our things from the house.

"Relax in the hammock. Take a nap. Naked." He waggled his brows. "I'll be right back."

As much as I liked the idea of a naked hammock nap, I didn't quite have the nerve without Levi. So, I picked up a little and straightened the bedding, then stood in the open sliding door, staring out at the pale blue sky and sea. One more night would only make it harder to give him up, but I couldn't bring myself to change my mind.

What started as a fling became so much more. And now I wanted to keep him. Tell myself we could do long-distance, that this time would be different. Tell myself that Levi wouldn't grow frustrated with the challenges of time apart. That *he* wouldn't refuse to move to be with me. That *he* wouldn't ask me to sacrifice the best thing in my life, my patients, to be with him.

But he would. Because orgasm or not, I wasn't the woman a man changed his life for.

A knock came at the door.

Expecting housekeeping, I fixed a smile in place and opened it.

"Janie." I gaped. "How did you … oh, Levi."

"Don't be mad. I made him tell me because I come bearing ice cream." She raised the Styrofoam cooler in her hands.

I gestured for her to come in because ice cream was ice cream. And maybe because I needed a sister right now. Janie was the only choice.

I motioned toward the small sofa while I sat in one of the club chairs.

"Let me say, first, I'm not here to tell you to forgive Jill. I get that love is love, but you deserve to be treated better."

I cleared my throat, a bit surprised. "I appreciate that."

"I came because I care about you. And to prove it, I brought Mango Fizz from Potter's." She patted the cooler.

I furrowed my brow. "How?"

She smirked. "Overnight shipping and rush fees."

"Since last night? Shit, Janie. How rich *are* you?"

She waved a hand. "I ordered it yesterday when we were still at the spa. Before five PM in Arizona, and Fed Ex had it here by ten AM." She sang at the end like it was a jingle and opened the lid. Inside were six small cartons of Potter's ice cream, the familiar white cow and barn logo, the same as when I was a kid.

"Wait, did you know about Troye and Jill?"

She shook her head, and relief coursed through me.

"I didn't know," she said, removing two cartons of my favorite dessert and handing me one along with a spoon.

"And this ice cream is not about Jill's shitshow last night."
She paused. "I ordered it because the spa was fun. The
day at the black sand beach was fun, and I wanted to eat
ice cream with my sister. As usual, Jill stole the moment."

I bit my lip, fighting a smile. "I thought she only did
that to me."

"No, I love her, but she is definitely the baby of the
family." She rolled her eyes.

"The spa *was* fun," I said. "And the beach … well,
before Jill tried to give me sex advice."

Janie huffed and opened her pint. "Talk about
awkward as balls."

I laughed. "You got that right." Pulling off the lid on
my pint, the light orange cream dotted with bits of pale
yellow ginger took me back to a simpler time when I
rode bikes with my sisters and bandaged my dolls' knees
with multi-colored Band-Aids and gauze. No sex talks,
awkward or otherwise.

"I'm glad I had the ice cream," she said, taking a
bite. "It got me in the door. I don't want what Jill did to
put you off the family completely." She paused, her gaze
intent and a bit cautious. She heard what I said to Jill
last night. She knew it wasn't my job that kept me away
from the family after all.

"I know Jill can be a lot, I know I can, and we all
know Mom can. But you're an important part of us, and
… we need you."

How long had I waited for one of the women in my
family to say something like that? Not sure I would have
guessed it'd be Janie. I swallowed the lump in my throat.
"It's not that simple. I can't be the one who always
bends, the one who smooths things over when we're

together. I've done it forever, and I won't do it anymore."

"Fair. It's time for us to move past that old pattern anyway, and I think *this* may just do the trick." Janie's eyes widened. "I do think Jill is sorry, at least for how it all went down. She wanted to tell you the truth once they were engaged, but Troye was against it until Steven figured it out at the rehearsal dinner. Then Troye assumed it was out and wanted to tell you before the wedding. Jill felt threatened, like he cared more about your feelings than hers, but Troye just wanted to marry Jill with a clean slate."

I nodded. "Makes sense, but I'm not sure I can trust her again, or him, with anything."

Janie sighed. "Also fair. She was shockingly decent at breakfast this morning and volunteered to load the dishwasher. On her wedding day."

I huffed. "That is surprising."

"Troye's still at the house. That's a good sign." She scooped up another bite and closed her eyes. "Damn, why is this so good?"

"You don't want to know," I said, taking my first bite and letting a single layer of butterfat coat the roof of my mouth.

She shook her head. "I swear, if he marries her after this week, they may have a real shot."

"I hope so," I said. "Their wedding is my limit. I won't be around if they break up."

"So, you will be around for their wedding?" She took another bite, then slowly pulled the empty spoon from her lips with raised eyebrows.

I huffed and considered my sister. "I thought you weren't here for her."

"I'm not. I'm here for you. You don't have to forgive her, but I think you'd regret missing the wedding. I know I'd regret it if you weren't there."

"You would?" I tried and failed to hide my vulnerability.

"Yes. I feel like this could be a turning point for this family, as messed up as it is. Mom and Dad are getting along. My kids are getting older and want more relatives in their lives. You and me … connecting, being real with each other. I could use more real in my life, Kate. I could." She sighed. "Come to the wedding. We'll get through it together."

32

LEVI

Janie asked for thirty minutes. I'd give her twenty. She wanted to talk about Jill and the wedding, and I wasn't sure Kate was ready for any of that. Caveman or not, I was protective of my girl.

Unbreakable and fragile, another duality I loved about her. I wanted to know all her contradictions along with all her curves, and I needed a lifetime to do it.

I had to convince Kate.

She had doubts, but I wasn't letting that scare me off. I liked a challenge and an adventure, and I was willing to do whatever it took. Now that I'd found her, I sure as hell wasn't giving up without a fight.

I checked my watch for what had to be the fiftieth time, ran a hand through my hair, and stood from the barstool overlooking the garden between the lavish hotel pool and its upscale restaurant.

At our room, I put my ear to the door. No crying or screaming, so that was good. "Kate," I said, slowly stepping inside, and a moan caught my dick's attention.

She and Janie were both lying back with their feet

on the coffee table, each holding a pint of ice cream and a spoon. "Pistachio chip is the damn bomb," Janie said.

"Totallllyyyy," Kate moaned again.

"Ladies," I said, taking in the open cooler and half-eaten pints. "Did you save any for me?"

Kate's head lolled to the side, her smile wide. "Come here and I'll put something delicious on your tongue."

I blinked.

"Annnnnd, that's my cue." Janie sat forward and set a couple more cartons on the coffee table.

"Thank you," Kate said. "For coming and for the ice cream."

"Don't go getting sentimental," Janie said. "When you're doing extra burpees next week, you'll be cursing me."

"I'll leave the burpees to you, but I'll walk an extra mile and think of you."

"Sounds good," she said and closed the lid on her cooler. "Maybe I'll see you tonight. Maybe I won't." Her expression warmed. "But I hope I do. It wouldn't be the same without you."

Kate nodded and gave me a quick glance. It was her call.

Janie turned to me. "Thanks for getting me here, Levi. I can get myself back."

"Need help with the cooler?" I asked.

"You can have this cooler when you pry it from my cold, dead hands."

I stepped back, and Kate chuckled.

With a wave and a wink, Janie closed the door behind her.

"So, this was good?" I asked, plopping down on the

sofa and stealing a taste from Kate's spoon. "Oh, damn, that is good."

"Right? This is why I fell in love with ice cream."

"One bite and I'm hooked. Kinda like one bite of you," I said and buried my face in her neck.

"Hungry?" she asked, gasping as I found those ticklish spots.

"For you, babe, I'm always hungry." I grabbed her hips and pulled her, guiding her to straddle my lap. Cowgirl was the next position I wanted to try. No time like the present.

Kate leaned back, scooped up a bite of her treat, and fed it to me. My mind whirred with ideas about ice cream and getting my girl naked, but I needed to check in first. "Are you okay?"

She sighed. "Yeah, and … I think I want to go to the wedding. What do you think?"

"If you go, I'm going. What did Janie say?"

"That she cared about me and didn't want me to drop out of the family. And … that Jill, for better or worse, is my sister. I told her I'm angry they cheated, but I'm not angry she's with Troye. Janie said showing up might make that clearer to everyone."

I squeezed her ass. "I think she's right about that. And if not, your hot boyfriend will be there to drive the point home."

She scooped another spoonful of the pistachio chip and raised it to my lips.

"You know, we could do all sorts of fun things with this," I said after I swallowed my bite of the sweet, almost cherry, vanilla flavor mixed with hunks of dark chocolate. I rolled her center over my erection. Around

Kate, I was always hard, but I wasn't complaining. She fucking turned me on, and I loved it, loved her.

"Oh, yeah?" she teased. She ate another scoop, tilted her head back, and groaned as her throat worked to swallow. It was like that first night with the gelato, except way hotter, and I wanted that mouth on my dick.

"Keep teasing me, Baby Girl, and see what happens."

She bit her lip and let it slip free slowly. Damn, those pornographic lips.

"Teasing you like this?" She ran the clean spoon down her chest, edging it to the shallow valley between her breasts. The fabric of her tank dipped lower, exposing more skin and the absence of a bra.

"Exactly like that, babe," I said and took the pint of ice cream from her hand.

ONE STICKY, fuck-hot hour later, I led her to the outdoor shower to clean up, and we settled in the hammock on our lanai for an afternoon snooze. Naked. It wasn't sunset like I'd imagined, but it was pretty spectacular, anyway.

The wedding festivities started at five, and she wore an emerald dress, as the orange or coral one had been delivered to the house with the others. I'm sure Kate would have been stunning in it, but this one wrapped around her body like a glove and elevated every sweet curve. I wanted to pull her to bed and lick ice cream off each one again, but I also wanted to show her off.

She was doing something brave, showing up, and my job was to make it easier. So, I dressed in my tailored navy suit and escorted my girl to a wedding.

It was nice, as weddings go. Cliquish in ways like a high school dance. The groom's side and the bride's side separated as if they were ready to rumble in sport coats and dresses. Kate and I were directed to sit close to the front, and I led her to the end of the row, sat, and pulled her close. Nothing to see here.

I wondered about a wedding with Kate. It wouldn't be like this. It would be on a beach or on a zipline platform. I smiled to myself at the image.

I'd imagined marrying someone before, so it didn't freak me out, but I'm not sure it ever felt like this. Right and solid from the word go. That freaked me out more than a little. What if I couldn't convince Kate we could work? I thought women in my past had broken my heart. I didn't want to imagine what losing Kate would do to it.

A surprising number of people were here for a destination wedding, and her family was quietly elated that Kate came. Even Troye's parents grinned widely as everyone posed for a quick round of photos with the happy couple when the deed was done.

Jill's first approach to Kate was tentative, possibly contrite, and I don't think she wanted me there, but fuck that. I stayed close to my girl. She apologized, and Kate agreed they could talk, but it wouldn't be soon. She needed time, and both Jill and Troye agreed to follow her lead for a change.

Another beautiful sunset filled the back of the house with a golden glow as we sat at the family table, my hand resting on Kate's thigh as much as possible.

"Still okay?" I whispered when the conversation took off with a story about Jill in college.

"Yeah. It hasn't been too bad. Thanks to you."

"I'm glad." I winked. "My job was to make it easier."

She paused, her expression intent. "You did your job very well."

"You take care of everyone. I like being the guy who gets to take care of you."

They cut the wedding cake, and Kate's dad slid an envelope across the table to her. "You're all set. It's the early flight on Sunday, but it'll give you one more sunset."

"Thanks, Dad," Kate said and smiled at me. One more sunset … at least.

"Thanks for changing the tickets," I said when I pulled her close on the dance floor set up on the lawn where the rows of chairs had been.

"I wanted it too."

"Knowing I have you here for an extra night is making it a little easier to stay. I enjoy dancing with you, but I'd rather be doing it naked."

She chuckled against my shoulder. "Now who's insatiable?"

"Ahh, Kate. A potential downside to the no inter-course thing is that I want to be inside you all the time now."

She laughed. "It could make our jobs tricky."

"I'm willing to try if you are." I held her gaze, my expression serious. "I want to try Kate. I want to figure this out with you."

She glanced around at the other dancing couples. "Can we talk about it tomorrow? I'm here in this dress. You're here in that suit. The stars are coming out in paradise. I don't want to think about the real world, not yet."

There was a pleading there I couldn't deny. "Tomorrow. After everyone is gone and, it's just you and me. Dinner at the fancy hotel restaurant. We'll talk about how I'm not those other guys, and how you're worth whatever it takes."

She sniffed, and I noticed the sheen pooling in her eyes. "Please, Levi."

I nodded my agreement and held her close. I wanted to wrap her up and squeeze the way she liked. The way that settled whatever scary voice was in her head. The way that helped her let go of so much and be my adventurous, vulnerable, wonderful Kate.

That was the Kate I'd made love to last night. Because that Kate loved me back.

Steven asked to cut in, and I reluctantly let her slip out of my hold. I wove through the other couples, past Sam, who was spinning Jill and making her laugh like a would-be stepfather, while Cher watched alongside Phillip and Mei.

"Loving a Wells woman isn't for the weak," Troye said and handed me a beer. "But you seem like a guy who's up for it."

I took the beer and frowned at the asshole. "Thanks for your blessing. Since I've proved I'm not a sex worker or a criminal."

Troye sighed. "Kate and Jill will eventually forgive each other."

"What does Jill have to forgive Kate for? You two are the assholes here."

Troye held up a hand. "Okay, Kate will eventually forgive *us,* and there will be those family Christmases. The least you and I can do is get along."

"You're asking a lot. I'd like to punch your face in for

hurting her, and I'd like to buy you a car for not marrying her. Let's call it even, for Kate's sake. And no more fishing expeditions about our sex life. You fucked up. I didn't. Do better with Jill. I'll give you some books."

He said nothing, and I knew I was right about his insecurities. The minuscule part of me that felt bad for him grew, but only by the tiniest fraction. Considering the discussion done, we each took a pull from our bottles and watched our girls dance with other men.

My phone buzzed in my pocket. Nicole from work. It was nearly midnight at home.

I stepped away from Troye's prying ear. "Nicole?"

"Levi, we have a problem. When are you back tomorrow?"

"I changed my flight. I'm not back until Sunday."

"Shit," she said. Nicole didn't swear, usually. "Do you have your computer with you?"

"No. I'm off grid … as much as I can be. What happened?"

It had to be a breach. Blood pounded in my veins. I set my beer on a nearby table.

"Ransomware attack. It started this afternoon, and Jerry can't figure out how it's working. Patient care is not in danger, thanks to those changes you made last year, but we're locked out of the business office system, including patient financial records. The board is going nuts. The hackers are asking for two million dollars, or they'll release the personal information to the public."

Shit. SHIT. "Smart not to ask for too much money. They think a small hospital can't afford to fight and would rather pay than risk lawsuits. How much time?"

"Sunday at noon." She inhaled.

"What else?"

"Some of the board members … think you left a hole … on purpose."

I exhaled. "Shit."

"It's not everyone. It's some of the … more frustrating ones. The lady with the huge endowment who can barely use her cellphone. It's mostly her. She said the hospital should never have taken the risk on you. Another guy, I can't remember his name, but he has that company that does the private jet interiors for people like Oprah."

"Nicole, is this relevant?"

"Yes, the guy says there's a jet that took some doctors to the Big Island for a conference, and he said it can have you back here by morning."

My mind raced. Kate. But what other choice was there? This was *my* responsibility, and mine alone. They got in because I must have let them. I must have left a hole. It was my job to keep the system secure. I had to be the one to fix it.

"I've heard of hacks like this. I've seen online forums with … we'll call them *hypothetical discussions* about how they do it. Don't mention that to anyone. It won't look good. But I have some ideas." I ran my hand through my hair. "Where's the plane?"

33

———

KATE

"You look lovely," Steven said as he twirled me away from Levi's retreating back.

"Thank you, as do you."

He preened.

"Oh, please. You know you're handsome. To what do I owe the pleasure of this dance?"

"So formal." He nodded. "One of Troye's young stud friends asked Janie to dance, and she was so excited, I didn't have the heart to stand in the way, but I didn't want to watch. I figured another pretty Wells girl will do."

I huffed. "Contrary to what Troye thinks, we aren't interchangeable."

Steven threw his head back with a laugh. "It's good you can joke about it."

"Oh, I'm still pissed … but I'll get over it." It was true. It had been surprisingly easy to watch my ex marry my sister. And I had Levi to thank for that. His attention, not to mention the way he looked at me in this dress, pushed all the self-doubt and insecurity away. I was beautiful and sexy, just as I was.

"You always do." Steven met my eyes. "I see you, Kate. It's a lawyer's job to notice the little things, the details. And I see the times when you hold this family together. But maybe you shouldn't. We're all adults. Let the chips fall as they may and focus on you and him." Steven nodded behind me to Levi. I wanted nothing more than to focus and me and him. He stood with his broad back to me, his phone to his ear, causing his biceps to bulge.

"You've been talking to Janie," I said.

"She's my wife. We talk … among other things."

"Yuck," I said and made a face. "She said the same thing, about not holding everyone together anymore."

Steven gave me a pointed stare. "You should listen to her. She's wise."

I smiled.

"So, you and him, it's the real deal?"

"Real feelings, yes. Real logistics problems, also yes."

"Problems can be solved, Kate. Talk to him."

My gaze found him standing farther away now, stiff. One hand still holding the phone. The other in his hair. Something was wrong.

"I agree. Excuse me," I said and released Steven.

"I didn't mean right this second," he called as I headed straight for Levi.

I placed my hand on his arm, and he jerked around to face me. His eyes were wild.

"Text me the information. I'll be there." He ended the call.

"What is it?"

He looked me over. "Goddamn, you're hard to leave,

especially in that dress." He shook his head. "But I have to. There was a breach, well, not yet. It's complicated, but there's a plane at Kona airport, and I have to be on it tonight."

"A plane? Tonight?"

"I'm the security guy. I have to go. Plus, the board thinks I'm involved. I have to figure out how to stop it. If I do, I can't be involved, right? Or if I stop it, I had to be involved to know how." He shoved a hand through his hair. "Fuck my friends and the shit they pulled. It feels like the witch trial all over again."

"I'll come with you," I said.

His eyes softened. "Kate ..." He cursed under his breath and glanced away. "Stay here. I'll be useless to anyone until I fix this."

I tried not to hear that as him not wanting me. I had to do something. "Let me drive you."

"I'll get an Uber."

"Up here and then to the hotel and then the airport? No."

I drove. I told Janie I'd call later and explain everything. Levi was quiet as he scrambled to pack at the hotel.

"If you miss something, I'll bring it to the hospital," I said without thinking. I'd see him at work every now and then, or I could. I wasn't sure if that was good. It wouldn't be the clean break of a vacation fling, and I feared the jagged edge of this one would bleed and bleed.

On the tarmac of the smaller facility next to Kona airport, Levi dropped his bags and kissed me.

"This is all so affected," he said with a laugh. "I'm

not going off to war, but I don't know what happens if I can't fix this. I'll know more by Sunday."

He took a deep breath. "Also, we're not done. We agreed on a week. I still have one more night. I need that night to get some things right. I want a do-over. You, me, this dress. You don't believe this can work, but it can. Give me one more night."

I nodded, then he pulled me in, cupped my face, and kissed me again, hard. He placed kisses on the tops of my cheeks and then jogged up the steps into the jet.

AN AIRPORT EMPLOYEE shuttled me back to my car, and I left, feeling numb. He was gone before we could talk. I agreed to one more night. That night would happen back in the real world.

Levi said he loved my body. He said I was worth *whatever it takes*. But I wasn't. I never had been. Not in the real world.

After a restless sleep in a bed that smelled like him. And then a shower that smelled like him, because he had forgotten his bodywash, and I was a weak woman, I let Janie into my hotel room.

"It sounds like a James Bond movie." She and the kids were heading back to LA today, and Steven was off to Japan on business. "At least you get to stay here another night. If I didn't have Amelia and Carter, I'd stay too."

I smiled. "Next time."

She pointed at me. "There will be a next time, Kate. Family Christmas and a trip to your islands, where it's cooler. Get out of the summer heat."

"They aren't my islands," I said, staring out at the ocean.

"Close enough." She blinked. "Have you heard from him?"

I shook my head. "He texted he'd landed, but that was it."

"Why do you look like Potter's announced they're closing? You'll see him when you get home."

I exhaled a deep breath. "I don't know. First, we were fake, then we weren't. He has a career he loves. I have a career I love. We live hours apart, and every time I've tried long-distance, it failed. It's a big risk." The biggest one. "I'm not sure I can handle another devastation to get over when it doesn't work."

She nodded her understanding. "Like the one with Troye?"

I shifted in my seat. "Well … I was sad about Troye, but not … *devastated*."

"So, with Nate, the mechanic? You guys really had a connection."

I paused. "Well, no. Not really."

Janie's expression was more confident than necessary. "The fisherman?"

I sighed, getting her point. "Okay, not devastated by any of them, but it hurt. I know you think landing a man is important, but no one changes their life for *me*, and if I learned anything this week, it's that I can't be the only one changing."

"Looking back, did you want them to change? Or is it possible you dodged a bullet? And I think landing the *right* man is important. Otherwise, don't bother." Her expression eased. "Have you considered that this thing with you and Levi could be right? That it could be worth a risk because otherwise you *would* be devastated?"

She held my gaze until I looked away.

All my breath whooshed out with a sigh. "I think I love him, and I'm not sure I've ever loved anyone like this. It's been a week." I shook my head. "I'm scared."

She nodded. "Yeah, it's scary loving someone like that. Knowing that as bad as it got with the others, you've never really felt devastation because he's the only one who could do it. You almost wish you didn't know he was out there. Because now you have no choice but to try … to take the risk. It's terrifying." She placed her hand on mine. "But that, my darling, is what ice cream is for."

I chuckled and lowered my head to my hands. "Janie, what am I gonna do?"

She looked around as if seeing the room for the first time. "You're going to stay one more night in this *freaking phenomenal* hotel. You're going to give your man the space he needs, and then you're going to tell him how you feel."

"What if I quit my job, move near him, and he figures out I'm not enough?"

"What if you are? All we can do is strive to be perfect and accept that we're close."

"You have an interesting relationship with perfection."

She shrugged a single shoulder.

"I'm sorry about your mantel photo," I said earnestly.

"Oh, screw my photo." She waved a hand. "Levi didn't bring a gray suit, so there went the whole gestalt."

"You wanted Levi in the photo?"

She leaned close, her grin sweet and, yes, wise. "Kate, it may have only been a week, but he's in love with you. We all watched him fall. So, tell him he better bring a gray suit to Christmas because we're taking that photo. Orange dresses and all."

JANIE and her layers gave me a lot to think about. I spent hours in the hammock doing just that, this time alone and dressed, and the experience was all the poorer for it.

Did Levi love me? It felt like he did. I'd never felt anything like it before. But was love enough? Trying to build something with him in the real world, with its stresses and the added challenge of a long-distance relationship, was beyond risky, especially if love was involved. But Janie was right. Not trying guaranteed devastation. I had no choice.

I didn't know how to try, but I knew I had to. He was the great white whale, but I was the one who got hooked.

My parents and their partners each stopped by in the afternoon for goodbyes and words of wisdom about Levi and love. Mei and Dad had suspected since the first day that our relationship was new. Him playing it up so well made them both like him more. They were also certain he'd genuinely fallen for me. I confessed I had for him.

Sam and Mom stopped by on their way to take a second look at a house they liked, and they were so confident in me and Levi that they insisted on hosting us for a "do-over" trip once they were settled.

The air cooled, and I headed to the hotel bar for dinner, a final Mai Tai, and the sunset. Memories of the week flooded in, conversations and touches and fantasies with Levi.

"Is this seat taken?" A man asked, and for a second, I thought it was him. It wasn't.

"No. Please, sit," I said and flashed a quick smile.

"How's the Mai Tai here?" he asked, and I detected the hint of an accent, British possibly.

"Great," I said. "This is actually a Mai Tai spritz with soda. Not as strong and not as sweet."

"I'm more of a whiskey and soda guy myself. Simple."

I looked at him. It was like my first coffee conversation with Levi.

He placed his drink order, and I caught his eye. "Can I ask you something … probably inappropriate?"

He grinned. "You're the first pretty woman to ask me that. I'm intrigued."

He used the word *pretty* like Levi had that day, too.

I squinted and bit my lip. "Are you hitting on me?"

He glanced at his hands and gave me a sheepish grin. "Not yet, but yeh, you could say I was working up to it."

"I'm not great at reading those signs. It's been mentioned."

"Well, you read mine. So, this fella who mentioned, where is he?"

I smiled. "He had to leave. But I'm …"

"His partner." My bar-mate lowered his chin.

"I think so."

"You don't know?"

"It's complicated. Everyone says that, but yeah, I'm with him, or I want to be."

"What about him?" he asked as the bartender delivered his drink. "He left you. And leaving a beautiful woman in a pretty dress watching the sunset wouldn't be my best choice."

"It was an emergency, life or death. His work."

"He's a physician?"

"No, but just as important."

"Well." The man straightened. "Since I'm a surgeon here for the cardiology conference, I may have to disagree with you. I hoped you were here for the conference, too. You have that dedicated carer vibe."

"I'm a nurse practitioner." I bit my lip. "Why did you want to hit on me?"

He coughed and smacked his chest as he set his drink on the bar. "You don't really expect me to answer that. Won't make me look like the upstanding fella I'm meant to be."

"What?"

"You're beautiful and … sexy. Mister important-as-a-doctor didn't tell you?"

"No, he did. Just hard to believe."

"Well, do. So, can I buy you another drink?"

I laughed. "I'm really with him."

"I got that, didn't I. Crashed and burned is what I did. But your burger looks good. I could order one. And as I may have said, the view could be worse." He grinned in a way that had me fearing for the ladies in this hotel.

Alec, the surgeon, was from Australia and made bungee jumping and black water rafting, which is white-water rafting in a dark cave, sound completely normal. What was it with me and these adventure dudes? But he was fun to talk to until a woman with light brown hair cut short touched him on the shoulder.

She was another surgeon, and the sparks between them made it pretty clear Alec was glad I'd turned him down, or he wouldn't have run into her. The entire interaction had been like a live-action re-enactment of the day in the coffee shop with Levi. He'd said he saw me that day and wanted to know me. That day had been in the real world. So, it wasn't *all* a vacation fling …

My FLIGHT WAS UNEVENTFUL, though the absence of Levi was most acute there. Had it only been a week since I fell asleep on his arm and possibly drooled?

After grabbing my bags, I took the long ferry ride to Coho Island and the winding road to my little house on a cliff at the edge of town, and I was home.

The sunset on this side of the Pacific was beautiful but not quite like Hawaii.

Levi texted while I was on the ferry to see if I'd made it back. He said he'd stopped the breach, but there was a lot to review with the police and the board, and he needed to sleep more than anything.

He asked when I'd be in town, and I told him I'd be at the hospital Friday for a staff meeting. He said we'd get together then. He said he wanted to see me. He said he'd call.

34

LEVI

I DIDN'T CALL.

I didn't wake up again until Monday afternoon. By the time I'd figured out how to unlock the system and identify the source IP address of the attackers, it was early Sunday morning. I'd been mostly awake for two days, running on *Starbucks' naps*, which was sleeping between shots of espresso.

The rest of my week consisted of meetings and debriefs, and what felt like a repeat of that long-ago interrogation. But this time, there was Kate. Someone who believed I could never do this, and though it may have seemed like nothing, it was everything.

I did text a few times. I told her I'd tell her everything on Friday and that I was thinking about her, that I missed her, missed waking up with her. It was the best I could do short of telling her I loved her over and over and begging her to give us a chance.

I wasn't a hacker anymore. I still read the blogs and plotted hacks in my mind, like a choose-your-own-adventure book, working through all the scenarios, but that was it. The scan of my computers and devices showed nothing, as expected. However, the potential breach highlighted a weakness. I was the single sharpest point of defense, and I wasn't enough. A single person working alone was bound to leave weak spots. It was only human. They needed a team, multiple sets of eyes watching for those holes and filling them.

One of my mountain biking buddies had a brother who owned a tech consulting company, and I recommended the hospital consider contracting with them. Turns out, the cost was actually less than a full-time employee. They would save money and get better support, but it would put me out of a job.

I hated not sharing every detail with Kate, but my life felt up in the air, and I needed a plan. She deserved a man with a plan. She promised me one more night. It had to be good enough to get me another and another until we figured out how to share them all.

On Thursday afternoon, less than twenty-four hours until I saw Kate again, I was still dangerously short on that plan.

"Join me for a coffee," my buddy's brother, Lucas, said as we left the hospital board room with decisions made and my signature on the separation agreement still wet.

"After last weekend, I'm taking a break from coffee," I said.

Lucas laughed. "Then a drink at The Boathouse. On me."

I had nothing else to do besides clean out my cubicle and make a plan to keep Kate. Maybe Lucas could help. He was a happily married man. "Why not?"

"That's the spirit."

We settled in a booth in the back of the sailing-themed bar where I'd spent many nights during the last couple of years meeting women who weren't Kate. Lucas rapped his knuckles on the heavily shellacked wood table and startled me out of my apparent daze.

"What's your plan?" he asked.

I blinked. "See her, kiss her, beg her to stay while I figure my shit out. I've got money for the short term. I'm not moving back to Seattle. That could put me even farther away from her."

"Who?" Lucas furrowed his brow.

"Kate."

"A girlfriend?"

I nodded. "It's new. She's a nurse, but she lives on Coho Island and has had … some bad experiences with long-distance relationships. I need to convince her to give us a chance, anyway."

Lucas considered me. "Coho. That's far, and you're right. Seattle wouldn't be good either."

"I gotta figure this out. Computers are all I know, but with my history … it's tricky." Shit.

"Hmmm," he said with every ounce of calm I didn't feel. "You know … my company has a new contract with the hospital here to take point on their IT security." I huffed like *duh, I was just in the meeting that made that happen.* "We have enough contracts in the compliance space now to need someone to manage the work and the team."

I stared at him.

"They'd have to be great and willing to connect in some *legally gray* areas to be sure we stayed current on the trends. Completely backed by the job, of course. The pay's good, but we don't have dedicated offices. My workspace is in a barn on my family's farm." He smirked.

"Everyone is fully remote. As long as there's reliable connectivity, I'd say the right candidate could work from just about anywhere in the area. I'd need them to come to town occasionally for meetings, but otherwise, they could live on a deserted island for all I care."

He sipped his beer and grinned. "Do you know anyone who'd be interested?"

Me: Lunch in the cafeteria?

She would be on the early ferry now unless she'd stayed in Perry Harbor last night … with her friend Kristen, possibly. I thought about texting my friend Chris to ask about it but didn't. There was *anxious-to-see-her*, and there was *stalker*.

Her response was quick. Thank fuck.

Babe: [thumps up emoji] We're doing case reviews and those can run long, but I'll be there. Do you have a hard stop?

Me: Nope

I was free and clear with a bag packed and a willingness to travel.

The three dots appeared, followed by a heart emoji. That had to be a good sign. I smiled like a fool.

I finished the paperwork Lucas sent last night, hit send, and headed out for a quick bike ride. Being in the woods on my favorite mountain trails restored something the potential breach had taken. Maybe it was the very real insult to my skills that rocked my confidence or the look of suspicion on some of the board members' faces that rocked my sense of self, but I was glad to put it all behind me. The familiar burn in my quads and glutes on the uphill and the tension in my hamstrings and shoulders on the down restored my center and clarified my thoughts.

After, I showered and shaved. I'd shaved at the start of the week for all the board meetings. Gone was the softer stubble Kate liked. I'd have to check with her about growing it back. Whatever she preferred between those lush thighs, she'd get.

I made a huge omelet with every vegetable in my fridge. Kate and I needed to have that talk, and I wanted no more interruptions, especially due to hunger.

Dressed in my standard jeans, T-shirt, and hiking boots, I strolled into the hospital lobby like any other day and wound through the short corridor to the cafeteria. I didn't work here anymore, and it was a strange sensation.

"Levi, you're back." A nurse stopped me in the hallway. Kimberlee *something*. She was blonde, wore too much makeup, and always flirted. I doubted she suffered for male company.

The two women with her were the same. I didn't return their interest. No medical staff. But even without my rule, I wouldn't have done it. Those three had *mean girl* written all over them. I went to high school. I had a sister. It wasn't hard to spot.

"You're tan. A vacation somewhere sunny?" Kimberlee asked with a twinkle in her eye.

"Hawaii," I said, shifting my weight toward the food smells wafting down the hall.

"Are you heading to the cafeteria?"

"Yeah—"

"Us too." She gestured to her friends. "You can walk with us."

Okay.

Kimberlee sighed. "Hawaii's amazing. Which island?"

"The Big Island."

"Oh, I haven't been to that one yet. A colleague just got back from there, I think."

"Kate Wells?"

She looked at me, surprised. "You know her?"

Moment of truth. Do I tell? What if Kate decided not to give us a chance and didn't want anyone at the hospital to find out about us? Particularly considering any gossip about me and the breach.

Too late. We entered the cafeteria, and there was the only woman I wanted. On the other side of the room, she leaned against a wall in the same blue scrubs Kimberlee wore. Except on Kate, they were sexy. She was typing on her phone near a bright beam of sunlight streaming through the windows, and she was even more beautiful.

There was no way people wouldn't know about us zero point five seconds after I reached Kate, because I needed to kiss her. I needed to kiss the hell out of her.

"Yeah, I know Kate," I told Kimberlee. "I was with her."

Kimberlee's face froze. "Like on the same plane?"

"No. *With* her. She's my girlfriend."

"She's your—"

I heard nothing else because Kate pushed off the wall and started toward me, her smile bright and her body looking like everything a man could want. I took two gigantic strides and swept her up in my arms, crushing my mouth to hers.

"Hi," I said when I let her take a breath of air.

Her eyes flicked back toward Kimberlee, and a few others focused on us.

"I hope you don't mind," I said, lowering her. "But there was no way I could keep from kissing you."

She bit her lip.

"Kate," Kimberlee said from behind me.

I shifted next to my girl and rested my arm on her shoulders.

"You and Levi?" Her eyebrows were at her hairline. "When did this start?"

Kate straightened, showing off her pretty neck, and I wanted to kiss her there where her skin would be silky and warm and smell like coconut.

"A while ago," she said without hesitation and glanced at me. I loved it.

"We kept it quiet because of work. You understand," I said, grinning with confidence like I did that day with her parents. "But I just couldn't hold myself back anymore."

"Right. Well, good luck, I guess," Kimberlee said and walked off, possibly in a huff.

"Thanks," I called after her and looked at Kate. "You must be hungry, babe. Let's get you fed."

35

KATE

THAT DIDN'T HAPPEN IN THE REAL WORLD. THE PRINCE sweeps in and kisses the girl in front of her rival?
No way.

But Levi did. There may not have been balloons falling from the ceiling or glitter in the air or the surge of movie-magic music, but it was still pretty magnificent.

"I can't believe that happened," I said as we made our way toward the food line.

"Why?"

"You're the great white whale, and I'm … not a Disney princess."

"I'm … what?" he asked, smiling and furrowing his brow.

"The *great white whale*. The catch of a lifetime."

He pulled me close. "Nah, babe, that's you."

Ugh. How was I supposed to stay clear-headed when he said stuff like that? At the cold case, I grabbed a ready-made Asian salad, my favorite, and met Levi in the checkout line. He held an electrolyte water and a protein bar.

"That's all you're having?" I asked.

"I had a late breakfast." He pulled out his credit card as we reached the register. "I've got it."

"Employee discount?" the usual Friday checker asked.

"No," Levi said and placed his card on the reader.

"I can pay if you don't have your ID," I said. It surprised me he didn't, especially being the "security guy" he was.

"I asked. I pay." He nudged me, and I rolled my eyes.

The hospital cafeteria looked out onto a landscaped garden with flowering trees and green bushes. Levi nodded for me to follow him, and we stepped out into the sunshine of what was finally a warm day in June.

He gestured to a small sofa with a coffee table, set back and edged with potted plants for privacy and shade. "This okay?"

"Sure." It was as good a place as any.

I'd practiced what I wanted to say, telling him about my fears and capping it off with how I loved him and wanted to make it work. I wanted to set expectations upfront and make plans. If he could come to Coho some weekends instead of me always traveling to Perry Harbor, that would help. It wasn't a brilliant speech, but it was my speech. My best hope for avoiding devastation.

"I missed you," he said after we sat, and the familiar zing shot through me. He set his drink and energy bar on the table, his expression casual as he angled toward me and stretched his arm across the back of the sofa. His entire demeanor screamed *ready to talk*.

I placed my lunch next to his and leaned against the

cushion, my hands in my lap. "I missed you, too," I said, trying to keep the nerves out of my voice. "And there are things to say."

"I agree," he said with a slight curve to his lips, his tone light and airy as his fingers toyed with a lock of my hair. It was possible the timing wasn't right for serious and heartfelt. I'd paraphrase.

"Levi, you said you want to keep seeing me, and you must have meant it because no one misinterprets that kiss."

He smiled. "I meant it."

"I want that too."

His smile grew.

"But we need to set expectations first."

He tilted his head to the side. "Expectations?"

"For dating long-distance. I want it to be different with you. I want it to work."

"Ah," he said and sucked in a deep breath. "Thing is, I don't want long-distance."

Oh. All the air left my lungs.

He leaned closer. "I want more. I want to wake up with you and make breakfast and figure out a daily routine together."

God, I wanted that. Another hope-laced zing hit me. I needed to focus.

"That would be amazing, but …" Okay, heartfelt or not, I'd put it all on the table. "I love you. And I'm certain it's the first time for me. But we both have great jobs, and I'm not ready to quit mine to move to Perry Harbor. Not yet. It has to be long-distance right now."

"You love me?"

I swallowed. "That's all you got from that?"

He chuckled. "No, it was just my favorite part."

"Well, I do. I love you."

His expression sobered, but a light still danced in his eyes. "I don't have a job at the hospital anymore."

Wait. The love discussion paused. "They fired you because of the breach?" My voice suddenly rose with outrage, the words coming out faster. "You stopped it. You left your vacation to come back here and stop it."

He flopped his head from side to side. "Not exactly fired. I was, let's say re-org'd out of a job."

"That's bullshit. You did nothing wrong."

He took my hand in his. "It's okay. I got another job."

"Oh, well … good."

"Problem is …" he said, hesitating, and my pulse jumped. It was in Seattle. It was across the country. It was on the moon. "They don't have office space. I'll have to work from home."

Whew. "Is that bad?"

"My place is small. I'll go stir-crazy there. You know me. I need outside and trees and water. So, I'm thinking of moving."

What? *Don't hope. Don't hope. Keep it locked up.* I chanted to myself, ignoring how much I wanted that sparkle in his eyes to mean something good for me.

"My sister's getting married soon. She and my nephew don't need me as much. But I don't want to go too far. I'm considering one of the outer islands. Get a place with a view and easy access to bike trails."

Time slowed. I could actually hear my heart beating in my chest, and hope, having sniffed out a possible escape, was jiggling the door of the cage I kept it in. Coho was a big island. Lots of trees and water and trails for bikes.

"Did you have one in mind?"

A smile broke across his features like the sun, and that zing became a world of butterflies as hope flung its cage door wide open.

"As a matter of fact, I do." He was closer now. Cardamom and leather. His thumb stroking the back of my hand. His blue-gray eyes trained on me.

"We're talking about Coho, right?" I held my breath, my free hand gripping the edge of the sofa cushion.

"Whatever island you're on."

Oh god. I whispered, "You'd do that?"

"Move somewhere to be closer to you when I could move anywhere I wanted? Yes, Kate. I'd do that. Why would you think I wouldn't?"

I covered my mouth as tears threatened. "Because …" I hauled in a breath. "Because … I'm not the woman a man changes his life for."

His expression warmed, and he glanced at my lips before meeting my eyes again. "Turns out, Kate, you are."

"Why?" It came out on a shaky exhale. I hadn't meant to say it out loud.

He straightened. "In a word, loyalty. It's more than that, too, but it's that. I know you'd have my back the same way I have yours. I don't have a lot of experience with that kind of loyalty. My oldest friends could have landed me in jail. The woman I thought I loved abandoned me. College professors I considered mentors suggested I could do something illegal. The feds didn't believe me. My parents …" He shook his head.

Levi hadn't shared about his parents other than his

dad's job and his mom's desire to make everything beautiful. His sister and his nephew were his family.

"My dad's not a doctor. He's a surgeon. There's a difference. Ask him. I was supposed to be a surgeon. I had the grades. I had the financial resources to get through med school without going into debt. I had a renowned father who could pull strings for internships and residency placements. And I didn't want to be any kind of doctor. I hung out with skinny dudes and 'played video games' into the wee hours. Wasting my life, he said. And because I didn't do what he expected, he cut me off emotionally. When everything went down with the case, he offered to get me a lawyer. That's it."

"Levi …" The tears now threatening, were for a different reason.

"There are people in the world who are supposed to be loyal, supposed to love you. It's hard to be loyal to people who aren't loyal to you. It's hard to love people who don't love you back. I think you know what that's like."

I looked at our joined hands.

"I can trust you to not take it for granted. And I want that in my life more than any job."

A single tear fell, and then another. I wiped them away and sucked in a breath, fighting the others. But plenty of people cried on this sofa for many reasons. Why not me?

I let them fall.

"Too much? Too soon?" he asked, his brow furrowing as I wiped my face and sniffed.

"No, not too much." I shook my head, call it, aggressively. "If I were a little drunk, I'd tell you to move in with me."

He grinned. "Let's start with this weekend. We'll go to Coho. Make that breakfast together and walk on the beach. We'll see how it goes when it's just us … in the real world."

Hope was flying away now and taking the flood of butterflies with it.

"This is crazy," I said. "It was a week."

"It was a *big* week."

"Do you have a car here?" Levi asked, collecting our trash from lunch and sorting it into the correct bins for recycling, composting, and the landfill. He'd shared more about the breach and his new job, and I'd shared my history with Kimberlee and the mean girls.

"When I come to town for meetings, I usually walk on and grab an Uber," I said. "It's easier than bringing a car."

"Then I'll drive. I need to swing by my place for a few things." He winked at me. "We can stop on the way to the ferry."

"You have a truck," I announced when we made it out to the hospital parking lot.

"Yeah. It's a hybrid and gets great gas mileage." He hit the fob to unlock the doors.

"I've only ever seen you on a bike. I never thought about what kind of vehicle you drive."

"A truck's good for hauling gear." His eyes got that naughty gleam. "And it's good for going to far-off places. Throw down some thick camping mats in the bed and watch the stars come out."

"Or cuddle," I said after climbing in on the passenger side.

"Naked cuddling, absolutely. Nothing better than naked cuddling under the stars."

"Nothing?" I asked in a teasing tone.

"Well … maybe a couple of things are better. Are you looking to do some research tonight?" He flashed his dimple.

My inner walls spasmed like he'd kissed that spot on my neck, and I sucked in a quick breath.

"What?" he asked, checking traffic and pulling out onto Commerce, the main road in Perry Harbor.

"I … I got a little charge when you asked if I wanted to do *research*. I think I may have a kink for sex outdoors."

"Don't tease me, Kate." He glanced at me.

"Surprisingly, I'm not."

His smile was huge as he shook his head. "I love you."

I bit my lip.

"That's a big smile," he said.

"I'm glad you said that. It was daunting to say it first, and then you didn't say it back."

He frowned. "Say what first?"

"I love you."

"You didn't say it first. I did." He kept glancing between me and the road.

"You did?" What had I missed?

"In Hawaii. I said I loved your thighs and your smile and everything about you."

"I thought you meant my body since you were about to fuck me."

"What? You didn't hear *I love you* in there?"

"No, Levi. I did *not* hear you say *I love you*. I would remember."

He looked over again, as if he expected me to say "gotcha" or something similar, then checked his mirrors and turned into the lot of a church. He put the truck in park and got out.

I sat still for a moment. What?

I opened my door to step out, but Levi was already there on my side, blocking my way. Instead, he pushed in and notched between my knees. He put his arms around me, grabbed two handfuls of my backside, and hauled me against him. In a church parking lot.

"Levi, what—"

"Katherine Elizabeth Wells, let me be clear. I love you. I'm *in* love with you. It was a week, and I was always the guy who believed you couldn't fall in love in days. But I was wrong. So fucking wrong. I don't know where this adventure will take us, but I know I only want to take it with you."

And then he kissed me.

LEVI

Kate was an adventurer who liked sex outside. Exactly like me. And now that I'd made it clear I loved her, and she loved me back, I imagined us following the sun around the world and *enjoying* the great outdoors on all seven continents.

At my place, I grabbed my large gear bags and the cooler I'd packed earlier.

"What are you bringing?" she asked, laughter in her voice.

"You'll see," I said and flashed my dimple.

Kate had shown me pictures of her house when we were in Hawaii. It was perched on a low cliff overlooking the ferry dock on Coho. She had a view of the Salish Sea and other islands, and giant, old-growth trees separated her from the neighbors on both sides. It was perfect.

"You don't like fish," I said once we were on our way. "What about crab?"

"I like it. One of my patients gives me a few from

each of his summer catches. It's work, but the meat is an excuse to eat drawn butter, so it's worth it."

"My sister makes great crab cakes. She offered me a bag from her freezer if I brought you by to meet her."

She looked at her scrubs. "Like this? You want to introduce me to your supermodel sister dressed like this?" She sat tall in the seat, released the elastic holding her hair, and fluffed it around her shoulders. A familiar hint of coconut laced the air in the cab of my truck. Her. Here.

"Kate, you're beautiful. And Ione won't care. You'll see." She shot me eye daggers, clearly not believing me.

I pulled into my sister's driveway and realized I was nervous. I hadn't introduced anyone to Ione in years. Her fiancé Travis was shooting hoops with my nephew as usual.

"Hey, man," Travis said and loped over for a back-slapping hug with Rory trailing behind. "You had quite the week. It's good to see you."

"Yeah, happy ending, though. All good." I took Kate's hand. "This is my girlfriend, Kate. Kate, my sister's fiancé, Travis."

"Girlfriend," Travis said with a sly smile. "Can't say I've heard that one from him before. Good to meet you."

"You too," she said and shook his outstretched hand. "And this must be Rory."

My nephew nodded, one arm holding a basketball against his hip like an appendage.

"Thanks for the phone conversation a couple of weeks ago. You were right about your uncle."

Rory grinned at me, looking less like a tween every day. "She's pretty. Don't mess it up."

"Watch it," I said, wrapping my arm around his neck and mussing his hair.

"Ione's inside," Travis said and nudged Rory, gesturing to return to their game.

"Hey," I called into the entryway.

"Hey," Ione called back, stepping out of the kitchen and wiping her hand on a tea towel. As usual, she'd pulled her hair back and wore casual tan shorts with an old T-shirt from the bike shop in town. The giant shirt had to be Travis's.

"Look at you," she said. "All sun-kissed, and maybe just plain kissed." She flashed a smile at Kate. "I'm Ione. It's great to meet you officially."

"You too," Kate said.

"So, this guy minded his manners in Hawaii after all?"

Kate laughed.

"Don't answer that. Okay, you're in a hurry. Crab cakes." Ione headed back to the kitchen and returned with a small bag of frozen patties.

"Let's pick a date for dinner soon. Get here early, and you, Travis, and Rory can ride while Kate and I have a glass of wine on the deck." She waggled her brows at my girl like the conversation would include every embarrassing tale of my boyhood and dating history.

"Yeah, we'll get right on that," I said, taking Kate's hand and waving the bag of crab cakes toward my sister like goodbye. But she knew I wouldn't stay away for long.

"She's your home," Kate said as I piloted the truck into the standby ferry line.

"She's my family. Not my home. She's found hers

with Travis. I'm still looking. The one on the horizon seems promising, though." I winked, and she grinned.

The road to her house curved through town, and I noted it would be an easy bike to the ferry terminal. Bikes on ferries meant no lines. It was the best way to commute.

The house was one level, painted gray with white trim. It had a two-car garage on the end and two concrete steps to a dark-stained wooden door. Inside was a mostly empty room to the left with wood-paneled walls, a single chaise, a side table, and a standing lamp. The built-in bookshelves above an old brick fireplace were full, though. This had reading room written all over it, but there was a corner by the window with a view of the nearby woods in front that could fit a desk and monitor … should one be needed. I grinned to myself.

The eat-in kitchen stretched along the back, with a den and hallway leading to her bedroom and the spare. A door to the single full bath was that way, too. Definitely a house from the seventies, mid-update. Definitely her style, with walls painted in different muted colors flowing together and furniture with colorful throw blankets inviting you to sit and stay.

"Are you doing the remodeling?" I asked, about to be even more impressed with my girl.

"No," she chuckled. "Some of my patients have a construction business here. They've done most of it the past two winters. I always get a screamin' deal since it's the off-season." She shrugged a shoulder like *you know, everybody gets a break on construction costs in the winter*. They did not.

"Any chance these patients are single guys?" I may

have to do a little staking my claim around here. No problem. I was up to it.

Kate bit her lip. "Well, one. He's super cute too, all lean muscles and confidence."

I cleared my throat and possibly puffed out my chest.

"He's also sixteen." She grinned. "His dad and his uncles own the business. And those guys are all happily married fathers of teenagers. I don't date patients."

I pulled her in for a hug. "Free crab and construction."

"Not free construction. Discounted."

"Whatever," I said. "I can see why you care for them so well. They care for you too. But tonight, it's my turn."

The back deck was thin and stretched nearly the length of the house. New wood marked places that were recently repaired, and it needed a good sanding and a fresh coat of paint everywhere. Something I'd do in my spare time, staking that claim.

Today was the summer solstice, and although there was no official pagan tradition of celebrating naked, I intended to make it a tradition for Kate and me.

She headed back to shower, and I got to work. I laid the dark tarp down first, then the thick, self-inflating camping pads, and then the plush, old-style sleeping bag, unzipped and spread out over both mats. I covered it all with a fitted sheet to help it stay in place and set the blankets I brought to the side. I snagged a couple of throw pillows from the sofa, set out candles for later, and opened a chilled bottle of wine from the cooler.

I was in the kitchen loading groceries into the fridge when Kate appeared in a plush robe. Her hair was wet and hung around her shoulders in loose waves.

"What's all this?" she asked with a knowing smile.

"A solstice celebration. The sun is high. It's warm. A good night to be outside."

"Naked?"

Ah, my sexy adventurer. "It's the best way to enjoy a massage."

"If anyone has binoculars on those boats in the harbor, they'll get an eyeful."

She headed back toward her bedroom and returned to spread a giant blanket along the railing, blocking the view from below, and added soft pillows to the bed I'd made. She stood barefoot in the middle, faced me, and slowly undid the tie of her robe, owning it, and me with every breath.

I didn't move. I loved her unveilings.

She rolled her shoulder, and the robe slipped off, exposing her to my hungry eyes. She did the same on the other side, and the fabric pooled at her feet. "When does this massage start?"

"Right now." I closed the lid on the half-empty cooler and walked toward the woman I loved, shedding all my clothes on the way.

"Lie down on your stomach," I directed and opened the tropical-scented massage lotion I brought.

She relaxed on the cool sheet with a deep sigh, and my inner caveman noticed. All that skin and curvy soft-ness. So utterly female.

I spread her legs enough to settle between them on my knees and set to work, massaging with slow strokes up her calves to her thighs.

"Beautiful," I whispered more than once as I toured my favorite landscape. Her moans and sighs were subtle, and I caught the scent of her when I leaned close to leave a tender kiss on each of the dips at the base of her spine. I knew if I touched her, she'd be wet.

"You shaved," she said as my cheek brushed against her low back.

"I did. Board meetings. But I can grow it out again if you prefer."

"Hmmm," was her only response.

After long minutes with her shoulders and neck, I stretched out at her side, propping my head with my bent arm and smoothing my fingers down the column of her spine.

She wriggled her hips. "Levi?"

"Yeah, babe?" I leaned down to kiss her shoulder.

She hesitated, her breathing deep, before she rolled to face me. "You make me feel sexy."

"You are sexy."

She grinned and reached for me. "You make me feel like I can do things."

The spark in her eye flashed. This was going somewhere good.

"What do you want to try?" I was up for almost anything.

She rose and brought an arm and a leg over me. She was on all fours with me flat under her. It was a very good look.

"Cowgirl?"

Hell. Yes. We didn't get to it that day with the ice cream.

"Babe, that's a question I will never say no to." I found the sleeve of condoms I'd placed under the edge of the camping mat earlier, and Kate shifted pillows behind my back.

I rolled on protection while Kate reached into the

pocket of her discarded robe and produced her pink vibe. My girl came to play.

She switched the vibrator on and clicked the controls until it emitted a pulsing pattern of short buzzes and breaks. With our gazes locked, she lowered herself onto me, and I nearly lost it from the sight alone. Kate, her hair tumbled, all that creamy skin flushed pink. The scent of her. The heat of her. All of her here with me in the wide open air. It was nearly too much.

She set the toy below her pubic bone, and the buzz hit the base of my dick. *That* was good.

"Mmm," she hummed and arched as my dick swelled inside her. I needed to move and thrust and fuck, and feared that if I did, I'd come.

I groaned when she squeezed her legs and lifted, dragging her walls against me. As we found our rhythm, one hand kept that vibe pressed to her center, and the other teased one peaked nipple. My mouth went dry.

Kate was a goddess above me in the late afternoon sunshine. I may have told her. I may have said a lot of things as she rose and settled over and over while my hands gripped her curvy hips and thighs.

She was in the driver's seat, and I followed her lead, thrusting to meet her, deepening our connection as she literally rode me to the maddening edge.

"Levi …" she panted, her eyes hooded and dark. She was close.

"You're so fucking sexy." The beast in me growled. "Give it to me. Let me feel it."

I pulled her down hard as I thrust up, and her walls fluttered. It was the lightest spasm and then another. Her pants came faster. She rode me harder. She worked the vibe between us with focused intention before giving herself over to it all with a keening cry.

I watched, transfixed, as her stomach muscles lurched and her inner walls gripped my dick. Definitely not fake. Definitely no way I didn't join her in release.

Her body trembled as she settled into the aftershocks and leaned forward, resting her head on my chest. She switched off the vibe and tossed it aside. "That … was incredible. Thank you, Levi."

I chuckled. "Thank *you*. That's a vision I'll keep for a long time."

She kissed me and rolled off me.

I took care of the condom, tying it and setting it out of the way. I'd get rid of it in a minute. I needed to do some cuddling with Kate first.

KATE

Cowgirl. Imagine that. This man was magic. No wonder I loved him.

I snuggled close to his side and sighed, his hand coasting along my back. "I love your Goldilocks dick."

His movements froze. "Um, what?"

"Your dick. Not too big. Not too small. It's *just* right. The perfect size for a boyfriend."

He paused. "That's a compliment, right?"

"Absolutely," I said, drawing back to see his face. "Big dicks are all the rage, but I'm not a fan."

He winced. "Good?"

"The fisherman I dated, he was a traditional guy with a big one he was really proud of."

"I'm not sure my Goldilocks dick wants to hear this."

I chuckled and spoke quickly, "No. Don't worry. It's not scary."

"Says you."

"That dick did not work for me. He thought all he had to do was thrust. Not so much. It was too much sensation where I didn't need it and not enough where I did. I like sex. I like morning sex and marathon weekend sex."

"Okay, this part of the story is better," he said, pulling me close again.

"The next day was usually a no-go. It felt like I'd pulled a muscle down there, and on those mornings, I couldn't even tolerate it long enough to fake it. Forget marathon sex. That wasn't happening."

"I like marathon sex," he said like a kid would say *I like puppies*.

I laughed. "Yes, I know you do." I crawled over him. "And good news, you have the perfect dick for it. And you fit so well in my mouth."

The body part in question jumped, and I raised my brow at Levi.

His cocky grin returned. "Yeah, I remember."

"I could take you deep and tease your perfect boyfriend dick for a long time … if that was something you wanted."

He groaned and rolled on top of me, pinning me under him. "Did I mention I love you?"

I giggled and wrapped my legs around his middle. "Is that a yes?"

"It's a hell yes." He did a push-up above me and stood.

"Where are you going?" I asked. Or possibly whined.

He turned back. The sexy beast was there. "Dinner. I need to feed you so I can fuck you again."

My pussy spasmed, and I swear he knew it. His grin promised all kinds of dirty things, and I couldn't wait for him to get started.

"I'll help," I said, reaching for my robe as Levi pulled on a pair of loose sweatpants and nothing else. "It'll go faster."

He sautéed chicken breasts and made fresh pesto sauce for pasta. I pan-seared grape tomatoes and buttered hunks of warm bread. I lit the candles he'd set all around while he poured two glasses of a tart white wine. Then we ate, sitting on the camp bed, resting against outdoor sofa cushions propped along the back of my house.

If I hadn't already decided to give us a chance, this would have done it. Everything was perfect.

"If I wasn't clear earlier, I'm in," I said, setting my empty plate aside and reaching for my wineglass.

Levi looked at me.

"You had me at 'Hi,' but if you only had this one night, you nailed it."

He grinned.

"Do you worry real life won't be the same as the vacation in paradise?"

He set his plate down and reached for my hand. "I can't say we won't have problems. I promise we will. I also promise the only person I want to get through them with is you. No relationship is perfect, but when you find the perfect person, you figure it out."

That was true. My dad and Mei. Mom and Sam. Janie and Steven. Even Jill and Troye. Their relationships were all unique to them, and they were happy. Levi and I would be too, because it was us.

"Problems come and go. Kates don't. You find a Kate, you hang on."

I kissed him then, because how could I not?

Food forgotten in the pink twilight, he pulled me

down to my back and held himself above me on his elbows. He smoothed his lips along my collarbone, my jaw, and across the tops of my cheeks.

"Your freckles were the first thing I wanted to kiss when I sat next to you in the coffee shop," he said.

"I can't believe that was only two weeks ago."

"I also may have thought about your nipples."

Now it was my turn to ask, "What?"

"Legend says the color of a woman's lips is the same as her nipples. I wondered if yours matched." He lowered one side of my robe below a breast. "They do."

His sly grin bloomed right before he kissed me there, biting and laving the swollen bud. He knew it would make me crazy for him in seconds.

"You're fantastic at that, babe," I said.

Levi looked up. "That's the first time you've used a nickname."

I gave him a saucy look. "No, it isn't, *Daddy*."

"Oh, *Baby Girl*, there you go, asking for it again."

I laughed, but a shiver ran through me. I wanted whatever Levi wanted to give me as long as he was naked.

He kissed his way to my mouth, and the tip of his tongue caressed my bottom lip. I pulled him closer, taking the kiss deeper. He had one hand cradling the back of my head while the other stroked down the side of my body, opening my robe completely and setting off fireworks along the path.

On and on, he kissed me, his fingers only nearing the part of me that burned for him until, finally, a soft slide right where I needed it. Electricity shot through me. He went lower, pressing against my swollen folds, making me squirm as my inner walls contracted. He made another pass over my clit and down to do it all again. The magic figure eight.

"Levi, please." I tugged at the waistband of his sweats.

"Not many words better than those," he said and finished removing his pants while I pulled my robe all the way off.

He was on me again, skin to skin in the deepening twilight. He held my gaze and stilled except for the slow caress of his thumbs at my temple. "I love you."

My heart swelled. "I love you too."

His kiss was tender and slow, but not teasing. Perfect. I stroked my hands along his back, soaking in the feel of his strength. I loved him more than I ever imagined possible. I didn't know where this adventure would lead either, but like Levi, I knew I wanted to figure it out with him.

When he reached for a condom, I stopped him. "I'm good. You're good. I have an IUD. We're out here naked in the open, starting something new. I want you to love me like this tonight."

"Are you sure?"

"I'm sure."

The silence between us was heavy. Then, with whispered words of love and tender caresses, he filled the place that ached for him. The one in my center and the one in my heart.

Slow and gentle became more. Hands clutched, lips met. When we both let go, all that remained was love and candlelight under a sky turned evening purple.

Levi breathed above me, the hand buried in my hair gently massaged, and he made no move to leave me. The distant hum of boat motors settled to the chirps and calls of night birds in the quiet, and I reveled in the closeness. I wanted it for a lifetime.

We eventually cleaned up the deck and kitchen and made it to the shower, where I'd put the bottle of body-wash he'd left behind at the hotel. His smile was knowing as he tested the weight.

"So, I used it this week. I missed you, your smell. I'll buy you some more."

He laughed and kissed me.

"It's like showering outside," he said, taking in the wide skylight covering the entire top of the space. "I think this is destiny, Kate. You're an outdoor adventurer who's spent too many years inside."

I laughed.

We settled in my bed, and Levi pulled me close. He told me about all the adventures he wanted us to take. Kayaking, hiking, biking, camping. He waggled his brows about the camping, and I knew I'd love that adventure the most.

We made plans for summer trips and into the fall when the forest floor would be damp and blanketed with leaves, the smell of wood smoke a hint in the air.

"I want a do-over with the dress and the beach and sunset," he said. "I want to go back to Hawaii."

"Me too."

"There's a lot to plan. A ton of stuff we didn't get to." The low growl of his sexy beast had ideas fizzing in my mind.

I grabbed my phone and started a new group chat, for just me and Levi this time. I sent him the first text and heard it ding. "Hawaii for Two."

EPILOGUE

Levi

We started this Hawaiian journey in Hilo, the rainforest side of the Big Island. We did my favorite ATV tour, which included a stop at a waterfall for a swim and a catered lunch.

Kate wore her purple bikini. I'd seen her in it fifty times since that first day, but its power hadn't diminished. Nor had my desire for her in it and out of it. I wanted to put my hand inside those little bottoms and watch her squirm, trying to stay quiet out in the open.

She'd grown more adventurous over the last year, and I fucking loved it. Sneaking off to private outdoor spots as much as possible had become our thing. We always found a way to explore our mutual kink. Even during a late spring back-country hike in the mountain snow a couple of months ago. Kate was my adventure.

After lunch, as folks splashed in the pool below, others hiked the forest trail to the top of the waterfall.

"You want to go?" I asked, gesturing at the people heading up.

"Yeah," she said with a gleam. I wasn't sure if that was for the potential view or for the thing we did on hikes whenever we got the chance. I'd find out.

I waited so that Kate and I would be last in the line of hikers, and I took her hand as we climbed. Water squeaked in our rubber trail sandals as we dripped along the path.

"It's like I'm hiking naked," she said.

"You practically are babe. I like it. You should wear that bikini on all our hikes."

"Could make Mt. Rainer a little tricky this fall."

"I bet I could warm you up." I turned and dropped a kiss on her strawberry lips.

I kept my eyes open and soon pulled Kate a few steps off the trail to a spot blocked on three sides by boulders.

"Levi, this is a family event. Kids are here," she said, but there was that gleam again.

"If you'd rather not—"

"I didn't say that," she said with a smirk. "Since you went to all the trouble of finding a private place."

I leaned in and channeled the inner beast with a low growl. "You'll have to be quick and quiet."

Her eyes flared, and I moved right to that spot on her neck. I bit and soothed the mark with my tongue while I plucked a plump nipple through her bikini top.

"Yes," she said and shifted against me.

I pulled the wet fabric away from her body and set my mouth there with warm kisses on her cool skin before I drew back, blowing air across the peak.

She gasped softly, and that flare in her eyes became a smolder.

I had to kiss her. She was always greedy for my kisses when she got that look. Another thing I loved, and when I slid my hand inside those bottoms, she was drenched.

"This rock is rough," she panted. "Can't fuck me here. Have to use your fingers."

I hummed in her ear and slipped a single digit inside her warmth, then another, and pressed the heel of my hand to her clit, stroking her in all the places she needed it.

That's when she fell on me with open-mouthed kisses, panting breaths, and quiet sighs. Her body was always so responsive, and she sank into the pleasure I was giving her.

"Can you come for me?" I whispered into her ear. "Squeeze my fingers and make my dick ache for you?" My girl liked a little dirty talk.

"Yes," she said with a quick exhale. "And then I'm going to suck you dry."

My dick got harder. Seems I liked a little dirty talk too.

I kissed away her moans and sighs, holding her steady against the rough rock. I didn't stop until she was on the edge. When I pressed my thumb to the spot and rubbed the way she liked, she came.

When she settled, she still vibrated with energy. That was one thing about these outdoor quickies. They made her hungry for more. She dropped to her knees, yanked my board shorts down, and wrapped those sweet lips around me.

No teasing. All business. Her head bobbed in the rhythm she knew would get me there fast. Hell, with

Kate, I could always get there fast. The issue was holding back.

I growled low, and she added a tongue swirl along my crown before taking me deep again. She knew all my secrets and tells. My blood burned fast. My skin was too tight. My balls drew up close to my body, and she knew. She gripped my base and squeezed, and I was over the edge, all the way down, breathing hard with my release.

She stood and pulled my shorts back into place with a smirk.

I looked at my watch. "Seven minutes, Kate. That has to be a new quickie record."

"I want to finish that hike. Let's go, sexy beast."

Kate

The waterfall pool had cooled my heated skin and body, so I resisted attacking him again until we got back to our hotel. Hilo was on the other side of the Big Island and received much more rain than the Kona side. The landscape was lush and filled with all the shades of green, dotted with bright tropical flowers in orange, red, pink, and yellow.

Our room wasn't as private as the Grand Hawaiian, where we would be for the second half of the week, but last night, we still found our way to the outdoor shower and the lounge chairs on the lanai.

Standing on the next-to-the-last platform on another frighteningly beautiful zipline tour, I yearned for more of that adventure spirit. "Yes, you can do this," the guide had said at the beginning. "Keep saying it."

"Yes, I can do this," I now chanted under my breath.

This tour was advanced. The platforms were higher

and smaller, and I'd had to summon all my courage to glance at the valley floor hundreds of feet below and tell myself *yes*. Levi had wrapped me tight in his arms once already to calm my heart, and I feared he'd have to do it again.

"This one is steep and fast. Possibly scary. It is for me too, if I'm being honest. But this is you and me, Kate. We got this."

I nodded and swallowed as I watched the man I love leap off the platform, drop a bit, and sail away on a thin wire of steel.

"You can take a minute," the guide said. "Since you're the last one on this jump, it's okay to take in the view."

"I'm trying not to be frightened."

"Nah, no reason to be frightened. The hardest part of this one is the landing, and you've got your man down there ready to catch you. All good."

"Yes," I laughed. "I couldn't do this without him. He's … well, he's everything."

The guide chuckled, and I felt the blush rise. "Do you get a lot of over-emoting up here, or is it just me?"

He shook his head and grinned. "Not just you."

His radio squawked, and he hit the button to silence it. "Time to go. You ready?"

"Oh god."

"You got this."

I sucked in a deep breath and squeezed my eyes shut.

"Keep those eyes open, Kate. Life-changing thing, this view."

I wasn't sure I believed him. I nodded anyway. "Eyes open. Think yes."

"That'll do it. Now jump."

I did and screamed with the drop. Then I sailed. I flew. The sky above the deep chasm was so wide and bright blue. The sun was warm in a world full of wonder again on another adventure in paradise. It *was* life-changing, just as it was the first time.

As I neared the lower platform, Levi was there, ready to catch me. Behind him was a big white sign with red letters, but I couldn't make it out. And then I did. It said *Marry Me* in bright, unmistakable script.

I screamed and landed in his arms. "Oh, my god. Levi, is this real?"

He held me tight. "I fell in love with you on a zipline. It seemed only fitting." He leaned back and kissed my cheek.

"But how did you arrange it?"

He shrugged. "Turns out, I'm not the first to ask for the proposal package."

Laughter bubbled out of us both.

Levi pulled a box from a zipped pocket on his shorts and opened it. "Marry me, Kate?"

Oh, this man. My man. The bright sparkle of diamonds flashed as tears burned. I threw my arms around him. "Squeeze me tight again," I said. "Tighter."

He did. When I stepped back, I looked at him, and all the love and loyalty I never had was right there, waiting for me to claim it.

"We got this, Kate. All you have to do is say yes."
His eyes held mine, and his heart held mine, too.

"Yes."

.   .   .

THANK you for reading *Hawaii for Two*. I hope you loved Levi and Kate's story of family, adventure, and passion. If you did, please leave a review on Amazon, Goodreads, or Bookbub to help other readers find characters and stories they will love.

WANT to know about the do-over at the Grand Hawaiian Hotel? Check out the steamy Bonus Scene and all the sexy Bonus Scenes on my website at www.christinabraver.com/bonus/

WHAT'S the story with Levi's sister Ione? Her journey to happily ever after is Book 6 in my Perry Harbor series of interconnected standalones about strong heroines and the swoony men who fall hard for them. These books can be read in any order.

Your Hero (Perry Harbor Book 6)

They have nothing in common. Except how much they want each other.

Ione Abrams has everything except the perfect dad for her son—and so far, the dating pool has been shallow. When she accidentally gets doused with water at a youth basketball game, and the soaked shirt leaves her ample curves on display, it's not the attention she needs. But it's not like the world hasn't seen her body before.

Travis Gray was calling foul on a layup gone wrong when his friend's sister came into focus. Incredible. Practically naked. In public. Whipping off his referee jersey to cover her was only the first time he saved her. He didn't mean to make it a habit.

Now, preparing for the presentation of his career, he's the one who needs saving. But Ione's help is dangerous with her curves, her smile, and her smarts. Travis may have shoulders that could hold up the world, but she needs a partner, not a hero. And as much as he wants to, he can't be either.

A STEAMY, strong single mom, starting over, slow burn romance with light suspense and a protector hero who falls hard. It's about getting what you want and finding out you deserve it after all.

TW: The FMC is briefly attacked on the page.

ORDER *YOUR HERO* TODAY.

WANT the inside scoop on my misadventures in writing along with freebies and real sex positive info from my reading and research? Sign-up for my newsletter via my website:

www.christinabraver.com. Unsubscribe at anytime.

As MUCH AS I TRY, I'm not perfect. If you find an error, please email me at:

author@christinabraver.com.

ALSO BY CHRISTINA BRAVER

Want more stories about independent women making their way in the world and the sexy men who fall hard for them?

Scan the QR code below for the full list of Christina Braver novels. Or head to the Books page of my website, christinabraver.com.

ChristinaBraver.com Books Page

ACKNOWLEDGMENTS

Thank you to all the wonderful people who made this book possible.

To Ann B., Kim S., and Maryanne K., my beautiful book betas who bravely read this entire manuscript first. Their feedback, comments, and support make my books better.

To Brent Archer, my fabulous writing sprint partner who helped me plot and kept me writing.

To my Editor, Lynne, for her continuous support, talking me off more than one "ledge" with this one. I appreciate you.

To my designer, Amy, for your professional insights and advice.

To Lauren and everyone at ECRW for being the best writer community.

To all my friends, with or without glasses of wine, who encouraged me when I felt like giving up.

To my kids for believing in me, and putting up with all my sex positivity talk.

To my husband and very own beta hero who makes this work possible and first said the words "You should write a book."

ABOUT THE AUTHOR

Christina Braver writes steamy, small-town, contemporary romance usually set in the Pacific North-west. Her stories are about strong heroes with softer sides, independent heroines with a bit of sass, and the guaranteed happily-ever-after we all need.

She has a master's degree in clinical psychology and uses that knowledge to create well rounded character driven stories described as "a little bit nerdy and a little bit dirty." Influenced by books and information from prominent sex therapists, her novels bring toe curling spice and real-life sexy tips, as well as address deeper issues such as women's sexual health and sex positivity for everyone.

She lives outside Seattle, and when she isn't writing, Christina can be found biking with her husband, laughing too loudly with friends, sipping wine, or reading.

www.ingramcontent.com/pod-product-compliance
Lightning Source LLC
Chambersburg PA
CBHW071348300726
48976CB00006B/1810